ISBN 1-890768-45-6

First Printing, December 2002

This book is a work of fiction. Names, characters, places and incidents are either the product of the author's imagination or are used fictitiously. Any resemblance to actual events or locales or persons, living or dead, is entirely coincidental. Although the author and publisher have made every effort to ensure the accuracy and completeness of information contained in this book, we assume no responsibility for errors, inaccuracies, omissions, or any inconsistency herein. Any slights of people, places or organizations are unintentional.

Library of Congress Cataloging-in-Publication Data
Brewer, Steve.
    Cheap Shot : a Drew Gavin mystery / by Steve Brewer.
        p. cm.
    ISBN 1-890768-45-6 (alk. paper)
    1. Sportswriters--Fiction. 2. Albuquerque (N.M.)--
Fiction. 3. Basketball teams--Fiction. I. Title.

PS3552.R42135 C47 2002
813'.54--dc21

                                                20010525213

10 9 8 7 6 5 4 3 2 1

To Kelly, who makes all things possible.

ONE

The telephone jangled Drew Gavin awake.

He checked his glowing alarm clock—3:04 A.M.—then snatched up the phone on the second ring. Good news never arrives at three o'clock in the morning.

"Hullo?"

Silence. Drew's thoughts raced, first to his father in the nursing home, then to Teresa, then to what story might've broken in the night, one important enough to awaken the *Albuquerque Gazette's* sports editor at this ungodly hour.

"Drew. Man, I'm in trouble."

The halting voice on the line was slurry, and it took a second to register as his best friend, Curtis White.

"Curtis? What's wrong?"

Curtis moaned.

"What? What's the matter?"

"The girl, man. She dead."

Drew sat up. "What girl?"

"That cheerleader. Fontanelle. Dead."

Drew's heart thudded. He didn't know any cheerleader by that name, didn't know what the hell Curtis was talking about. But "dead" came through loud and clear.

"Dead how?"

"Somebody killed her. Oh, man. Shit."

"Where are you?" Drew snapped on a lamp and fumbled among the magazines and fat books on the bedside table, hunting a pen.

"I don't know, man. I don't know what happened—"

"Curtis! Pull your shit together. Where are you right now?"

"In her bedroom. I woke up and here she was. Cold and naked and dead. I gotta get the fuck outta here."

"Don't move. Just tell me where you are. I'll come there."

Curtis moaned again. He sniffed loudly into the phone, and Drew realized he was crying. That was hard to picture. Curtis White was a smooth ladies' man, a gazelle on the basketball court, a competent sportswriter at the *Gazette*, but he wasn't the sentimental type. Most of the time, he wore his "game face," a lazy smile and confident eyes that betrayed no emotion. Drew had known him for over a decade, and the only time he'd ever seen him weep was when they both lived in the athletic dorm at the University of New Mexico, and Curtis had gotten a phone call from East St. Louis, informing him his grandmother had died.

"What happened, Curtis?"

"I don't know. I'm fuckin' dizzy."

"Come on, get a grip. You're at her place? Give me an address."

"I don't *know* the address. I don't even know how I got here."

"You've got to tell me where you are. I can't help you if I can't find you."

"She got a fuckin' pompon stickin' outta her mouth."

"What?"

"A pompon, man. I told you, she's a cheerleader. Her uniform's all tied around her neck. Somebody choked her."

"You're sure she's dead."

"She's staring up at the ceiling. She don't move."

Drew tried to take a deep breath, but it felt as if his chest had been wrapped tightly in panic.

"She's a cheerleader for the Rattlers?" An irrelevant question, but it was all that came to mind.

"Yeah . . . yeah." Curtis sounded groggy.

"Curtis! Go outside, get an address, come back and tell me."

"I got no clothes on."

"Grab some pants and do what I told you."

"I should go out that door and keep going."

"No, you don't. Come back to the phone. I mean it, man."

"Okay, okay."

Drew heard a clunk as Curtis dropped the phone. He waited through an anxious minute or two, wondering whether Curtis had fled for his car. He didn't sound like he was in any condition to drive.

Just as he'd convinced himself Curtis wasn't returning, he heard, "Five-eight-oh-four. Apartment twelve."

"Good," Drew said as he scrawled the numbers on the margin of a page ripped out of a *Sports Illustrated*. "What street?"

"San Mateo. Up by those car dealers."

"Okay, Curtis. Just sit tight. I'll call the cops and then I'll be right there."

"The cops?"

"Come on. Of course I'm calling the cops. Somebody's been murdered."

"Fontanelle," Curtis said absently. "Her name's Fontanelle

Harper."

"You were in bed with her?"

"When I woke up. But I don't know how that happened. I don't—"

"Hang in there," Drew said. "I'm coming."

He disconnected and dialed 911.

TWO

Drew raced out of his small house to his Jeep. The neighborhood—his old neighborhood, the one where he'd grown up—was dark and still. Even the homeboys who usually hung on the corner in their long flannel shirts, drinking beer out of sack-wrapped bottles, had called it a night.

He didn't have much time. He'd thrown on his clothes while on the phone with the police, and now he needed to get halfway across town to Curtis. He wanted to be there when the squad cars arrived. Curtis didn't sound like he was in any condition to talk to cops.

It was chilly for mid-May, and the stars were sharp pinpricks in the black-velvet sky. Drew tried to button his shirt with one hand while he steered with the other, urging the Jeep toward Interstate 25. The canvas-topped Wrangler was drafty, and early-morning air stung his face.

He blew through red lights crossing downtown, then rocketed up onto I-25. Huge banks of white lights illuminated the freeway, and he squinted against them as he sped along the broken road, weaving between concrete barricades. Construction crews worked nights reconfiguring Albuquerque's main crossroads, where I-25 and I-40 meet, a tangle of ramps and interchanges the locals call the "Big I."

Usually, the construction area crawled with cops working radar guns, but none were around now. Probably all racing to the murder scene.

Drew wondered who the dead woman was, and how well Curtis knew her. Might be a simple pick-up. The Rattlers played Thursday night. Curtis might've gone home with her after the game. It wouldn't be the first time he'd found himself in bed with a strange woman after a night of too much bourbon and too little discretion.

And it wasn't the first time he'd called Drew for help when a rendezvous went sour. Drew couldn't count the number of times that Curtis had phoned him over the years, needing a designated driver or a ride home from some woman's apartment. And there was that time a year ago, when a jealousy-crazed boyfriend treed Curtis in an upstairs bathroom, ready to kill him. Curtis had been in his underwear, locked in the bathroom with the boyfriend pounding on the door, but he'd had the woman's cell phone. He'd guessed correctly that the boyfriend would settle down once a man Drew's size arrived for a calming talk.

So it wasn't surprising that Curtis would turn to Drew now that a dead cheerleader had turned up. But it was surprising that she'd been murdered. Drew couldn't picture Curtis killing someone. He'd never seen Curtis lay a hand on any of the women that had passed through his swinging life. Curtis was too laid-back for violence. He didn't care enough about anything to fight about it.

He would've mentioned, though, if he'd gotten involved with a Rattler cheerleader, and Drew wouldn't have forgotten a name like Fontanelle Harper. So this probably was a one-night stand. But how did she end up dead?

The Jeep weaved between the few cars that dotted the early-morning freeway, the speedometer pushing ninety. Drew slowed as his exit approached.

The familiar exit wasn't far from the *Gazette* building, and the thought of the newspaper chilled him. The brass at the *Gazette* would go nuts when they heard about Curtis and the dead woman. And Drew would be back in a familiar place—taking heat to protect Curtis' ass.

But before he could brood too much over that, another thought jarred him.

"Sweet Jesus," he said aloud. "This could be *my* fault."

Drew, still uncomfortable at being his friend's boss, had insisted a week earlier that Curtis get close to the Rattlers. He wanted him to learn more about the franchise, how it was financed, if it had any chance of success. Could Curtis have been seeing the cheerleader as a way to get back-stage with the team? Maybe he'd somehow translated Drew's orders into "go bed down the cheerleaders." Sounded like the kind of "mistake" his buddy would make. Drew could be indirectly responsible for Curtis waking up next to that dead woman.

It was the debut season for the Albuquerque Rattlers and their parent league, the Western America Basketball League, or WABL, which the wags in the newsroom pronounced "Wobble." The league was the brainchild of a local software tycoon named Scott Cerf, and was doomed to be a money-losing proposition. Minor-league teams came and went in New Mexico all the time. Basketball, hockey, baseball and soccer teams all had called it quits here in the past. And WABL's timing was lousy. Albuquerque recently had come close to getting its own NBA franchise, a sneaky plan that Drew and the *Gazette* helped shoot down. The NBA gave the expansion franchises to two other cities, which hadn't helped Drew's popularity around basketball-mad Albuquerque. To most fans, the Rattlers seemed a poor consolation prize.

Curtis hadn't said much about the story since it was assigned, and Drew wasn't sure he'd made much progress on it. Probably didn't matter now. The story definitely had taken a different direction. The news would sort itself out later. The main job now was getting Curtis out of trouble.

He zoomed down a ramp off the freeway and through a hairpin turn onto San Mateo Boulevard. San Mateo's six lanes were lined by fast-food joints and chain restaurants and car dealerships and shopping centers. Tucked behind them to the east were sprawling apartment complexes surrounded by asphalt moats. Albuquerque's version of "living over the store."

Drew heard sirens approaching as he bounced over speed bumps into the parking lot of the two-story apartment building. It only took a moment to locate Apartment Twelve among its darkened neighbors on the ground floor. The windows were ablaze with light, and Curtis had left the door standing open. Drew hoped he was still in there. Fleeing would only make things worse.

He slammed the Jeep into an empty parking slot and sprinted to the apartment door, his gimpy ankles twinging with every step.

He stopped at the doorway and peered inside. Curtis sat alone on a sofa, wearing only a pair of jeans, his skinny arms propped on his knees, his dreadlocked head in his hands. Empty glasses crowded the tabletops, ashtrays overflowed and a couple of booze bottles stood open. The dregs of a party.

"Curtis?"

Curtis lifted his head and tried to focus his bloodshot eyes. "What's the matter with you? You drunk?"

"I don't know, man. I feel fucked up. I'm dizzy."

"Where's the woman?"

Curtis pointed to where a hall split the space between a tiny kitchen and a cluttered dining room. "Down there. On the bed."

"You move anything?"

"I didn't touch her," Curtis said. "I mean, I don't think I did. I can't remember shit."

Tires squealed and Drew turned just as two uniformed cops bailed out of their car. Flashing lights bathed the parking lot in red and blue.

The driver put his hand on the butt of his pistol and shouted, "Hold it right there!"

Drew raised his empty hands and said, "It's okay. I'm the one who called."

"Step outside! Away from the door!"

He did as he was told. The cops ordered him to put his hands on the wall and he assumed the position, the rough stucco digging into his palms. One cop patted him down while his partner peeked around the door jamb into the apartment. Drew hoped Curtis was coherent enough to sit very still.

Two other squad cars shrieked into the parking lot and spilled more officers. Lights flicked on in nearby apartments.

"Okay, you're clean," the cop said. "Turn around."

Drew faced the cop, a middle-aged sergeant with sun-leathered cheeks and a rutted forehead. He was stocky, but at least six inches shorter than Drew's six-foot-four. His name tag said "Griggs."

"I'm Drew Gavin, the one who called 911. The guy inside works for me at the *Gazette*."

Griggs squinted up at him. "You reporters?"

"Sportswriters."

Griggs' expression softened a little. People figure sportswriters won't cause trouble because they only care about one thing— sports. And, Drew thought, that's pretty close to the truth.

He could hear other cops ordering Curtis around inside the apartment, and he badly wanted to go in there and help him. At least be by his side, keep him from making things worse.

"He called me a few minutes ago, said there's a dead woman here. In the bedroom."

"You see the body?"

"Never made it past the front door. I got here seconds before you did."

"All right. Stay here."

Griggs hurried inside. Drew waited on the sidewalk, worrying. He glanced through the door and saw the cops had Curtis standing unsteadily, his hands on top of his head, mashing the four-inch-long dreads that rose from his head like the tendrils of a sea anemone. His lean, dark body looked like a shadow against the sunny yellow wall.

Griggs had disappeared, but he came out of the hallway as Drew watched. The sergeant's mouth was set in a tight line.

"She's dead all right," he said. "Get on the radio. Get Homicide over here."

Drew felt a pain shoot between his temples, a warning shot of headaches to come. Regardless of whether Curtis had anything to do with the murder, his presence here would mean a scandal. If there was one thing the top dogs at the *Gazette* couldn't abide, it was a staffer who made the newspaper look bad. At minimum, Curtis' job was on the line, he figured. Mine probably is, too. Thanks a lot, Curtis.

Griggs gestured him into the living room. Drew stepped through the door and nodded as the cop warned him not to touch anything. He followed Griggs down the hall. They stopped just outside the open bedroom door and Drew looked past Griggs' head to see inside.

On the bed, a young woman lay on her back, naked except for a blue-and-gold leotard knotted around her throat. Her legs were bent and the covers were bunched around her feet, where she'd kicked as she died. Her skin was the color of mocha, a couple of shades lighter than Curtis', and her body was trim and firm. Her black hair fell in ringlets around the pillow and into her dark eyes, which were wide and unfocused. The lower half of her face was covered by a pompon, rain-slicker yellow and neatly spread over her jaw.

"You know her?" Griggs asked.

"Never seen her before."

"That thing in her mouth, is that what I think it is?"

Drew nodded. "My friend told me she's a cheerleader for the Rattlers, that new basketball team? Looks like the handle of her pompon was stuffed down her throat."

Griggs studied Drew's face for a second, then looked back at the woman. "Why the hell would he do that?"

"You mean the killer?"

Griggs' eyes narrowed. "I mean your friend. You don't think he did it?"

Drew shook his head. Curtis was no murderer. But he couldn't explain how he'd ended up in bed with a corpse.

Griggs stared at the dead woman. "Looks like she's got a

flower blooming out of her face. A big goddamn flower."

They returned to the living room, where Curtis was back on the couch, his hands cuffed behind him. His eyes looked wild and red and there was a glob of thick spittle in the corner of his mouth.

"Curtis?" Drew said. "You all right?"

Curtis didn't answer. Drew tried to approach him, but the cops waved him away, ordered him to wait outside. He looked back over his shoulder as he went. Curtis seemed bewildered and bleary. Was he stoned on something?

Neighbors in bathrobes swarmed the parking lot, attracted by the commotion. A couple of cops moved them back to make way for an unmarked Chevy that screeched to a stop near Drew's Jeep. From behind the wheel climbed a big, square-shouldered Hispanic wearing a white guayabera shirt. An eager young cop ran over to him.

"Lieutenant Romero?"

The square man nodded once and said, "Where's the body?"

"In the bedroom."

Drew knew Lieutenant Steve Romero well. He'd seen a lot of him during the past eight months or so, during two murder trials in which Drew was a key witness. The *Gazette* naturally led the way in covering the headline-grabbing cases, winning awards and raising Drew's currency around the newsroom. But he still wished none of it had happened. People had died, and many of his illusions had gone with them. Only in the past few weeks had he put it all behind him. Now here was the homicide lieutenant, back in his life.

Romero had hawk's eyes and they lit on Drew. "What are you doing here?"

"One of my reporters is inside. He called me. I called 911."

"You been in there?"

"Yeah. It's ugly."

Romero hitched up his pants and strode into the apartment. As he passed Drew, he said out of the side of his mouth, "Stick around. I'll need to talk to you."

Romero disappeared down the hall without another word to anyone. In the living room, Curtis was babbling, incoherent, but the cops standing around him seemed a rapt audience. Griggs was taking notes. There was a good chance Curtis was digging himself deeper.

"Curtis!" Drew shouted through the open door. The cops swiveled their heads toward him. He waited until Curtis met his eyes, then said, "Shut up. Wait for a lawyer."

The cops scowled, but Curtis got the message. He clamped his mouth shut and bowed his head.

THREE

Curtis White felt shaky as the jailer led him into a large interview room. The walls and ceiling were painted baby-shit green, and a long brown table divided the room, lined on either side by gray plastic chairs. Curtis' head pounded and his vision kept blurring. Fucking table looked like it was swimming around the room.

He'd been questioned for two hours, fingerprinted and issued an ill-fitting orange jumpsuit, but it all seemed cloudy and scattered now. His only concrete memory was the look on Fontanelle Harper's face, the surprise in her dead eyes.

His hands were cuffed in front of him, and the beefy guard grabbed them to turn him around. He pushed Curtis into a chair and told him to wait there.

The room had a narrow window covered with heavy wire mesh. Sunshine poured inside, making Curtis wince. He scooted the chair up to the table and rested his aching forehead on his chained wrists.

What am I doing here? he wondered. What happens now? How can those cops believe I killed Fontanelle? He shivered as the next question arose in his muddled brain: *Did* I kill her?

He couldn't remember. His head felt like it was full of pudding.

He looked up as a door at the far end of the room opened.

Drew, *Gazette* editor Bob Goodman and the newspaper's lawyer, Manuel Quintana, marched inside.

Oh, shit, he thought. Here we go.

The men took chairs across from him. Curtis noted that Goodman's bald head was bright red—never a good sign. Drew looked weary and worried, a muscle twitching in his big jaw. Curtis didn't really know the hatchet-faced attorney, but he'd seen Quintana around the newsroom. The little man had a reputation as a tough customer.

Curtis felt as if the three pairs of eyes were boring holes in him. The silence weighed heavily until Drew finally said, "How you feeling?"

"I don't know, man. How am I supposed to feel? I've never been locked up before."

"Did you talk to the cops?"

Curtis shook his head, which made him feel woozy. He closed his eyes for a second until his equilibrium returned.

"They asked me about a million questions. That one guy, the boss—"

"Romero?"

"Yeah, him. He looked pretty mad because I wouldn't say nothing. I thought he might slap me around."

Quintana sat up straighter. "Did anyone harm you?"

"No, man. They didn't touch me. Just said I was being charged with murder and turned me over to the jailers. I haven't even been to a cell yet. They brought me here."

Quintana nodded curtly. "Standard procedure. They have to let you see a lawyer. You did the right thing not talking to them."

"They said I'm a killer! That's not me, man. I never hurt nobody."

Quintana nodded again, but he seemed preoccupied. He opened a thin briefcase he'd carried into the room and fished out a yellow legal pad. Curtis noticed the man wore an olive-green suit, not a color Curtis would ever be caught dead in, though it looked a sight better than a fucking orange jumpsuit.

"You're in a lot of trouble, Curtis," Goodman said, his deep voice sounding like it was arising from Hell. "Particularly since you can't explain what you were doing in the dead woman's apartment."

"I'd like to explain it. I just can't remember."

"What *do* you remember?" Drew asked. "What were you doing earlier in the evening?"

Quintana cleared his throat. "If you don't mind," he said stiffly, "I'll ask the questions here. I don't know how much time we have."

Drew nodded and clammed up. He looked pissed, a familiar crease pulling his eyebrows together.

"That's a good place to start, though," Quintana said. "Back up to whatever you can remember and we'll work forward from there."

Curtis lifted his cuffed hands and rubbed at his face. He didn't feel like talking. His head throbbed and his mouth was dry.

"I was at a party," he rasped. "With the Rattlers. I filed my story after the game, then went to the dressing room to get some quotes. One of the players, Michael Bonner, told me they were going to a party. He invited me."

Quintana scribbled on his notepad. Curtis craned his neck to see what the attorney had written and saw Bonner's name in block letters, along with a bunch of words he couldn't make out. Having Quintana taking notes made him uneasy. Felt like being on the wrong end of an interview.

"Then what happened?" the lawyer asked.

"I went to the party, had a few drinks. Talked to the players."

Drew asked, "This party, was it at Fontanelle's place?"

Quintana frowned at the interruption, and Drew explained. "Looked like there had been a party there. Lots of liquor and dirty glasses sitting around."

"I guess it was," Curtis said. "Yeah, I remember now, sitting on that sofa in her living room with Bonner and Raj Davis, that big power forward. I didn't know it was her place at the time. I just went to the address Bonner gave me."

"Okay," Quintana said, "that establishes why you were there. That's important. And we can talk to the players, get them on record about inviting you. Do you remember seeing Fontanelle Harper at the party?"

"Yeah. She's Raj's girlfriend. She was sitting on his lap and they were laughing about something."

Curtis could picture the moment in his mind, but it was like a snapshot. No context.

"Who else was there?" Quintana asked.

"Some other guys from the team. Rogers. Mustafa."

"Women? Were there women present other than the victim?"

Curtis gulped at the word "victim," the sight of the dead cheerleader flashing in his mind.

"Yeah, there were women. Couple of cheerleaders, some others I didn't know."

"Do the Rattlers and the cheerleaders often party together?"

"I don't know, man. I've never been to one of their parties before."

Quintana made some more notes.

"Forgive me for asking," he said after a moment, "but was everyone at the party black?"

Curtis felt himself bristle. "What the hell difference does that make?"

"Sad to say, it could affect the investigation."

"Cops handle it different if it's just a bunch of niggas killing each other?"

Drew reached across the table and rested a hand on Curtis' arm. "Take it easy. If the man says it's important, then it is."

Curtis tugged his arm away and ran his hands over his face. With his eyes closed, another scene from the party flashed into his mind. People laughing, drinking, smoking cigars.

"No, man. There were white folks there, too. Think that'll impress the cops?"

Goodman scowled, but Quintana ignored Curtis' tone. "Can you name any of these people?" he asked. "We need to talk to them all."

"I didn't know most of 'em. Just the players, couple of the cheerleaders. I had a few drinks, playing along and all, but mostly I was just watching."

"Watching?"

Another memory jolted Curtis. He looked at Drew. "That's right. I was watching, trying to get a feel for the team. Remember? You wanted me to get close to them, find out about the money."

Quintana cut in. "What money?"

"The money behind the Rattlers," Drew said. "I'd assigned Curtis to do a story about the financing for the team. They'll lose money for the first few years at least. I wanted to know how much Scott Cerf could afford to pour into them."

Cerf! The name caused Curtis to sit up straight.

"That's right. I was asking around about Cerf, trying to see if anybody at the party knew anything about him."

The men across the table exchanged looks.

"Who did you ask?" Quintana said.

"Couple of the players. I talked to Fontanelle for a minute, too. In the kitchen. She acted like she knew Cerf, but she wouldn't say anything about him."

"You had a conversation with the victim?"

"Guess I did, though I didn't remember before now."

"How did she seem?"

"What do you mean?"

"Frightened? Worried? Any indication she was in danger?"

"No, man. Nothing like that. We just talked a little. Flirted."

"You flirted with her?" Quintana asked. "While her boyfriend was present?"

Curtis closed his eyes, tried to sort through the fluff that had replaced his brains. "He musta been in the other room or something. Wasn't like I was hitting on her. Just friendly, you know."

Quintana furiously filled the page of the legal pad and flipped to the next one.

"Do you remember having any other conversations?"

Curtis closed his eyes, trying to remember.

"I don't know, man. Everything's a fucking blur."

"What about that, Curtis?" It was Drew's voice. "Why are you so woozy? Did you take some pills or something?"

Curtis opened his eyes. "No, I would remember that."

"He said he'd had several drinks," Quintana interjected.

"This is Curtis we're talking about," Drew said. "He could

drink all three of us under the table and never feel a thing. I've seen him do it. But I've never seen him like this. Think somebody slipped you something?"

Curtis shrugged. "If they did, I don't remember it. But maybe that was the idea. Maybe they wanted me to pass out, so they could set me up."

"Why would someone do that?" Goodman asked. "Anybody there have a grudge against you?"

Curtis shook his head, trying to think.

"Maybe because he was asking questions about their boss," Drew offered. "Maybe somebody there planned to kill the cheerleader anyway and thought they could set Curtis up for the blame."

"Nice conjecture," Quintana said brusquely, "but we don't have anything to indicate that's true."

Curtis stared at Drew, his mind nibbling away at the edges of something. Something he couldn't quite dredge up. And then it came to him. The heavy jaw, the icy blue eyes, the thin gray hair slicked into a desperate comb-over.

"Otis Edgewater," he said, prompting all three men to say, "What?"

"Cerf's right-hand man. He was at the party."

"He was?" Quintana's pen was poised over the paper. "What's his name?"

"Otis Edgewater. Older guy. Used to be in the military or something. He's chief of security for Cerf Software."

"And he was at the team's party?" Quintana looked dubious.

"He told me he likes to keep an eye on the team."

"What else did he say?"

A drop of sweat burned Curtis' eye and he brushed it away.

It wasn't that warm in the room, but remembering was a strain.

"I asked him some questions about Cerf, but he wouldn't talk. Just told me to drink up and enjoy myself."

Drew grasped Goodman's shoulder and whispered into the editor's ear. Quintana ignored them, his attention on Curtis.

"Did Edgewater pour you any drinks? Give you any drugs?"

"No, man, he left soon after that. I remember seeing him go."

"But you stuck around?"

"I had another drink or two. Decided to stop asking questions and just have fun."

"And then what happened?"

Curtis closed his eyes and thought hard. When he opened them again, the three men were staring at him, waiting.

"I can't remember anything else."

"Do you remember going to the woman's bedroom?"

"No."

"Taking off your clothes?"

"No. I'm telling you, man. There's nothing there. It's like a fog."

Quintana glanced over at the other two. They were frowning.

"We'll file a request with the police to have his blood checked," the lawyer said. "Maybe something will show up and we can prove someone drugged him."

"They're probably checking Fontanelle Harper, too," Drew said. "Maybe they'll turn up something during the autopsy."

Curtis caught himself before he groaned. He hadn't considered an autopsy, that somewhere Fontanelle was stretched out on a cold steel table, a coroner opening her up with a scalpel.

"What about in the meantime?" Goodman asked. "Can he get bail?"

Quintana shrugged. "An open count of murder, it's going to be tough. The D.A.'s people file it that way so the judge will know they're considering a first-degree murder charge. Buys them some time to make their case. Until a final charge is filed, they won't like bonding him out. No judge wants to be the one who turns a killer loose on the city."

Curtis felt a scowl creep onto his face.

"Sorry," Quintana said. "Just telling you the way they think. I don't usually handle criminal cases, but I've got people who do. I'll get my associates to pursue bail, but don't get your hopes up."

The beefy jailer flung open a door. All heads turned toward him.

"Homicide's calling for the prisoner. More questioning."

"Aw, man," Curtis said. "I can't face any more right now. I can't see straight."

Quintana quickly rose to his feet. "I'll tell them you're ill. Maybe we can at least put this off until after the bail hearing."

Drew and Goodman stood, too.

"This is a nasty business," Goodman said. He waited until Curtis met his eyes before adding, "I want you to know the newspaper is behind you one hundred percent. Manuel's firm will handle the legal stuff. Let us know if there's any other way we can help."

Curtis nodded. "Thanks, Bob."

"You need anything?" Drew asked. "Anything we can do?"

Curtis stared at him a moment, wondering how to answer. "Just get me out of here," he said finally.

"We'll do everything we can," Drew said. "You get some

rest. And keep trying to remember what happened. The cops will drop the charges against you if we offer them something better. A lot's riding on what you can recall."

The men turned to leave. Curtis would've loved to walk out with them, out into the harsh sunshine, away from the clanging doors and pungent smells of the jail. But he stayed at the table, watching them go.

Drew turned and looked back at Curtis. Gave him a little wave.

Curtis tried to wave in return, but his wrists were cuffed, manacled like a slave's. His hands clenched into fists and he very deliberately set them on the tabletop. He stared at the handcuffs until the jailer called his name.

FOUR

Scott Cerf's shiny black Range Rover glided into the parking lot of Cerf Software and practically steered itself into his reserved parking space. Cerf shut off the engine with a satisfied sigh.

It was a beautiful day. The sun had melted away thin morning clouds and the empty blue sky glittered with that magical New Mexico light that attracts artists from all over the world. The silvery light glinted off cars and pickups that crowded the employee parking lot. Gangly young catalpa trees edged the asphalt, their crinkly white flowers making Cerf think of popcorn.

The building fairly glowed. A mass of pale green concrete and brushed stainless steel, it gave off all the right visual cues for a software company—solidity and speed, modernity and money. Emblazoned across the front was the company slogan—"Cerf the 'Net!"—that was well on its way to making him a household name.

Cerf popped open the Range Rover's door and climbed out, his sleek stainless steel briefcase in hand. He hadn't even opened the briefcase before he left the house. Hadn't perused his e-mail or answered his phone or checked in with his staff. The morning had been too pleasant to burden it with business. He'd spent the past two hours in solitude, grooming and exercising on his Stairmaster and drinking lattes on the balcony of his streamlined mansion in the foothills of the Sandia Mountains.

A perfect morning, really. One that promised to get only better as he entered his building for a day of making money.

Cerf whistled merrily as he passed the security guards at the door and the phalanx of secretaries and assistants who already were hard at work, pecking away at keyboards and talking into headsets. He waved and nodded as he moved among them, smiling at the familiar faces and feeling the eyes of the women follow him across the bustling room.

They always watched him, drawn by the smooth movements of his taut body, still as trim as when he played basketball in high school. Silver touched his black hair now and his lean face had a few lines on it, but aging only made him more attractive. A local magazine recently had declared him "Albuquerque's Most Eligible Bachelor." The notion made him chuckle under his breath. Eligible for what? Marriage? At forty-three, Cerf felt no more urge to settle down than when he'd been a frisky sophomore at Stanford. Not when he could have his pick of women, not when life was this good.

His personal secretary, a curvy redhead named Ramona, greeted him with a fistful of pink callback messages. She swung open one of the heavy mahogany doors that sealed off his office from the rest of the company. He thanked her as he strolled inside, just as he did every morning, and the door closed behind him before he realized that his perfect day had just taken a turn for the worse.

Otis Edgewater sat in Cerf's leather swivel chair, his spit-polished combat boots up on the granite top of his boss' desk.

He held a sheet of paper in his hands, waiting.

Cerf frowned. He set his briefcase on the desk and said, "I believe you're in my chair."

Otis didn't even blink his pale eyes. Just sat there, an inert lump of muscle. Cerf noted the way he filled the big chair. The man was broad, his neck wider than his jawline, his shoulders stretching the seams of his standard security man's blue blazer. His legs, crossed and elevated, were like fat pythons encased in gray polyester.

Cerf always thought Otis looked as if someone had screwed an old man's head onto a young weightlifter's body. His doughy nose was embraced by deep lines that ran down to the corners of his thin-lipped mouth. His tiny, battered ears resembled wads of chewed gum stuck to the sides of his head, and his eagle eyes peered out from nests of lines and pouches. Mostly, though, it was the hair, or the lack of it. Otis combed his gray hair over in long strands to cover up some of his shiny baldness, and the arrangement of those ropy clumps mesmerized Cerf. They were like seaweed arranged by tides on a beach, ever-changing, but never seeming to move on their own.

"You seen this?" Otis held up the paper.

"What is it?"

"See for yourself, chief."

He tossed the page onto the desk and waited a few beats before dropping his feet to the floor and moving from the chief executive's chair. He wandered over to the large windows, which looked out over the office park where Cerf Software had staked its claim.

Annoyed, Cerf walked around the desk and sat down before picking up the paper. If Otis had something to tell him, why didn't he just come out and say it?

The paper was a short article printed from the Web page of the *Albuquerque Gazette*. The headline: "Rattler Cheerleader Found Murdered."

Oh, shit. Not today, when everything had been going so well.

He skimmed the brief article, which said cheerleader Fontanelle Harper, twenty-four, had been strangled in her Albuquerque apartment. The name gave Cerf a chill.

The article said police had arrested a Curtis White, a thirty-two-year-old sportswriter for the *Gazette*. Cerf didn't know White, but he'd seen his byline. A final paragraph said the death had followed a party for the basketball players, cheerleaders and others. Investigators planned to question team members today.

Cerf tossed the paper onto his desk.

"Goddammit, how did this happen?"

Otis shrugged his beefy shoulders without bothering to turn from the window.

"Not sure," he said. "Wasn't what I had planned."

"Did you talk to her?"

"Some. Didn't get much of a chance. Too many people around at that party. After a while, I left."

"She was still alive then?"

Otis turned toward Cerf, stared at him with blank eyes. Looked like he was trying to keep from smiling. "Sure, chief."

"Then what happened? How did she end up dead?"

"Maybe the reporter killed her. That's what the cops think."

"Why would he do that?"

"Good question." Otis scratched his head, then patted his

combed-over strands to make sure they still were in place. "Maybe she wouldn't tell him what he wanted to know."

"The hell is that supposed to mean?"

"The guy was asking questions at the party, trying to find out about you."

"Me?" Cerf felt something drop away inside him, that here-we-go feeling of a swift elevator.

"Yeah. Your finances. Your business dealings."

"You *heard* him asking these questions?"

"I was one of the people he asked. Maybe he talked to Fontanelle, too."

Cerf rested his elbows on his desk and massaged his forehead with both hands. This he did not need.

"Think she told him anything?" he asked.

"Nah. Why would she? She had nothing to gain, talking to a reporter."

Cerf looked up. Otis was sucking on a tooth, watching him. He seemed unmoved by the bad news, which infuriated Cerf.

"Damn it, we don't need this! I told you to take care of things, but I never said I wanted her dead. Now we'll have cops and reporters sniffing around. The hell do you plan to do about it?"

Otis casually studied his fingernails while Cerf ranted.

"Don't imagine we have to do much of anything about it, chief," he said when Cerf finally ran out of steam. "The cops have their suspect. They'll ask some questions, but that's all. Long as we make sure they get the right answers, we're in no danger."

Otis' cool made Cerf madder. He took a deep breath and told himself to calm down, study the situation, examine it for pitfalls.

"Won't our new partners worry about the media attention?" he asked after a moment.

Otis shook his old head, and drawled, "Nah. This thing's purely local. They won't care about it, long as the feds don't get involved."

"What about the Rattlers? This isn't the kind of publicity the team needs."

Otis chuckled, and Cerf felt his blood begin to boil again.

"Seems to me we could use any kind of publicity. Way the turnout's been so far, a little bad publicity might be just the thing."

"A dead cheerleader? Think that'll help ticket sales?"

Otis shrugged. "Couldn't hurt. Hell, some people are attracted to disaster. That's why so many people go see them goddamn car races. They're hoping for a crash."

Great, Cerf thought, I've got a murder on my hands, and this goon's psychoanalyzing the unwashed masses.

"What about the reporter?" he asked. "What if he tells the police he was looking into my business dealings?"

"So what? Part of his job. Nothing to connect you to the killing. The cops'll dream up some motive for him, but it won't have anything to do with us."

Cerf sighed heavily. "How can you be so sure?"

Otis gave him an insincere grin.

"You're worried about him, we can get rid of him. Newspaper says he's still in jail. Be pretty easy to arrange his unfortunate demise. Wouldn't cost more than a few cartons of cigarettes."

"Jesus, no, that's not what I want. Is that your answer to everything? Kill the problem?"

Otis shrugged again, still smiling. "Worked with

Fontanelle. She's not a problem anymore."

Cerf caught his breath, but said nothing for a minute. Thinking: I wouldn't be surprised if Otis strangled that girl, even if he denies it now. He's certainly capable of killing. Hell, he'd probably enjoy it.

"She's *more* of a problem now," he said finally. "Before, we could handle her. Now, the media's involved."

Otis grinned but said nothing.

"Leave Curtis White alone. I'll make some calls, make sure he stays in jail. You talk to the team, be sure they say the right things to the cops. And make absolutely certain nobody talks to the media."

Otis nodded. "You got it, chief."

He turned and sauntered toward the door, seemingly in no hurry to do Cerf's bidding. God, the man could be irritating.

"And Otis?" Cerf called. "See if you can find anything that'll help this mess go away faster. I don't need the distraction."

Otis made his huge hand into a pistol and clicked off a round at his boss. He winked and went out the door, closing it behind him.

Scott Cerf turned slowly in his chair until he was facing the windows and the sunny day beyond. And he wondered who else might have to die before this was over.

FIVE

Drew Gavin yawned and stretched his arms straight out to the sides—a crucifixion pose that seemed particularly apt as he sat through his fourth meeting of the day with the *Gazette* brass. He'd had only a few hours' sleep before Curtis called, and he'd been stuck in meetings ever since.

Sitting in meetings sometimes seemed like all he'd done since agreeing to the promotion to sports editor eight months earlier. Before that, he'd spent as little time as possible meeting with editors, figuring little good could come of it. No real work gets accomplished in meetings. But since becoming a department head himself, he'd taken up permanent residency at the long table in the *Gazette* conference room.

This latest meeting was on how the newspaper would cover the murder of Fontanelle Harper and the arrest of Curtis White. The city desk had rushed an article onto the newspaper's Web site, but full-blown coverage was needed for the next morning's editions.

Bob Goodman sat at the head of the long table, looking as tired as Drew felt. Drew sat to his left. The city editor, Don Elliott, glowered opposite. Elliott always looked as if he'd just eaten something that disagreed with him.

Drew rubbed his scratchy eyes with his fists while he

listened to Goodman.

"I hate to put this thing on the front page, but I don't see how we can avoid it. We bury it inside, and everyone will say we're covering for Curtis."

"I don't know, Bob," Elliott said in his hoarse smoker's baritone. "Anybody else was arrested, we wouldn't necessarily play it out front. In some ways, it's a routine murder."

Drew blinked his eyes open to find Goodman shaking his bald head.

"A cheerleader gets strangled with her own uniform? A pompon stuffed in her mouth? We'd run it out front even if Curtis wasn't involved. We've got to play it big."

Elliott coughed twice, quick barks, then swallowed and said, "The publisher won't like it."

"I'll handle the publisher," Goodman said, then had to fight back a smile. The publisher, a bow-tied gnome named Parker Warrington III, was widely regarded as a corporate dickhead. Saying he would handle Warrington was like saying, "Oh, look, a grenade! Let me throw myself on it. . . ."

"Who've we got working it?" Goodman asked.

"Quattlebaum's asking around, seeing if she can come up with anything. The basic cop story's being handled by Mike Burns."

"Burns? Isn't he a little green for this?"

Elliott shrugged his narrow shoulders. "He's doing cops this week. You want somebody else?"

"Where's Teresa?"

"She's off today and most of next week," Elliott said.

"Vacation? Is it something she can cancel?"

"I asked the same question, but she couldn't change her plans. She was pretty mysterious about it."

The editors turned to Drew. His romance with Teresa Vargas was the worst-kept secret in the newsroom. They'd started dating right after the murders that had resulted in him spending so much time in courtrooms the past few months. Teresa had covered the murders for the *Gazette* and had won a fistful of awards for her work.

Drew shrugged his shoulders and kept his mouth shut. He knew where Teresa was going, but he was sworn to secrecy. He'd been so busy all day, worrying about Curtis, he'd hardly given her plans a thought. Teresa was flying out to Los Angeles in the morning for a four-day tryout with the *L.A. Times*. It was a great opportunity for a young reporter, but the thought of her leaving meant Drew had to fight to keep a frown off his face.

Goodman said, "Guess it's Burns. Can he handle it?"

"Teresa's been training him on the cop beat," Elliott said. "I'll keep an eye on him. He'll just handle the basics. Quattlebaum will see if she can come up with any angle the cops don't have. She's good at that sort of thing."

Drew thinking: There's an understatement. Felicia Quattlebaum was probably the *Gazette's* best reporter, a tiny woman with the personality of a hungry bulldog. If anyone could dig up who really killed Fontanelle Harper, she'd be the one.

"What about sports?" he said. "How can we help?"

Elliott shifted in his chair. He was a lanky man who rarely seemed comfortable sitting still. Drew had speculated before that he suffered from hemorrhoids, an occupational hazard for editors who spent all day every day sitting at computers.

"Don't know what sports has to do with it," Elliott said. "Purely a cityside story, far as I can see."

"The victim's a cheerleader for the Rattlers. The murder occurred after a team party. Seems like there's plenty for sports."

Goodman shook his head.

"Don't think so, Drew. You sic your guys on this, everyone's going to say they're protecting one of their own. We've got to look completely clean on this deal. Report the Rattler games, but that's all."

"Henry can handle the games," Drew said. "But she ought to talk to the Rattlers about the murder. At least do a sports story on whether the team will be distracted by the death, that sort of thing."

"No, we'll leave it to Don and his crew for now. Once things simmer down a little, maybe you can do something for the sports page."

Drew cracked his knuckles. The sound was like gunshots in the close room.

"Somebody needs to look into Scott Cerf," he said. "Curtis was sniffing around the team's finances. I think there could be some connection to the murder."

Elliott ran his hands over his face, clearly running out of patience. He had a plan for the coverage, and he didn't want Drew mucking it up.

"I'll tell Quattlebaum to check him out," he said. "But I can't promise anything. You know how she is. I try to tell her how to report the thing, she'll hand me my head."

Goodman laughed nervously. A lot of veteran reporters were tough to handle. They had personalities suited to their jobs: cocky, inquisitive, fiery. The traits that made them good reporters made them horrid employees. They questioned everything, especially instructions from their bosses. Felicia

Quattlebaum was in a league of her own, the queen of bad attitude. Drew remembered once when she hurled a telephone across the room during an argument with Elliott's predecessor. That guy left the business not long after, a nervous wreck. Which made Felicia something of a hero, since nobody liked him anyway. Elliott was better-regarded, partly because he refused to tangle with her.

"Don't worry," Elliott said. "If there's anything there, she'll find it."

"I feel like *I* should be doing something," Drew said. "I'm the one who ordered Curtis to look into Cerf's business. That's why he went to that party in the first place."

Goodman leaned over and clapped a hand on Drew's shoulder.

"I know that. But it's going to be all right—"

The door swung open and Goodman turned to see who was interrupting the meeting. Manuel Quintana stood there, his hand still on the doorknob.

"A bad time?"

"No, Manuel, come on in."

The little attorney sat next to Drew. He still wore the same green suit he'd worn when they'd met at the jail early that morning. Drew wondered how the lawyer could look so crisp eight hours later.

"We finally got a bail hearing for Mr. White," Quintana said. "I'm afraid it's exactly as I predicted. No judge wants to turn loose a murderer. Particularly not in a case like this, where it might look like kowtowing to the newspaper."

"So Curtis stays locked up?" Drew asked. The words tasted bad.

"I'm afraid so. We'll try again once the DA files formal

charges, but I doubt we'll get any movement from the court unless new information is uncovered."

"What you mean is he's stuck in jail until the cops come up with something better."

Quintana nodded. "So far, your friend looks like a pretty good suspect. He can't explain what he was doing in the victim's bedroom. No sign of anyone else in the apartment at the time of the murder. The police seem to think they've got him red-handed."

Drew looked around the table at the others. "Then let's hope we find some way to help him."

Goodman cleared his throat.

"We'll do what we can," he said. "But our first job is to cover the news. Sounds like Don has that part well in hand. Let's get back to work. I need to talk to Manuel in private."

Drew and Elliott got to their feet and gathered up their papers and headed for the door. Before Drew could close the door behind him, Goodman called his name.

"Yeah?"

"Stay out of it. I know Curtis is your pal, but let the cops and the lawyers and the city desk handle this problem."

"Sure, Bob."

Goodman gave him the hard eye. "You're a terrible liar."

"So I've been told."

"I mean it, Drew. Stay out of it."

SIX

Drew got home around sunset, dead-tired and muddle-brained. He'd finally stayed out of meetings long enough to get the next day's lead stories edited and ready to go, then he'd left the rest of the work to his staff. He had other plans.

But first, he needed to get in out of the wind and bring in the mail and have something to eat and take a shower. He needed more coffee. He needed to wake the hell up so he'd be alert for what was to come.

It still seemed odd to be pulling up to his father's house. That's the way he thought of it, though the small frame house belonged to him now—his name on the deed, the works. Drew's dad, Chuck, hadn't wanted to rent out the place after a stroke landed him in a nursing home. Better, he'd said, that Drew occupy the house until Chuck was well enough to come home again. Both knew that looked less likely with every passing day. He was paralyzed down one side of his body and couldn't take care of himself. The nursing home more and more looked like the last stop in his life.

I need to call him, Drew thought. Chuck listened to news radio much of the day, and Curtis' arrest had been trumpeted all over. He'd be worried.

Drew checked his wristwatch. He'd call soon, but first he

needed to calm his growling stomach. He went to the kitchen and set the coffeemaker to perking and prowled the refrigerator for something that looked edible.

The kitchen still was furnished with Chuck's things, his battered old pans and frayed potholders, the round-cornered Frigidaire and the chrome-legged dinette set. Drew had left a kitchen window ajar the night before, but he closed it now. The tree-rattling wind was coming from the south, from the direction of the Rio Grande Zoo, and it carried the whiff of exotic dung. Not the best thing for a fellow's appetite.

The zoo was larger now than when Drew was younger, and the neighborhood had changed during the years when he was in college and living on his own. The neighborhood, squeezed between the zoo and Albuquerque's once-bustling railroad yards, was known as Barelas. Albuquerque had grown into a thriving metropolis of half a million people in the past few decades, but Barelas in many ways remained a sleepy village where everyone knew everyone else, going back generations, and Spanish still was spoken in the *bodegas* and *panaderias*.

Parts of the neighborhood were on the rebound. Old storefronts along Fourth Street sprouted new businesses and the huge museums of the National Hispanic Cultural Center opened a year earlier to the south. Residents even started an annual Barelas festival, three days of *mariachis* and dancers and parades and pride.

Growing up there, Drew often had felt like an interloper, a big gringo out of his element along the northwest fringe of the neighborhood. He'd seen his share of fistfights as a kid, playing out on the streets, but things were different now. The tattooed toughs on the street corners were likely to have guns.

Cheap rents in the area around the zoo attracted sharp-eyed homeboys and money-hungry immigrants from Cuba and Central America. It was a potent mixture. Drugs were sold in the alleys and junkies whispered into pay phones deep into the night. Drew's sleep often was interrupted by gunfire.

Families lived on either side of him, good people, but he didn't know how much longer they could hold out against the changes in the neighborhood. Whenever he saw them, they had fear in their eyes.

Drew didn't know how much longer he could live here, either. He didn't enjoy the constant wariness, the way you couldn't make eye contact with guys on the street without worrying they'd take it as a primal challenge. But mostly the old house was getting him down. Living in his childhood home, with its faded wallpaper and creaking hardwood floors, made him feel like he was stuck in a high-school flashback.

He'd brought with him the important things from his apartment—his big reclining chair, his own bed, his TV and stereo and collection of pre-Beatles rock-n-roll records. But he didn't have a lot to show from a decade of bachelor living in his own place, and the rest of it now sat in boxes in what had been his bedroom. He needed to clean out some of Chuck's old stuff and finish unpacking and make the house his own. But who had the time? He worked sixty hours a week. He was busy with Teresa several nights a week. Hardly ever home except to sleep. He could live in a motel and barely tell the difference. He felt transient, unsettled all the time. Like Chuck was still living here, and Drew was just visiting.

He looked around the familiar kitchen, with its round clock and its wheezing appliances and the grease stain above the stove in the shape of angel wings. He was going in circles, as predictable as the ticking of the red second hand around the face of that clock. Thirty-three years old, and he was right back where he started.

He ought to paint the house, get some new furniture, something. Drew's mother had died in childbirth and he and his dad had occupied the house by themselves the years he was growing up. The place had all the personality of a locker room.

He sometimes fantasized about having Teresa move into the house with him, redecorating it together, giving it a makeover. But that looked less likely now. He knew the *Times* would offer her the job. She was a talented reporter and she was Latina. Newspapers around the country were bending over backward to increase the ranks of minorities in their newsrooms. The *Times* was no different.

And then what? Could he pull up stakes and abandon his father and the *Gazette* to follow her to California? Drew had never lived anywhere else, had never felt the desire. Albuquerque was his home, the site of his youthful triumphs on the football field, the place where he'd made his name as a sportswriter. His roots ran deep.

He finished off a ham sandwich he didn't remember assembling, and refilled his coffee cup and told himself to stop moping. His troubles meant nothing, not when Curtis White was facing a murder rap. He needed to do something to help. First, he'd have a quick shower, change into some fresh clothes, call his dad. Then he would do what he'd been doing all his life—he'd go to a ballgame.

☆ ☆ ☆ ☆ ☆

The Albuquerque Rattlers opened their season two months earlier, but Drew had yet to attend a game. Most days, he didn't get away from the office early enough to make the seven o'clock tipoffs. Ever since he'd taken over as sports editor, he'd spent less and less time actually covering sports. Sometimes he felt he'd been chained to his desk.

He enjoyed watching basketball, even playing pickup games with Curtis occasionally, but the Rattlers hadn't intrigued him. Like most local sports fans, he felt the minor-league team was a pale shadow of the NBA club the city had missed.

Tingley Coliseum, an old, round-roofed rodeo arena at the state fairgrounds, had been gussied up to host the Rattlers' games, but its aroma—dust and hay and manure—still was the first thing he noticed when he entered the building. He guessed the Rattlers wouldn't draw many people who suffered from hay fever.

He probably could've skated into the game on the strength of his press credential, but he bought a ticket instead. Better to sit in the crowd and get a feel for the team. Better, also, not to let Henry know he was there. She might think he was checking up on her, making sure she was up to filling Curtis' size twelve shoes. She also might let slip in the newsroom that she'd seen him here. Goodman had warned him to stay away from the Rattlers.

The arena was rigged to seat nearly ten-thousand people, including new bleachers installed close to the parquet floor that crews put down over the dirt of the rodeo grounds. Fewer than a quarter of the seats were occupied, and the empty chairs didn't bode well for the Rattlers' future.

Cheerleaders clad in blue-and-gold leotards pranced around the edges of the floor, trying to generate some excitement among the fans, but their jiggling and jumping only called more attention to the sparseness of the listless crowd.

Drew's seat was six rows up from the playing floor. The chair on his right was empty, but a middle-aged guy in a Rattlers cap and T-shirt sat to his left. He nodded a greeting when Drew sat down, but immediately turned his attention back to the game, clapping and exhorting the Rattlers.

Drew recognized him right away as a true believer, one of those ardent fans who attend every game. Hell, the guy probably went to every local hockey game and baseball game and football tilt as well. Probably had his whole house decorated in sports paraphernalia. Pennants and posters and coffee mugs and goddamn inflatable chairs shaped like football helmets, all covered with licensed professional sports logos. Drew regularly took irate complaints from such fans, who called about every trivial matter. The callers lived so deeply in the world of sports, they felt they knew everything already and the newspaper got it all wrong. The guys in the sports department had a generic name for these callers, a John Doe of sorts: Jim Shortz.

The Rattlers, who wore white uniforms edged in blue and gold, moved the ball upcourt against the half-assed defense of the visiting team, the Pueblo Warriors out of Colorado. The point guard spotted a big-shouldered forward open near the basket and fired a pass to him, but the ball slipped through his hands and went out of bounds. Jim Shortz loudly booed, which drew a scowl from the forward as he trotted back up the court.

"These guys can't do anything right," the fan said.

Drew looked him over. He wore thick glasses and a thin mustache and he had a large black mole on his cheek. He was slightly built and his chest looked concave under his loose yellow shirt. Drew couldn't help but smirk. Jims almost never were former jocks themselves, but they lived vicariously through athletes. This Jim, skinny little shrimp, no doubt would provide a running commentary on the game, pointing out every flaw, every error. As if he could do better, as if he'd last a minute in a game himself.

"You always come to these games?" Drew asked him.

Jim Shortz nodded without taking his eyes off the court. "Haven't missed one yet."

"First time for me."

"Really?" Jim glanced over. Drew worried briefly that Jim would recognize him from the photo that ran with his weekly column on the sports page, but the guy was too busy concentrating on the action on the court. "You haven't missed much so far. This team has been dragging its ass since Day One."

"That right? They got any talent?"

Jim Shortz smiled. People love to be asked their opinions.

"That guard's pretty good, Bonner. And Raj Davis, that big forward, could go to the NBA if he'd keep his head in the game."

"Which one is he?" Drew asked, though he'd recognized Fontanelle's scowling boyfriend from photos in the *Gazette*.

Jim Shortz pointed to Davis, who was trotting past as the team changed ends of the court. Davis took a nice feed from Bonner and launched toward the goal for a slam dunk, but a lanky white Warrior held his ground and Davis crashed into him. The referee whistled a foul against Davis.

"See what I mean?" Jim Shortz complained. "Easy shot there, but he goes for the dunk and charges the guy. Guy's got the tools, but he doesn't know what to do with them."

Drew studied the Rattler bench, trying to recognize players from photos filed in his mind. The coach, a young, ruddy, inept guy named Carl Moss, crouched by the sideline, the pants of his brown suit hiking up to show bare leg. *Gazette* copy editors loved Moss because they could sneak in headlines like: "Moss Grows on New Team."

The two teams' benches bracketed a long table where the scorekeepers and time clock operators and sportswriters sat. Henry was one of only two women at the table. She was hunched over her laptop, but he worried she might turn his way if his seatmate kept yelling.

"Hey, Cerf, you're late!" Jim Shortz called. "Couldn't bear to face it again?"

That got Drew's attention. He followed Jim's gaze and saw a tall, elegant man making his way to an empty seat behind the Rattler bench. Close behind Cerf, bulling his way past the audience's knees, came a watchful bodyguard, his biceps straining against a blue blazer. The guy looked as if his coat size and his age were about even—somewhere around fifty-six. Drew guessed the man was Otis Edgewater, the security expert Curtis had mentioned.

Cerf didn't acknowledge the jibes from the Jims in the crowd. He folded into his seat behind the players and focused on the game. The security guy squeezed in next to him, and Drew noted how Cerf leaned away.

"Hey, Cerf!" Jim Shortz screeched again. "When you gonna get some real players?"

Cerf didn't turn, but the bodyguard did. His ravaged head swiveled on his thick neck and he glared at Jim Shortz and Drew five rows up.

"Better cool it, man," Drew muttered.

"Aw, what's he gonna do?" Jim screeched. "Force me to watch the *Rattlers*?"

Heads turned at the scorer's table, and Drew looked over in time to meet Henry's eyes. She frowned, then looked away. He didn't know whether he was guilty of spying on her or failing to say hello when he arrived, but he'd have to make amends later. For now, he needed to get the hell away from Jim Shortz.

He went to the nearest aisle, then made his way down the steps toward the floor. Raj Davis managed a backboard-rattling dunk that made the crowd go "oooh." Drew sensed the discontent of those behind who couldn't see past him. He bent at the waist and sidled down Cerf's row, saying "excuse me" over and over.

Already bent over, Drew was near Cerf's ear by the time he reached him.

"Hi there," he said. "Could I have a word with you?"

Cerf's eyes narrowed, but he said nothing. The bodyguard leaned across Cerf's lap and held out a thick hand in the universal gesture for "halt."

"What you want, son?" he asked Drew.

"Just some brief conversation."

"And who would you be? You a friend of that asshole up there?"

Then Drew understood. He'd been mistaken for a Jim Shortz himself. The big, bald guy had seen him with the unruly fan and had assumed he was one, too.

"My name's Drew Gavin. I'm with the *Gazette*."

Cerf cocked an eyebrow. The big guy didn't move his distancing hand.

"What does the *Gazette* want with Mr. Cerf?"

"I had a few questions about the Harper death. The party last night."

"Mr. Cerf has no comment."

Drew glanced at Cerf, who kept his eyes on the court, as if he could ignore two huge men leaning across him.

"Mr. Cerf can't speak for himself?"

"Not to you, he doesn't," the bodyguard said. "But I can tell you this: Mr. Cerf doesn't know anything about the party. He wasn't there."

Drew was ready for the opening. "But *you* were, right?"

"What?"

"Isn't your name Edgewater? You were at the party where the girl was killed."

The fans nearest them were busily listening in. Edgewater noticed, too.

"This isn't the time or the place," he snarled. "You want to talk to me, call my office."

"Easier to get rid of me that way, right? Just hang up? Not have to face me?"

Edgewater's face relaxed, but his eyes were cold. "I'll get rid of you right now, if that's the way you want it."

He still held his arm across Cerf's chest, and the hand slowly curled into a fist. Drew's heart pounded. He didn't like the looks of that scarred fist. It looked experienced.

Cerf's pale hand came up from his lap and grasped Edgewater's forearm.

"Cut it out," he said tightly. "People are watching."

Drew sighed. He needed a few minutes alone with Cerf, just to get a reading on the man, see if he was one of those brittle business types who'd crack when challenged. But that clearly wasn't going to occur as long as Edgewater was in the way.

"Now, son," Edgewater was saying, "I'm putting it to you like this: You can walk out of this arena right now, and I mean without looking back, or my security guards can show you the door. What's it's going to be?"

Drew started to say something more, but he could see it would do no good. He clamped his mouth shut and turned away. Better to not make a bigger scene than he already had.

He kept walking until he was outside in the cool evening air.

Two hours later, the noisy crowd spilled out the exits at Tingley Coliseum. Drew had made good use of the interim, prowling the outside of the arena, keeping to the shadows in the gathering darkness, avoiding roving guards. He'd determined the location of the VIP entrance and had figured a way to watch it from behind the wheel of his Jeep in a nearby general-parking lot. The general and VIP lots emptied into the same exit from the fairgrounds. If he timed it right, he could follow Cerf right onto Louisiana Boulevard.

The departing crowd had thinned, and he was beginning to fret, by the time Cerf finally appeared in a shaft of light from the VIP door. He had his arms around the shoulders of two Rattler cheerleaders, and he was smiling broadly. The cheerleaders were still in uniform, and overnight bags swung from their hands. One was taller than Cerf's shoulder and wore her icy blond hair long. The other looked Hispanic, shorter and rounder and dark. They both returned Cerf's hundred-watt smile for all they were worth. Edgewater followed them through the door, glowering while Cerf and the two women climbed into a black Range Rover. He slapped the hood twice—contact!—and the headlights came on and Cerf pulled away. Drew waited until Edgewater went back inside before he cranked up the Jeep and followed.

It wasn't easy. Cerf drove his dark truck speedily and well, going east on I-40 toward the looming bulk of the Sandias. Drew followed him north up Tramway Boulevard, a fast-moving thoroughfare that slices the throat of the mountains, whose craggy faces tower to a mile above. Then it was into a serpents' nest of residential streets that slithered and dipped through the foothills. No way Drew could keep much distance between them without losing the Range Rover. But apparently Cerf was too busy chatting up the cheerleaders to watch behind him. He steered into the driveway of a modernistic house that thrust up from a hilltop. Drew stopped on the shoulder of the road and killed his lights.

Cerf emerged from the car snickering about something, and the cheerleaders' musical laughter danced up the driveway. The women met Cerf at the front of the Range Rover and he snaked his arms around their waists and led them into the house. They still carried their overnight bags. Looked like they had a big night planned, one that could last until morning.

And it wasn't a night of mourning for Fontanelle Harper.

SEVEN

Teresa Vargas was nearly finished packing when her doorbell rang Saturday morning. She skipped to the front door, anticipation putting spring in her legs. She flung open the door and found Drew leaning back against a white column on the small porch. He was unshaven and dark circles underscored his bloodshot eyes.

"You look like you just rolled out of bed, tiger."

"Pretty much." He closed his eyes and let his head tip back to rest against the column. "I was up too late."

"Come on in. There's coffee."

She grabbed his sleeve and tugged him into the apartment, his big feet slow and reluctant. Once he shut the door, she snuggled against his chest and stood on tiptoe to be kissed. Then she pushed him off toward the kitchen in search of a caffeine jolt, and returned to her bedroom to finish packing.

Teresa traveled light. Never more than one carry-on bag. When on assignment for the *Gazette*, she had to lug along a laptop and a cell phone and God-knows-what; her clothes and shoes and make-up had to be kept to the minimum. This time, she'd packed light blouses and one pair of heels and a slinky black dress in case an occasion arose. But mostly, she'd wear her usual stuff: Doc Martens boots and jeans and black

T-shirts. No sense putting on the dog for the editors in L.A. They'd take her as she was, the whole package, or not at all. She stuffed a hair dryer in on top of everything else and zipped her black duffel bag closed. She slung the strap over her shoulder and hefted the bag and marched into the kitchen to see if her ride was awake yet.

Drew slumped at the kitchen table, a mug of steaming coffee at his lips. She wished she were leaving him in better shape. She knew he was torn up over Curtis' arrest—they all were at the *Gazette*—but he still needed to sleep and eat and take care of himself.

"Ready to go? I need to get to the airport early. With all the new security precautions, you have to leave time for the strip search."

He squinted at her. "You'd probably like it."

Teresa ran a hand through her spiky black hair, then let it trail down her neck. "You'd like to watch."

Drew cleared his throat and sat up straighter. Some things work better than caffeine.

She caught him under the jaw and held him there as he rose, so it seemed as if she were lifting him from the table by his chin. Before he reached his full height, she planted one on his lips that made him blink a few times.

"Sure we need to leave right away?" he asked.

"Yup. Let's go. I've got to go wow them out on the Coast."

Drew asked three times, "You got everything?" while Teresa went around the house, turning off lights and unplugging appliances. Then they went out to the Jeep and she pitched her bag into the back.

They were underway before he said, "You *are* going to wow them, you know."

"Who? The Coast?"

"You bet. They get one look at you, and they'll offer you the job."

"On the basis of my looks?"

"Nah, I don't mean that, though it can't hurt that you look delicious. But you've got what it takes, Teresa. The energy. The personality. They'll see that right away."

"Thanks, tiger. I need to hear that. I'm a little nervous."

"Don't worry about it. You'll wow them, I promise. The hard part will come after."

She felt the smile slide off her face. She knew this was coming. He'd been quiet about it ever since the *Times* called, but the job prospect raised all sorts of questions about their future. Why the hell did he have to mention it now? On the way to the airport? No way to resolve anything in the few minutes they had left. Why even bring it up?

Drew must've read something in her face, because he quickly changed his tune. "We don't have to think about that part yet. Go out there and do your best to impress. Once they make the offer, we can sort out the rest."

Teresa exhaled loudly. She hadn't even realized she'd been holding her breath.

"I just want to take things one step at a time."

"That's the best way to handle them," he said.

They both stared ahead at the road, lost in their thoughts, until Teresa changed the topic.

"Listen, I'm worried about you. You've been running hard ever since Curtis woke you up yesterday. You need to take it easy. This thing isn't going to get sorted out right away. We might be in for a long haul."

He nodded, his lips pressed together.

"I thought about delaying this trip," she said. "Thinking maybe I should stick around, help out with Curtis, look after you. But it could go on for months. Who knows when I could get free again?"

"Don't worry about it. Curtis will be fine, and so will I. We've got the lawyers and the whole staff working it. Somebody will come up with something to get him off the hook."

He drove up a ramp marked "Departing Flights" and swung the Jeep over to the curb outside the American Airlines door.

Teresa leaned into his arms.

"Thanks for the ride. Get some rest. I'll call tomorrow and let you know how it goes."

He looked deep into her eyes, and she felt a little flutter inside her chest.

"L.A. is the big time, Teresa. Go out there and take your best shot."

"I will."

She kissed his warm lips, then quickly got out of the Jeep with her bag. She had a gritty lump in her throat and her eyes felt hot, but she turned away before Drew could see. As the entrance doors slid open for her, she glanced back over her shoulder. He still sat there in the Jeep, watching her, looking glum. She waved and walked inside, pausing only briefly when the automatic door closed behind her. Was that the sound of one life slamming shut and a new one beginning?

EIGHT

The cigarettes caught Curtis White's attention first. Two blue hardpacks of Gitanes. The guard carried them into the visiting room as Drew Gavin filled the doorway behind him. The guard slapped the cigarettes onto the table, then turned back to his post by the door. Drew pulled up a seat across from Curtis. The plastic chair sagged under his weight.

"Brought you some smokes," he said, a weak grin on his face. Looked like he was trying to put on a happy façade, and it was a strain.

"Thanks," Curtis said. A crumpled pack of Winstons sat beside his cuffed hands, and he scooped them off the table and into the pocket of his jail coveralls. "These American cigarettes are good for barter, but they taste nasty."

Curtis opened a pack of Gitanes and removed a squat cigarette and ran it under his nose, inhaling the aroma of the strong tobacco.

"Hey, guard, can I get a light?"

The guard didn't even look at him. "No smoking in here."

Curtis sighed and carefully put the cigarette back in the pack.

"Thanks anyway, Drew. These will help me get through this, man."

"Sure." Drew's grin had slipped until it hung crooked on his face. He tried to prop it up, and said, "I'll bring you some more in a couple of days. Hate contributing to your bad habit, but I'm afraid to see what you might do in here without your nicotine."

Curtis grunted, which he recognized as a jailhouse sound. Goddamn, was he already acting like a con? He sat up straighter and said, "How're things at the paper?"

"We've mobilized. City desk is running the show, trying to report the story and find the killer at the same time. Goodman's going around with this fake smile on his face, like everything's fine, fine, and no, the publisher isn't eating my ass off, why do you ask? Henry's covering the Rattlers. Otherwise, the sports department is ordered to keep out of it."

Curtis kept his face impassive as he took in this news. Drew looked weary. Anxiety crept under his upbeat demeanor, showing itself in the tightness at his jaw, his flickering eyes, his wavering smile.

"So," Curtis said, "what have *you* been doing to investigate it?"

"Who, me?"

"Yeah, right. I know you, man. You been out there sticking your dick into everybody's business. Up all night, moping and pacing. That's you, man."

Drew's face split into a grin. This time, it was genuine.

"I've been sniffing around a little," he said. "Getting nowhere fast."

"I knew it. You can't stay outta trouble. You're a fuckin' busybody, man."

"Lay off me. I'm trying to help you."

"You want to help, get yourself one of these jumpsuits and come inside with me. I could use somebody watching my back in the dayroom. I don't like the way some of those boys been lookin' at me."

Drew paled. White boy's always so easy to read.

"Anybody threaten you?"

"Naw, man, I'm okay. Long as the cigarettes hold out. Word's out I work at the newspaper. All my fellow inmates want to chat me up and bum smokes. I'm a fuckin' celebrity, man."

"Nothing like the limelight."

Curtis felt a smile flash across his own face. Hadn't had that sensation in a while.

"I'm so busy talking with my new friends," he said, " I can't concentrate on remembering what happened at that party. I've been trying here and there, but nothing's coming back."

"Nothing?"

"Oh, little snatches, you know. Something somebody said or the way some woman laughed. But, mostly, it's like I just woke up in jail. It's like a bad dream, man. I need to wake up again."

Drew frowned. "Drink a lot of water. Maybe it'll flush out whatever they drugged you with."

"They took some of my blood for a drug test." Curtis pushed up his sleeve to show the round "flesh-tone" Band-Aid on the inside of his elbow. "Said they wouldn't have the results for a week or two."

"I'll see if Quintana can speed that up," Drew said. "In the meantime, I want to find out more about Scott Cerf, see if he's somehow involved in this. You got a lot of his financial records, right?"

"The ones that were public. They're in the bottom drawer of my desk."

"Don't guess you got a chance to look them over?"

"No time."

"I'll get them. Maybe there's something there that could help the lawyers or Quattlebaum."

Curtis felt a little bubble of hope well in his chest.

"They put Quattlebaum on the story?"

"You bet. She's out there now, chewing up sources."

"That's good news. That woman's spooky. She'll tear somebody a new asshole."

Drew laughed and nodded.

"Two minutes!" the guard shouted, which pissed Curtis off. He swallowed the emotion, tried to remember the jailer was just doing his job. His second day in jail, and he already regarded his keepers as the enemy. That's thinking like an inmate. He should be thinking like an innocent man, a citizen, a fucking taxpayer. Keeping his head up. Trying to clear his foggy mind.

"You look tired, man," he said. "Go home and get some sleep."

"Sleep? I've got to go to the office, make sure they get the damned paper out on time."

"It's Saturday, man. They can get by without you."

"I'm behind on my own stuff. I spent all day yesterday in meetings with Goodman, thanks to you."

"My pleasure."

"I can catch up today, try to keep my mind off things."

"What things?"

Drew circled a forefinger in the air, a gesture that encompassed the jail and everything that led there.

"Don't worry about me. I'm surviving okay. We'll get this straightened out."

Drew nodded and got to his feet.

"I know we will. It's just going to take some time. You can help it along by remembering what happened to Fontanelle Harper."

"I'm working on it, man."

"Okay. I'd better get going then."

"Hey, Drew? In that same drawer, in with Cerf's financial stuff, are a couple of notebooks, stuff I've been collecting on the Rattlers. Look those over, too, if you can read them."

"Will do. See you later."

Curtis could see something in Drew's eyes. He was holding something back. But there wasn't time to pursue it, not with that jailer looking at his watch every few seconds.

"Thanks again, man. Tell everyone at the newsroom I said hi."

His throat suddenly felt tight. "Tell 'em all I'm doing fine."

NINE

The sports department was empty when Drew arrived, and he went directly to Curtis' desk and located the Cerf financial documents and the notebooks. He put the stuff in a file folder and carried it outside and locked it in his Jeep.

Before Drew could get back inside the building, Filthy Hogan rumbled into the parking lot in his latest junker, a thirty-year-old Cadillac landshark that lost its muffler twenty years ago. Drew waited for him outside the employees' entrance. The little copy editor came shambling up, mumbling under his breath, his thick, smeared eyeglasses halfway down his nose. His shirt looked like someone had wadded it up and carried it under his arm for a week.

"Morning, Filthy, how's tricks?"

"Bulls were ahead by three on the radio. UNM's making noises about Dengler's contract extension. TV led with Curtis this morning."

Drew grinned. "It's a beautiful day, too, huh?"

That pulled Filthy up short. He pushed up his glasses and looked around. "So it is. Lakers are on in five minutes."

Filthy hurried into the building, and Drew followed, smiling. A typical exchange with Filthy Hogan. The man had the personality of a news ticker. All sports, all the time, on Tunnel Vision.

Filthy was one of a trio Drew thought of as the Dwarves. Little, avid guys who'd never played sports themselves, but who could tell you who won the National League pennant in 1957 and by how many runs. The other two arrived shortly after Drew and Filthy had settled at their desks under the blare of crowd noise from a ceiling-mounted TV. Herman "Spiffy" O'Neil and Chris "Sparky" Anderson already were arguing some picayune point about the Tarkenton-era Vikings as they came through the door. Those two could go at it for hours, Sparky still too young and edgy not to take the bait offered by Spiffy, who was old enough to be handshake buddies with Moses.

Spiffy wore his usual black fedora and a skinny silk tie with the handpainted slogan, "I Like Ike." His pointy shoes were glossed to a high shine, and his clothes fairly glimmered. The man made Fred Astaire look like a clodhopper.

Sparky Anderson dressed like Drew and most other sportswriters in the free world: Jeans and a polo shirt and clunky white sneakers. Next to Spiffy and Filthy, he looked normal.

"Hey, boss man," Sparky said to Drew. "What're you doing here on a Saturday?"

"Just trying to catch up."

"Slow day. Mostly AP filling the pages tomorrow."

"I've got other stuff hanging fire while I've been stuck in meetings about Curtis. Things stack up."

Drew glanced over at Goodman's office, where the lights were off. He hoped the editor was home sleeping. It had been a heart-attack kind of week, and Goodman's high blood pressure was legendary. The last thing they needed was for something to happen to him. He was the buffer between the newsroom and the management weasels upstairs.

The mention of Curtis sobered the Dwarves and they settled at their desks and started to work. Sparky and Filthy scanned the wires and other news services on their computers. Spiffy got on the phone and talked too loudly for too long with a high school coach. Drew managed to clear some of the paperwork that had piled up on his desk, all the time serenaded by sportscasters marveling at Shaq and the Lakers murdering the hapless Trailblazers.

Drew's mind kept drifting. To Curtis, penned up in a cellblock, surviving on cigarettes. To Teresa in Los Angeles, maybe forever. To Scott Cerf and Otis Edgewater and cheerleaders and team parties.

"Hey, Filthy," he said. "When's Henry supposed to get here?"

"She's off today. Had to go to a wedding or something."

Drew frowned. He still needed to set things straight with Henry, make sure she hadn't misunderstood his presence at the Rattlers game.

"Aren't the Rattlers practicing today?" he asked. "Who's covering it?"

"Nobody. Goodman came by and said cover the games but otherwise stay away from the team. We figured that meant practices, too."

"Why didn't someone talk to me about it?"

"You weren't around. Goodman acted like he'd told you already."

"Yeah, he did. But not exactly in those terms. I think we ought to be at practice. I would've argued it with him."

Filthy leaned over and checked his desk calendar, which was so covered with coffee rings and black-ink doodles, Drew couldn't see how he made out anything.

"Too late now," Filthy said. "Practice started an hour ago."

Drew said nothing for a minute, then he stood and started gathering up notebooks and pens.

"Well, fellas," he said. "I think I'm all caught up. I'll leave the *Gazette* in your capable hands."

Spiffy eyed him, his pink cheeks glowing. "Got to be somewhere?"

"Things to do. I'll call in later."

The Dwarves grinned at him, not fooled for an instant. He scowled at them, but it didn't do any good. They smiled him out the door.

☆ ☆ ☆ ☆ ☆

The Rattlers were taking a water break when Drew entered Tingley Coliseum twenty minutes later. They stood around stomping and steaming, like horses eager to race. Their practice uniforms—plain gray shorts and T-shirts—were soaked dark.

Coach Carl Moss stood talking to two of the bigger players, and he looked like a yappy dog barking up at the taller men. One of the big men was Raj Davis, who ignored the coach, instead staring balefully at Drew as he approached.

Moss wore polyester shorts and a polo shirt and sneakers and a whistle on a cord around his neck. In short, he looked like every other coach in the country. Drew had spent so much time around coaches, including his own father, he'd recognize the type anywhere. They had a certain energy, a certain bluff command they couldn't disguise. Moss had it, too. He might be dumb as a bag of hammers, but he still exuded "coach."

"Hi, Coach. Drew Gavin of the *Gazette*. I'm filling in

today. Can I talk to you when you get a minute?"

Moss hesitated. "I guess so, if you want to wait around. We'll be done in an hour."

Drew was saying that would be fine when Raj Davis stepped between them and stood with his jutting chin three inches from Drew's nose.

"You gotta lotta nerve showin' up here at all," he said, fury making his low voice raspy. "One of you fuckers killed my woman."

Davis stood five inches taller than Drew, and he glared down into his face. His dark head was clean-shaven and sweat beaded on it like raindrops on a well-waxed limo. A heavy browline and hooked nose gave his face a reptilian cast.

Drew wanted to step backward, to get the man out of his face, but he wouldn't give Davis the satisfaction. Instead, he said, "I want to talk to you about Fontanelle. About the party."

"You ain't talkin' shit around here. And don't you dare say Fontanelle's name. Poor girl ain't even cold yet and you fuckers coming around here like buzzards—"

"Careful," Drew said flatly. "You'll hurt my feelings."

"*Fuck* you, man—"

"Raj!" It was Moss. He stepped between them and put his hands on Davis' chest. "That's enough. Hit the showers. You're done for today."

"I ain't done with this motherfucker—"

"*Now*, Raj."

Davis took a step backward and glared down into the coach's face.

"Don't know why you're protecting a fuckin' reporter. We been told not to talk to them. What's he even doing here?"

Drew spoke up before Moss could answer. "Who said not to talk to me? Cerf?"

"I did." The voice came from behind Drew, and he knew who he'd find before he turned around. Otis Edgewater, his muscles bulging, his thin hair arranged across his bald pate.

"Aw, shit," Drew muttered. "Here we go."

TEN

Otis Edgewater felt warmth wash through him, a tingle in his hands, a tightening in the groin. Delicious anticipation.

Lately, working for Cerf had been filled with such moments. Otis felt alive again, his blood coursing hot through his veins. Civilian life was going better than he'd expected.

A soldier's life is waiting. Waiting for the next skirmish, the next battle, the next war. Otis Edgewater spent thirty years sitting around barracks, lifting weights, waiting for the next thrill, the next jolt of combat in a remote desert or steaming jungle. But out here in the civilian world, he didn't have to wait. He could *make* things happen. And, sometimes, like with this reporter here, the challenges fell right in your lap.

This Gavin joker was a big old boy. Six-foot-four, maybe two-fifty, probably an old jock. He'd gone soft around the edges, a desk jockey now, and Otis knew he could take him as easy as a cat on a sparrow. Back home in Georgia, Otis had grown up on a diet of jocks, taking them down, feeding them their inflated egos, showing them the difference between the games boys play and the grown-up world of sudden violence.

"The hell you doing here, son?" Otis said when he was inches away from Gavin.

The players melted away, giving them room. Carl Moss, that idiot, stood his ground until he realized he was the only one within swinging distance and he quickly scurried off, too.

"I'm covering the practice for the *Gazette*," Gavin said. "I've got a right to be here."

"No, you don't. Practices are open only when I say so. And I told you nobody's talking to the newspapers now."

"You said Cerf was off-limits, but you never. . . ."

"Shut up, boy."

Otis couldn't stand backtalk. It detracted from the clarity of the moment. One man commands, the other performs or risks the consequences. Simple, beautiful. The way the world should always work. The only trick to it: You've got to be willing to kill to get your way, if it comes to that. Once you're past that, once you have no hesitation, other men sense it and know the consequences are real.

Gavin warned, "Watch out now."

The big jock wouldn't just take an insult and slink away. Jocks were like that, all that leftover testosterone and no way to expend it. They'd stand around talking about it for-fucking-ever, but eventually they'd rile if you pushed hard enough. Otis reached out and jabbed Gavin hard in the chest with his index finger.

"I said shut up, which means you'll shut up. And I'm telling you to leave now. There's the door."

The men held each other's gaze, the tension electric between them. Otis savored it, then poked Gavin again.

"Are you not hearing me, son? Is there something *wrong* with you?"

Gavin's hand came up and reached for the offending finger. Otis quickly grabbed Gavin's first two fingers and bent them back. Then he kicked him in the shinbone with the hard toe of his combat boot.

Gavin tried to dance around on one leg, but Otis' grip on his fingers was firm. Gavin's free hand doubled into a fist, and Otis exerted more leverage on the bent fingers, forcing the taller man to bend over. Otis clipped him a hard one behind the ear and Gavin went down on his knees.

A whistle shrieked and Coach Moss shouted, "Hold it! Hold it! That's enough."

Otis grinned at Moss. The worried little coach acted automatically, breaking up a scuffle the way he'd do when his players got in each other's faces at practice. Otis Edgewater didn't react to whistles, like fucking jocks and dogs. But Moss had distracted him. The moment was destroyed. He released Gavin's hand and backed away.

"You all saw it," he said, the grin tight on his face. "I had to defend myself. This son-of-a-bitch attacked me."

The players murmured among themselves, but no one called it any other way. Gavin lumbered to his feet, his injured fingers clutched to his chest.

Moss felt moved to speak up again. "You want me to call the cops, Mr. Edgewater?"

Otis glowered at him. "No need. This guy's not going to try anything else."

Gavin looked to be thinking it over, whether he wanted to take a crack at Otis and mend his wounded pride. Otis prayed he would give him another reason to exact some punishment.

But a door banged open at the end of the court, and two of Otis' security men burst in, nightsticks drawn.

Otis held up his thick hands to calm the guards.

"It's okay," he said. "This boy was just leaving."

Gavin saw he had no options. He tried to stare down Otis, who had to suppress a laugh. Stupid jock.

"I'll see you again," Gavin said, his voice low and shaky.

Otis gave him a big smile.

"You can count on it, son. And we'll have us some fun."

ELEVEN

Drew woke up stiff the next morning with a steady ache in the back of his neck. His shin bore a swollen knot. His hand was puffy and mottled purple. Every time he moved his fingers, his whole arm ached. He shuffled into the kitchen for coffee and aspirin.

He spent an hour thumbing through the Sunday *Gazette*, but kept coming back to the front-page story about the murder of Fontanelle Harper. Felicia Quattlebaum and Mike Burns shared the byline, and they'd done a nice job. All the facts were straight, though they weren't exactly news to Drew, who'd heard it all a hundred times in those damned meetings. The story played it straight down the middle, showing Curtis no favoritism. The words "taken into custody on an open charge of murder" looked just as harsh as they did in any other crime story. He wondered how many readers would simply assume Curtis was guilty. Most, probably. Even if somebody else eventually was convicted, Curtis' reputation would be shot. A man gets charged with murder, no matter how unfounded, and he draws a cloud that's with him for life.

Drew finally tossed the newspaper aside. He couldn't concentrate on it anyway. Turning the pages made his hand hurt, and every twinge prompted him to rerun the encounter with

Otis Edgewater, trying to see where he could've done better, how he should've protected himself. And he kept coming back to one answer: He shouldn't have been there in the first place. Or, at least, he should've walked out of the arena the minute Edgewater showed up. Once the confrontation was under way, there was no backing down.

Now, he just prayed Goodman didn't hear about it. The editor had ordered him to keep away from the Rattlers. His job was on the line.

Still, there was plenty he could do without coming into direct contact with Edgewater and the team. And the place to start was with the financial records Curtis had collected.

He spread the papers across the green tabletop and organized them into stacks—news stories, company handouts, stockholders' reports and Internet analyses of the company's financial performance. He stacked Curtis' notebooks separately, to be deciphered later.

It was an impressive collection of data, and he knew immediately that someone had helped Curtis gather it. Research had never been his buddy's strong suit; one of the reasons Drew had assigned him to look into Cerf's finances was to encourage him to do more with that side of sports journalism. He wondered which of the young women in the *Gazette's* news library Curtis might be seeing on the sly.

Curtis was the type of guy, in college, who got his girlfriends to do his homework. For him, it was always a net gain: more girlfriends than assignments to be completed. He could afford to parcel them out. Ten, eleven years later, at an age when most men have settled down, Curtis still went through relationships like a whiff of his expensive cologne. His languid manner and tall, slender frame and chocolate-drop eyes gave women temporary insanity. They'd do anything he asked. Then he'd drift on to the next, usually leaving smiles in his wake. The guy was the freaking Johnny Appleseed of Love.

Drew had no trouble imagining him putting a few moves on some young, underpaid library assistant to get the dope on Cerf Software, Inc. However he'd accomplished it, though, Curtis had given him plenty to study. He poured another cup of coffee and sat down to read.

First, he went through the news clippings and printouts from the *Gazette's* digitized library. These were the items he'd find easiest to understand; they were written in his native tongue, American Journalism.

The stories mostly were about Cerf himself and his successes. Scott Cerf had arrived in Albuquerque eight years earlier. He assembled software engineers in an empty warehouse and whipped them night and day until they came up with a new Web browser that was faster and easier to use. Cerf apparently didn't design much himself. He was the suit, the organizer, the man who put it all together and gave the company a handsome public face. He hit the venture capital market at exactly the right time, when flush investors were crazy to buy up any stock connected to the Internet. The company's initial public offering was a boom day on Wall Street.

Cerf took the gains and built an office-and-manufacturing complex near Interstate 25, the steel-rimmed green building that always made Drew think of money coming off a printing press. The articles reminded him that Cerf got a nice fat gift to build the plant. The city issued bonds to help finance the construction, and gave the company tax deferrals to last a decade. Albuquerque regularly gave such sweetheart deals to high-tech companies, so it wouldn't lose those jobs to some other city. Drew thought of it as corporate blackmail, but it seemed to be the way the world worked now. Cerf apparently was a master at playing the game.

Since then, Cerf had become a fixture of the society pages. He served on boards and commissions. He'd bought a half-interest in a fancy nightclub called Snake-Eyes. And he'd funded the Rattlers.

Drew stopped for more coffee. He stood at the back door and looked out into his weedy back yard, thinking about Cerf's expensive lifestyle. The man clearly had made a fortune—enough that he wanted to piss some of it away on a basketball league—but what had he done to earn the money? Near as Drew could tell, the Cerf browser had been only a moderate success. The company's stock had plunged, suffering from the same contagion that had hit other high-tech firms lately. The news stories said Cerf researchers were up to something else, high-tech stuff for the Department of Defense, but so far that was all hush-hush and apparently none too profitable.

No, what Cerf had accomplished so far was that he'd gotten people to give him money: investors, who now probably spent all their time wondering if Cerf Software would be the next Internet start-up to jump off the ledge; city taxpayers, through bonds and tax fixes that would cost them for years; and now, perhaps, the federal government, through a juicy defense contract with Sandia National Laboratories in Albuquerque.

Cerf was no computer geek. He was a salesman.

What's he trying to sell with the Rattlers? It seemed out of character for Cerf to waste money that way, when he was so good at raking it in from the suckers. Maybe he saw some new wave of the future that evaded Drew. Maybe Cerf believed that Internet success comes and goes, but sports hang around forever.

Drew shook his head and turned from the window. Cerf must be looking at the long term if he believed a basketball league would profit him. Drew had seen too many little leagues start up with great fanfare, only to vanish into bankruptcy after a year or two. Lot of competition for the sports fan's dollar. And most guys, hell, why would they spend a dime on the Rattlers when they could sit at home and watch the NBA on cable?

He returned to the table and picked up the stack of slick stock-offer brochures and corporate reports and dry financial analyses. Not pleasant reading by any stretch, but he had something in mind now, a direction to watch. He plowed through the documents until his eyes crossed, and he kept coming back to one thing: Cerf Software wasn't doing so hot. The company had debt up to its eyeballs, investors slinking away in search of bargains, and a long-shot chance at a defense contract that might take months, even years, to come together.

Throughout, Drew thinking: If I owned Cerf Software, I wouldn't be putting money down on a new boat, much less a sinkhole like a basketball league.

Cerf's annual salary as chief executive officer was five-hundred-thousand dollars, modest by CEO standards. Sure, he owned a lot of Cerf Software's shaky stock, but that money was only on paper. If he sold it, his company would fold up like a pup tent. So, half a million a year, plus whatever he makes off other investments. He wasn't sitting on any family wealth, that was for sure. All the business reporters made a big deal in their stories about how he'd come out of poverty, pulled himself up by his bootstraps, blah, blah, blah. So, the guy's got half a million a year, bunch of money on paper, expensive house and car and lifestyle, where's he get the four or five million he used to start the WABL?

The whole thing made Drew's nose itch. There was a scent there, something fishy.

He knew the reporter's creed: Follow the money. You got corruption or crime, you've got a money trail out there somewhere. And if large sums are showing up in other than obvious, public means, then you've got reason to be suspicious.

He wondered whether he should have given the documents to Quattlebaum. It was her story. But she'd probably assembled her own, similar stack by now. No, he'd keep them another day or two, give himself time to stew over the numbers. Maybe he was misreading the situation. He needed to think about it all some more.

Then he'd decide what to do next.

TWELVE

Chuck Gavin lay flat on his back in his hospital bed, glaring up at the steel triangle that dangled from a chain above his chest. The triangle was the latest indignity, put there by fool nurses who thought he needed help to sit up. Chuck hadn't needed such aid since those first weeks after the massive stroke crippled him. To have the triangle hanging over him now, like a goddamned noose, was a constant reminder that his condition was worsening.

Chuck thought a stroke was a terrible way to go, especially for an active guy like himself, a high school football coach, a man always in motion. He'd been in his mid-fifties, the prime of his fucking life, when the stroke cleaved him in half. He sometimes wished it had taken out his mind, like some of the poor drooling geezers he saw parked in wheelchairs in the halls of the nursing home. Might be better than recognizing every waking minute that your body was ruined.

He heard voices in the hall and recognized his son's baritone. He struggled to sit up, ready to greet Drew when he came through the door. And he didn't used that goddamned triangle either.

"Howdy, boy," Chuck said as Drew ducked through the doorway. "You bring me a treat?"

Drew had started the Sunday tradition of bringing sweets not long after Chuck was moved to the nursing home. Chuck had a ferocious sweet tooth, and the nurses were no help. They always told him to eat his vegetables, like that would make a damn bit of difference.

Drew held up a convenience store bag. "Oreos."

Chuck's mouth watered. He thanked Drew while his son took out the package of cookies and opened it. He was chewing before he paused to look Drew over.

The boy looked tired. That muscle twitching in his jaw. Probably hadn't been sleeping. Drew had never been a great sleeper, even when he was a little boy in Dallas Cowboy pajamas. Chuck had spent many a night sitting up with the boy, talking to him about football, waiting for his eyelids to grow heavy.

"You look like something the cat dragged in."

"Thanks, Pop. I can always count on you for the good word."

He fell into the ugly green chair that filled one corner of the room. Beneath his bulk, the chair practically disappeared, which suited Chuck fine. He hated looking at that chair almost as much as he hated the dangling triangle.

"You getting any sleep, son? This business with Curtis got you up all night?"

"Something like that." Drew folded his hands in his lap. Chuck noticed that one was bruised. "Just trying to help him out . . ."

"How's he holding up?"

"Okay, I guess. Jail's not the place for him, but he seems like he's trying to take it day by day."

"Only way to face anything."

"This is Curtis we're talking about, Pop. Discipline's never been his strong suit."

"That's the truth. I've always worried about him. He likes to party too much."

"This looks like a case of being in the wrong place at the wrong time," Drew said.

"That's what partying does. Puts you in the wrong place. People get drunk, make mistakes. Next thing you know, someone's in jail."

"He's innocent, Pop."

"Of course he is! Curtis is no killer. Even drunker than a skunk, there's no way he'd strangle that girl. The man's got no violence in him."

Drew nodded. "I think it might be something more than a party that got out of hand. I think someone killed that girl for a reason, and set Curtis up."

Chuck eyed his son. It wasn't just lack of sleep that made him look so drawn. The boy was working on something, like a hound dog on a scent. Chuck knew that look. Once Drew got obsessed with something, there was no stopping him. He'd worry it to death.

"I think somebody drugged him, Pop, and left him in bed with that dead girl."

Chuck hesitated before he said, "You know who did it?"

"I've got a hunch. The guy who owns the Rattlers, Scott Cerf, has this security guy named Edgewater. I've run across him a couple of times now. He sure seems capable of killing. I'm wondering if that cheerleader was somehow mixed up with Cerf. Maybe Edgewater needed to get her out of the way."

"This Edgewater, was he at the party where the girl got killed?"

"Yeah. Curtis saw him leave while she was still alive, but he could've come back."

"You told the cops any of this?"

"Not yet. I don't have anything but suspicions. But I'll go to them if I get anything concrete. That guy Romero, the homicide detective I've told you about, is in charge of the case."

Chuck smiled. "At least he's a familiar face."

"One I thought I was done seeing."

Chuck fished another Oreo out of the bag, and wagged it at Drew as if it were the point he was making. "This might all turn out fine. The cops will sort it out eventually and Curtis will be off the hook."

Drew shook his head. "You've got more faith in the police than I do."

"Why do you think that is?"

"Maybe because I've seen them in action more than you. They like simple solutions. Curtis is the easy answer. I'm not sure any of them, even Romero, will look beyond that."

Chuck watched Drew while he talked. His strong jaw. The worry groove between his eyebrows. The way he sat forward in his chair, stiff and awkward. The boy definitely was on the scent of something. Chuck just hoped it didn't turn around and bite him.

"You put it in the *Gazette*, they'll have to pay attention," he said.

Drew gave him a fatigued smile. "We've got good people working the story. I'm just nosing around a little on the edges."

"Just keep your nose clean," Chuck said. "Don't let Curtis take you down with him."

"I've got to help him, Pop."

"I know that, and I don't blame you. But be careful. Somebody's already dead."

"Don't worry. I'm not doing anything dangerous. I spent the whole morning going over documents about Cerf's company, stuff like that. Reading, that's all."

Chuck squinted at him. "That how your hand got all banged up? Reading?"

Drew covered the bruised hand with the other, as if he could hide it now.

"Just hyperextended some fingers, Pop."

"They broke?"

"Nah."

"You get an X-ray?"

"No."

"Then how do you know they're not broke?"

"I've had lots of broken fingers, Pop. I know how it feels."

Chuck could see Drew didn't want to talk about the injury, which meant he'd probably got it fighting. Just like when he was a kid. Chuck wondered whether he'd tackled this Edgewater fellow, but he didn't want to press it further. Drew would clam up if he did, and it would ruin their visit.

"Well, all right," Chuck said. "Your fingers are okay. You're being careful in this Curtis mess. How you doing otherwise?"

"I'm fine, Pop. I seem to spend all my time in meetings, but the job's going well."

"And Teresa? How's she doing?"

Drew's face stiffened. "She's all right. Out of town for a few days."

"Work or pleasure?"

"She's interviewing for another job. I'm not supposed to

talk about it. She's keeping it a big secret."

Chuck laughed. "Who am I going to tell? Think the damn nurses will be interested?"

That made Drew smile. He relaxed a little.

"*Los Angeles Times.* It would be a big step up for her."

"She going to get it?"

"Oh, yeah. The interview's a formality."

"And then what'll happen?"

The smile slipped off Drew's face. "I don't know."

"Maybe you'll have to follow her out there. Get a job somewhere in California."

"Aw, I don't think so, Pop. I can't see myself working in La-La-Land."

"Can you see living here without her?"

It took Drew a long time to answer.

"I may have to get used to it. We'll see. Maybe she'll decide to stay here."

Chuck waited, but Drew said no more. Looked like he was wishing it to be true.

"Hope you're right," Chuck said finally. "I like that girl."

"I like her, too, Pop. But she's got to put her career first. She's young and she's got the goods. She's got to make a run at the big time."

Chuck winked at him. "Sounds like you're talking about an athlete."

"Feels that way sometimes. The *Gazette's* a farm club for the big papers. They're always hiring people away from us. We've got a core of people, like me, who are rooted here. But a lot of the younger ones are just passing through."

Chuck felt a weariness creep over him. That happened a lot lately. It was the reason for the goddamned triangle, which bumped his head as he shifted on the bed.

"Which is it for Teresa? Staying or passing through?"

"She's the only one who can decide that."

Chuck leaned over until his head fell against his pillow, then used his good hand and foot to pull the paralyzed ones into place under the sheet. It took a while, and he was thinking the whole time, trying to find the right words.

"You might have to make her a better offer. Or you may have to follow her out there. If she's the one for you, you'll do what it takes to keep her."

Drew thought it over. "I could move to California, but then who'd bring you Oreos every week?"

"I'm not keeping you here, Drew. These nurses can look after me just fine."

"I know that. It's not just you. It's everything. This town is home."

"Good enough. Just so you know: I can make other arrangements to get my cookies."

Drew smiled, and Chuck said, "Now get on out of here. You've got things to do."

"I have?"

"Sure, you've got to go prove Curtis is innocent."

"Now, Pop . . ."

"Just be careful, son."

THIRTEEN

Otis Edgewater woke up early Sunday, still enjoying a little thrill from his encounter with Drew Gavin the day before.

He allowed himself one cup of coffee before he went to the gym at his apartment complex. There, he saddled up a weight machine and got to work. He pumped iron for an hour, but he was still thinking about Gavin when he was done. The man was trouble, asking questions about Fontanelle Harper and stirring up the team. Otis hated busybodies. The more he thought about Gavin, the more he wanted to watch him, see whether he was at all close to the truth.

He showered and dressed and looked up Gavin's name in the phone book. Sure enough, there he was, complete with his address. Idiot.

Otis drove to Gavin's ramshackle neighborhood near downtown. The sunny streets were mostly empty, the only sound the ringing of church bells. To Otis, the clumps of suckers outside the church entrances, smiling and spruced up in their Sunday best, looked like targets. A drive-by shooter could mow them all down in a heartbeat. And in this neighborhood, where bad boys in bandanas populated the corners, drive-bys might not be that uncommon.

Otis set up shop down the block from Gavin's place. The

house was a square, pitched-roof dump, looked like a house a child would draw. Gavin's black Jeep was parked in the twin dirt ruts that served as a driveway. Otis slumped down behind the wheel of his anonymous company sedan, sipped on a protein shake and waited. His muscles still were warm from the workout. He felt relaxed and ready.

He'd learned in Vietnam how to shut down his body, get total rest, while his mind stayed alert and his eyes watchful. Guys got killed all the time, dozing off in the bush. But Otis arrived in-country at eighteen, wide-eyed, and never got caught sleeping. Felt like he didn't even blink through two tours of constant firefights.

After that altered state, coming back to the States had been a letdown. No one to greet him, no hometown parades for the war hero. He didn't go anywhere near his hometown and the goddamned rubes who'd accused him of every pissant misdeed that ever happened there. Every small arson. Every dead cat. Every slick high-school boy who went home crying over a broken nose. Otis was blamed for them all. He'd spent more time with cops than he had with his teachers.

The Army had offered him a way out of that shithole, and Nam had shown him that it was possible to live at another level, a heightened existence where the senses are on red-alert and the body is a machine and life-or-death is the order of the day. Otis re-upped for another hitch and began waiting for the next war.

He settled into barracks life, worked at getting an education, craving combat all the while. He volunteered for Grenada, for Panama, but didn't see near the action he would've liked. And he kept getting promoted. Every step up the chain of command is one step further removed from the front line. The generals are so far back, it's a wonder they even know a war is going on.

Otis finished the protein drink and tossed the plastic bottle out the window. A light went out in Gavin's house, but Otis didn't move. Just stared at the house with unblinking eyes.

Fucking generals, he thought. Tie yourself to one of those suckers, and your career can take right off. Find yourself flying so far up the ladder you can't see the ground no more. Pretty soon, you're jetting all around the world, visiting embassies and whorehouses, the general's point man in his campaign toward the top of the Pentagon. And all the while, all you really want is a gun and an enemy to shoot.

It was all going fine, though, until Otis' general died. His black old heart gave out, and suddenly Otis was an orphan. He no longer had someone talking him up, carrying him. And the brass was no longer interested. He'd walked over too many people, cut too many corners, become *unpopular*, like the Army's a frigging country club. It didn't take him long to read the writing on the wall. He'd made major, but that was as far as it went. He rode along for a couple of years, but, shit, what was the point? His rank was too low to really matter and too high for them to let him go fight somewhere. Might as well retire. Go into civilian life, pander to a different sort of executive.

Sure, he was bitter about it, but he knew the Army had been good to him for thirty years. Given him a home. Given him a way of life. Given him a taste for war. The only thing it hadn't given him was a shitpile of money. And he was working on that now, thanks to his arrangement with Scott Cerf.

He wondered what Cerf was doing right now. Probably

lounging around in a silk bathrobe, sipping latte with some naked cheerleader. And here's Otis, sitting in a car on a Sunday morning, waiting for Gavin to come out of that house.

Just as Otis was entertaining fantasies of kicking in the door and dragging Gavin out, the bastard finally emerged, limping a bit—ha!—and got into his Jeep.

Otis followed him across town to a place in the Northeast Heights called the Mesa del Oso Retirement Village. He paused in the parking lot only a moment, just long enough to make sure Gavin was going inside. Then he wheeled the car around to hurry back across town.

Once he arrived at Gavin's house, he parked at the curb, then strolled around to the back door. The upper half of the door was glass—a burglar's dream. He could've just put an elbow through it, but he didn't want to leave any sign that he'd been there. He pulled a thin metal strip from the inside pocket of his blue blazer, slipped the strip between the jamb and the edge of the door and popped the old lock open.

Otis sidled through the door, casting a last look at neighboring houses. No one. Good. He wanted to look around Gavin's place, get a feel for the man. He didn't know how much time he had, and he didn't want to waste it persuading nervous neighbors he belonged here.

The door opened into a small kitchen furnished with appliances and a chrome dinette set that looked like they belonged in an antique store. He saw what he was looking for right there on the kitchen table, but he did a quick reconnaissance of the house first, making certain he was alone.

Gavin clearly didn't spend a lot of time reading home-decorating magazines. Or maybe he just didn't care about that shit. To Otis, anything beyond a bunk and a footlocker was a waste; maybe Gavin lived the same way.

A cramped living room fed into a tiny hall that separated two bedrooms. One bedroom was full of boxes, but they were covered by a layer of dust, and Otis didn't disturb them. Most of the furniture was gutshot and old. No wonder Gavin didn't worry about burglars. Wasn't shit here to steal anyway.

The dingy interior reminded him of poor folks' homes he'd known growing up in Georgia. Dusty relics full of hand-me-down furniture and tacky souvenirs and portraits of relatives nobody could even remember. Otis hated such clutter. It was one of the reasons he'd joined the Army fresh out of high school. Escape the poverty and disorder. See the world.

He returned to the kitchen and looked over the papers spread out on the table. Cerf Software financial reports. News stories about the company and the Rattlers.

Just as he'd thought. Gavin was snooping in Cerf's business, trying to tie in the Fontanelle Harper murder. That made him a danger, not just to Cerf, but to Otis as well.

He felt a little power surge within his chest. Gavin might be a handful. He was big and young and he wouldn't be fooled by a surprise attack again. Next time, it would be different. It would be more fun.

Otis smiled, lost for a moment in anticipation. Then he looked around the kitchen to make sure everything was the way he'd found it, and slipped out the door.

FOURTEEN

Drew was back at his kitchen table Sunday evening, trying to read Curtis' notes. The remains of a Hungry Man dinner sat at his elbow, and he'd nearly drained his third bottle of Heineken. No amount of nourishment could make deciphering Curtis' crabbed handwriting any easier, and the ringing of the wall phone signaled a welcome break.

"Hello, tiger. It's me."

"Hey. Nice to hear your voice. How are things in L.A.?"

"Great. The flight out here was the usual drag, but they put me in a nice hotel and a couple of the editors took me out to dinner last night."

"Did you wow 'em?"

Teresa laughed, and he thought she sounded a little too happy. Something inside him fell away. He'd stood to answer the phone, and now he plopped back down in his chair, the phone's curly cord stretched halfway across the room.

"You bet I did. I wore that little black dress you like."

"Oh, my."

"We talked for three hours! They have some very interesting ideas about local journalism, beyond the cop beat and stuff like that. I'd fit right in."

"They offer you the job yet?" Drew winced at the blue

note in his own voice. He sounded like freaking Eeyore. Not what she needed to hear.

"No, nothing like that. I'm having dinner with some other big dogs tonight. And then tomorrow I'm in the newsroom all day."

"You're in," he said, trying to sound upbeat. It wasn't easy. "Wait and see. The job is yours for the taking."

"If I want to take it," she said. "They have to win me over, too."

"How they doing so far?"

"Pretty damned good, I have to say. That dinner last night was out of this world. Fresh seafood."

"Can't get that here," Drew said. "Of course, you can't get fresh green chile out there, either."

"Ooh, tiger. You play rough. Life without green chile?"

"Be awfully bland, wouldn't it?"

"Guess I'd just have to console myself with beaches and palm trees."

"Sounds hellish. You getting any time to see the sights?"

"All day. The rental car's a convertible. I've been driving all over town with the top down and my sunglasses on."

"A California girl."

"I wouldn't go that far, but it's kind of fun to try it all on, see how it fits."

"Sounds like it."

"How's Curtis? Anything new?"

"No, it's all about the same." Drew thought about Cerf and his company and Otis Edgewater. He was tempted to tell her his suspicions, just to bounce them off somebody. Teresa had a quick mind. She made a terrific sounding board. He needed that more often than he'd like to admit.

"Oops," she said, "my message light just came on. I bet they're in the lobby."

"You'd better go then. Have a great time."

"Thanks, hon. I'll call you tomorrow."

"You'll be busy in the newsroom."

"If they hire me, they'd better get used to me calling Albuquerque all the time."

Drew choked up a laugh and they said good-night and he rose to hang up the phone. He looked at the clock, then forced himself to resume his study of Curtis' handwriting habits.

He stayed with it for a couple of hours, but his mind kept drifting west.

FIFTEEN

Curtis White lay on his bed in the jail cell, his hands behind his head, his cellmate blissfully snoring on the bunk above him. Lights out had been two hours earlier, and Curtis hadn't so much as shut his eyes since. Jail was a noisy place. Doors clanged and slippered feet shuffled in corridors. Drunks cried out in misery. Inmates called out for guards.

Curtis envied his cellmate, able to saw away through all the distractions. The boy's name was Eugene, and Curtis had him pegged as a kleptomaniac. Eugene was only twenty, but he was on his third bust for shoplifting. Poor bastard seemed doomed to a lifetime of sticky fingers and nights in jail. But his conscience sure as hell didn't keep him awake at night. How could such a scrawny little white boy snore so loud?

Could be worse, Curtis thought. I could be bunking with one of those bad boys from the dayroom, some experienced con with a taste for sodomy and the muscles to back it up. Eugene probably wouldn't top a hundred-and-twenty pounds after a big Thanksgiving dinner. He seemed in awe of Curtis, a black giant accused of murder, and Curtis did nothing to dispel that image. Better that the little man believe Curtis was dangerous. Maybe, as word got around, Curtis would get a reputation as a killer, someone to avoid. Then maybe he wouldn't have to worry so much about getting a shank in his gut.

A strange situation, he mused. Here I am, a newspaper reporter, a regular guy who didn't do anything but wake up in the wrong place. Lawyers working around the clock trying to prove me innocent. Friends backing me up. But in jail, it's safer to let people believe I'm a murderer. Feels like I'm straddling a pointy fence, afraid to tip either direction. Pretending to be what I'm not, just so I can keep my balance.

Fatigue seeped through his muscles, felt like it pulled him down through the flat mattress to the cold concrete floor. He knew he needed to sleep, needed to take care of himself while this ordeal unfolded. But sleep wouldn't come, not as long as he was in this place, with its sudden noises and its mingled odors of disinfectant and vomit and unwashed men.

Lying awake gave him time to sort through his scattered memories of that night at Fontanelle Harper's apartment, but he didn't feel any closer to remembering how he'd ended up naked in that bed with her.

Mostly, the memories that slipped through the fog were of Fontanelle. Her bright smile. The way she had of looking you right in the eye, a glimmer there of something wicked and knowing. Curtis remembered thinking she was smart as a whip, that every smile, every look, was part of a performance, one aimed at rocking you back on your heels, keeping you off-balance. Like she was standing outside herself, watching the game, toying with the men at the party.

Curtis would've liked to have known her better. Woman like that, full of mischief and pose, could be intriguing, at least for a little while. He might've enjoyed playing with her, dancing around, seeing who was better at the con job of flirtation. He'd never get the chance now.

His mind filled with Fontanelle the way he'd seen her last, dead and staring, the pompon blossoming from her mouth. He tried to drive the image away. Didn't do any good to think of her that way. He needed to remember her still alive, at the party, laughing and joking and popping off at her boyfriend. Maybe something would come from those clouded memories, something that would help him get out of this damned jail.

Eugene shifted above him and groaned. Then the snoring resumed, louder than before. Might have to do something about my cellmate, Curtis thought, reach up there and jab him in the ribs, tell him to wake up or roll over or stop fucking breathing. Something. Man sounded like a Buick without a muffler. Funny that his snores sounded such bass notes. When he talked, Eugene spoke in a nervous tenor, sounded like a teen-ager whose voice hadn't finished changing.

Curtis thought about voices for a while. The way Fontanelle's laughing, mocking voice sounded like water running. The way Otis Edgewater spoke in a nasal drawl, an air of superiority in every word and gesture. Dude always thought he was *in charge*. He remembered Raj Davis' voice, too, a throaty rumble, made you think of Isaac Hayes and "Hot Buttered Soul."

A memory flashed. Davis' deep voice clashing against Fontanelle's musical tones. The way the music vanished from her voice and her eyes flashed when she was angry. The memory jerked him upright and he banged his head on the underside of Eugene's bunk.

"Shit," he muttered as he swung his feet to the floor and leaned out so he could sit more or less upright. Eugene snored on, undisturbed.

Curtis closed his eyes, tried to picture Raj and Fontanelle, their voices clashing. Raj's expression hardening. The fire in Fontanelle's eyes. Something had gone down between them at the party, something that angered Raj and brought acid to Fontanelle's voice. He tried to replay the incident in his mind, but nothing more would come. He remembered a quick exchange of sharp words, shushing looks, Raj's scowl. But he couldn't put a script to it, couldn't recall what had sparked the conflict.

He worked at it until he felt the stab of a headache coming. He realized his jaw was clenched tight, that his muscles were tensed all over. He rolled back onto the hard bunk, let his head fall back against the thin pillow. Maybe he should bang his head on Eugene's bunk some more. Might trigger something. Or, maybe he should sleep, and let his subconscious sort out the snatches of memory.

Eugene rolled over and interrupted his snoring long enough to smack his lips and slur out a word. Sounded like he said, "Mine."

Curtis sighed and closed his eyes, but sleep would not come.

SIXTEEN

Another journalism rule Drew always followed: If you really want to understand somebody, talk to his competitors. Friends will feed you the same old chin music, but enemies often speak the truth.

From his Sunday reading, he'd gotten a sense of how cutthroat the software industry could be. Cerf had plenty of rivals. And one was right here in town.

Mertek Industries was the brainchild of Wally Mertz, a true computer nerd who'd known Cerf since college at Stanford. In many ways, their careers were parallel. Both had grown up poor in California. Both were big brains who'd gone to college on academic scholarships. Both had ended up in Albuquerque, the new Silicon Valley, running their own software companies.

Drew had seen an inkling in one of the articles, a snide comment from Mertz, who was identified as Cerf's chief competitor in the defense software arena. The reporter who'd written the story had done his legwork; he'd gone to the enemy for a quote. And Drew got the benefit.

First thing Monday morning, he showed up unannounced at the corporate headquarters of Mertek Industries, a sleek, black wedge in an office park on Albuquerque's booming north side. His arrival caused a stir among the armed guards in the lobby. He had no appointment. He had no clearance. At times like these, a press badge comes in handy. Phone calls were made. After an uncomfortable fifteen minutes of standing around the lobby, trying to look official, Drew was greeted by a harried young brunette who was as wide as she was tall. She introduced herself as Phyllis Gustafson, and said she was with the company's public relations office. He had expected her, or someone just like her, to take him to Mertz.

She led him through a maze of cubicles lit by the glow of computer monitors and down a long hall, all the while sputtering about how she would've been more prepared if she'd only known he was coming.

Drew said as little as possible, letting the little teapot of a woman steam. He told her only that he needed to see Mertz and that it was confidential.

The fact that he was the *sports* editor at the *Gazette* seemed to have evaded these people. All they knew was that he represented the newspaper, and they were ready to trot out whatever dogs and ponies he wanted in the show. Everyone wants publicity, even software magnates hidden away in the bowels of Death Star office buildings. And nobody likes to be surprised by the sudden arrival of a reporter. It suggests *60 Minutes* journalism, springing things on people, catching them in the act. Bad publicity can be a killer.

"You're lucky Mr. Mertz is even in town," Phyllis Gustafson said over her shoulder as she pushed through a set of double doors. "He's been traveling a lot lately. I'm surprised he could even work you in today, but he said he could spare a few minutes. I hope you weren't needing longer than that?"

She raised her eyebrows, still trying to get Drew to reveal

what he wanted with Mertz. He smiled at her.

"Shouldn't take long. He'll probably throw me out."

Her mouth went round in her round face, but she caught herself and turned a corner into a swank reception area starring a hip, black-clad secretary who had a ring through one nostril. Phyllis introduced her as Mr. Mertz's personal assistant, Cassandra. Drew shook the receptionist's limp hand and gave her a smile. She remained properly bored.

More reporter lore: Always be nice to the secretaries. They're the ones who really run things. You might need them later.

Phyllis Gustafson seemed a little flustered at letting Drew out of her custody, but Cassandra coolly led him through one last set of doors and into the inner sanctum of Wally Mertz.

It looked like a cross between Dr. Frankenstein's laboratory and Pee-Wee's Playhouse. The open room was maybe forty feet square and it reached up twenty feet to where orange girders held up the flat roof. The floor was scuffed oak parquet and somebody had used masking tape to mark off a shuffleboard court in the center of the room. A billiard table stood off to one side, buried under teetering stacks of computer printouts. Two dart boards decorated one windowless wall, and the wall showed the pincushion evidence of frequent play. A hat tree sported a dozen different baseball caps, topped by a plastic Darth Vader helmet.

Cables littered the floor, some bundled together like fat snakes, others slithering off singly or in pairs between overstuffed, cartoony armchairs that sprang up haphazardly in the room like fat blue mushrooms. Along the walls, tables and shelves held every manner of computer and monitor and digital device and electronic gizmo. Sitting at one of the long tables, pounding on a computer keyboard, sat the grand poobah of Mertek, Wally Mertz.

He looked like Alley Oop. A short, stocky guy perched on the lip of a steno chair that threatened to roll out from under him at any moment. Lank black hair that hung down past his ears. A square face and a heavy brow and a long upper lip. A jagged beard along his jawline. Big forearms, muscled up from typing. Not at all the nerd Drew had expected.

He dressed like one, though. A black Metallica T-shirt and ratty jeans and oversized running shoes. The guy had to be at least forty, but he'd skipped the suit-and-tie route in favor of life in a teen-aged version of virtual heaven. Drew half-expected to turn around and see bunk beds against a wall.

Mertz finished what he was doing—the frames on the screen flashing away so rapidly Drew barely got a glimpse—and rose from the chair. He wasn't much taller standing than he had been sitting down, and Drew tried not to loom over him as they shook hands.

Mertz dismissed Cassandra with a wave of his stubby fingers and led Drew over to two of the plump armchairs. The chairs didn't exactly face each other, but were more or less in the same quadrant of the big room. Drew pulled a notebook from his hip pocket before he sat down. Mertz took the other chair, pulling his feet up and sitting cross-legged.

"Taking notes, eh?"

Drew tried smiling. "Never can tell when somebody will say something interesting."

"Can't imagine what I might say that you could use on the sports page."

Drew cringed.

"I'm a big sports fan. I read your columns. They're good. No bullshit. I like that."

"Thanks. I didn't, uh, really mention that I was sports editor when I was trying to get in to see you."

"I know. A little subterfuge, eh? Shows creativity."

The guy talked in staccato spurts, hardly moving his wide, lipless mouth. The brevity made Drew think of e-mail. Mertz definitely spent too much of his life sitting at computers.

"Had to see what you were up to," Mertz muttered. "The sports editor! Probably not much interested in software, are you?"

"No. This is a personal matter."

"My life's an open book."

"Well, it's less about your life than somebody else's."

"Yeah? Who's that?"

"Scott Cerf."

Mertz narrowed his eyes. "What about him?"

"Most anything you can tell me would help. About his company and what it does. Or about him and the Rattlers."

Mertz stared intently for a moment, and Drew imagined circuits firing behind his dark eyes. He felt as if he was playing chess against a computer. Mertz stayed two moves ahead of him.

"This somehow connected to Curtis White?"

Drew nodded, but his neck felt stiff. This wasn't going the way he'd hoped. He wanted to ask his questions about Cerf, then get the hell out of there without talking about Curtis or the *Gazette* or who was really handling the Fontanelle Harper story. But Mertz was too astute for such half-assed attempts. Might as well tell him the truth.

"Curtis is my best friend," he said. "I'm also his boss. Before he got arrested, he was looking into Cerf's finances, trying to find out how he's funding the Rattlers."

He paused, and Mertz said, "You think Cerf had the cheerleader killed?"

Drew gulped. That's exactly what he'd been thinking, but he didn't want to say it out loud. It seemed ludicrous. Rich guys like Cerf almost always had better solutions to their problems. They could buy their way out of trouble.

"May be no connection at all," he said. "Curtis didn't kill that woman, but whoever did could be linked in some way to the Rattlers. And to Cerf."

Mertz scratched at the fringe of beard along his jawline. He looked like a dorm rat who'd overslept for his final exam. But the circuits still fired inside his head.

"So you come to me. Figure I'll give you all the dirt on Cerf."

"Not dirt. Just information."

"Try me."

"I was looking over a bunch of Cerf Software's financial papers, and it looked like they're not doing so hot."

"They're not." Merriment danced for a moment in Mertz's eyes, but he kept his expression deadpan.

"So how can Scott Cerf suddenly afford to throw millions down the Rattler hole?"

"He can't."

"Then—"

"Cerf's a gambler. He's gone deep in debt to start his basketball league. And he's spending like crazy to beef up his R&D department."

Mertz just let that hang there, but Drew could take a hint.

"Research and development, right? Why's he beefing that up?"

"To compete with me." Again, Mertz almost smiled. He looked like a kid caught doing something, trying to keep a straight face.

"For what?"

"For a thirty-million-dollar government contract."

"Damn."

"Lot of money. We're both bidding on the contract. Winner take all. Couple of California companies are after it, too, but Sandia would rather work with us local guys."

"What's the contract for?"

"Virtual reality software."

"For the military?"

"Sure. They use it all the time. Flight simulators, things like that."

"But you've got something new."

"Yep. Cerf's after the same concept, but we're getting there first. I'm gonna bury him."

Drew grinned, but Mertz let no amusement show on his face. He was serious.

"Hard words," Drew said.

"Just the facts, ma'am. Let me show you something."

Mertz uncoiled from the chair and hurried across the room to a computer terminal. He sat down and was pecking through commands before Drew caught up to look over his shoulder.

"Watch this."

Mertz hit "enter" and a landscape flashed onto the screen, a long stretch of pale desert, empty except for sandy hummocks of mesquite.

"Looks like southern New Mexico."

"It is. White Sands Missile Range. But you could use any landscape."

The view on the screen began to tilt, the land's surface lifting until it split the screen horizontally. The display showed as much of what was underground as it did of the upper world. The underground sections were colored to show different layers of sediment and stone.

Then the world blew up. An explosion roiled up within the center of the desert landscape, the air filled with dust and fire. Shock waves rippled underground, cracking the layers, rearranging the Earth.

"A nuclear blast," Mertz said. "Small one."

"Jesus."

"See how the force of the blast expanded from the center?"

"Yeah." Drew sounded hoarse.

"That's what we're trying to get at. What a bomb will do to the subsurface, how far will the destruction spread, radiation patterns, the works."

Mertz clicked a button and the original landscape was restored. Drew blinked at the virtual miracle.

"And this is it?" he asked, pointing at the screen.

"Shit, no. That's old stuff. Any eighth-grader could come up with a visual like that. The stuff we're working on, it's all top-secret material. But this gives you the idea. Simulated atomic blasts. Virtual reality."

"Why's it worth thirty million?"

"Ah, that's the other dimension. The third dimension, in fact."

Mertz got up from the computer and led Drew back to the armchairs. Drew realized he'd left his notebook sitting there, and he picked it up. He didn't have the first idea what to write, but it felt comfortable in his hand.

"We're doing these simulations in 3-D," Mertz said. "Look at the old stuff, and it's a pancake, flat to the limitations of the screen. Ours is a nice, round ball. We can show how far the blast will go in every direction, including how high up and how far underground. You can turn it around, study it every which way."

"And that's important."

"Sure. Scientists work on bombs, they need to know exactly what they'll do. They don't want to blow up their own soldiers. They don't want to unleash radiation into civilian areas. Any more than necessary."

"Don't they already have this information?"

"Some. But not for the new stuff. Years ago, they had a new weapon, they'd take it out to some atoll and blow it up, see how it did. Can't do that anymore. Test ban treaties. Environmental hazards. Bad vibes. It's all done with computers."

"And this is what Cerf's working on?"

"You bet. If he doesn't get that contract, his whole company goes down the tubes. He's overextended."

"And you're going to beat him out of it."

Mertz nodded.

"Here's the deal: My company's in good shape. Got a lot of different projects under way. We don't land this contract, maybe I don't get a bonus at the end of the year. Big deal. But if Cerf doesn't get it, he's doomed."

Drew studied the impassive little geek for a minute before he said, "Why do I get the feeling that his doom would make you a happy man?"

Mirth illuminated Mertz's eyes again, but all he said was, "For the record?"

"You see me writing anything down? This is to help my friend, not for a story."

"Don't see how it can help your friend." Mertz took a deep breath and blew it out his nose. "Don't see how it can hurt, either. Just don't repeat it."

"Agreed."

"I went to college with Scott Cerf. He was a showboat, a frat boy, always pulling pranks on people. I couldn't stand him. I made a pact with myself. One day, I'd best him. It's been a long time, but I'm finally there. We win this contract, and Scott Cerf won't be gloating anymore."

Drew said nothing for a moment, busy absorbing what he'd been told.

"You've built your whole life around a college grudge?"

"Not really. If Cerf had never existed, I'd probably be right here, doing what I'm doing. I'm good at it. It feels right. Having him here, at my mercy, that's just icing on the cake."

"A thirty-million-dollar cake."

Mertz finally allowed himself a smile. It made his mouth even wider, like a chimp's. No wonder he didn't do it often.

He said, "People should teach their children: Be careful who you torment when you're growing up. Someday, it might cost you."

SEVENTEEN

Drew reached the office shortly after ten, still early by morning newspaper standards. The sports department's desks were empty. No eavesdroppers around. Perfect.

He fell into his chair and got busy, flipping through his Rolodex while his computer booted up. He found the number he was seeking and dialed it.

"Paul Davenport, please," he said when a woman answered.

While he was on hold, he looked around the newsroom. Rows of beige desks and blank-eyed computers stretched away across the long, open room. A couple of reporters—Benjamin Dover and the ever-present Bill Morrison—already were drinking coffee and jawing around the city desk. Morrison saw Drew looking and they exchanged a little wave, but he kept talking with Dover at the far end of the newsroom. All the other desks were empty. Teresa's looked especially vacant.

Drew noticed that the light was on already in Bob Goodman's office. Goodman practically lived at the newspaper building, and his schedule no doubt was worse now that Curtis was in jail.

"This is Davenport."

"Hi, Paul. Drew Gavin here. How've you been?"

"Drew! Haven't talked to you in months. I'm doing fine. You?"

"Okay, I—"

"How come we don't see you at the poker game anymore?"

Davenport was one of a mixed bag of guys—a couple of journalists, an advertising exec, a college professor, a photographer—who met weekly for poker games that went deep into the night. Drew had been a regular for a while, but hadn't attended often in the months since he became sports editor. The new job kept him too busy. And his nights were mostly occupied with Teresa. He'd enjoyed the card games, but he didn't miss them much. Truth was, he wasn't a very good poker player. On more than one losing night, he'd offered to just mail his money to the other guys, but they insisted it was more fun to fleece him in person.

Davenport was an oddity in the group. An honest-to-God rocket scientist. A tall man in his sixties, he'd worked at Sandia National Laboratories for decades. The other cardplayers sometimes kidded him about building bombs, but Davenport would just smile his thin smile and keep raking in the pots. He never talked about his work. Drew wasn't sure Davenport could help him now, but he was one of the few people Drew knew from among the thousands who worked at the labs.

"I've been pretty busy, Paul. First, because of my promotion. And now one of my reporters has landed in jail."

"I heard about that."

"Well, this is kind of a long shot, but I think the murder might somehow be connected to Sandia."

Davenport let a low whistle escape into the phone.

"How's it connected?"

"I'm not sure yet. I need to find out about a contract that's floating around over there. Virtual reality software. My understanding is that it's a big contract and the competition for it is fierce."

"How big?"

"Thirty million."

Davenport whistled again, but Drew imagined that he kept his poker face on the whole time.

"How could that be connected to the murder of a cheer-leader?"

"Like I said, odds are it's nothing. But the contract's being sought by the guy who owns the basketball team. Scott Cerf. The timing seems funny to me. I was hoping to get some information about the competition for that contract."

He didn't answer right away, and Drew expected a "no" from his close-mouthed friend. Davenport finally said, "This isn't my area, but I may be able to steer you to someone."

"That would be great."

"There's an auditor over in Contracts, a numbers whiz named Sylvia Smith. I've met her a few times. Very smart."

"And this would be in her area?"

"Maybe. If not, she'll know where to turn. Only thing is, I don't know how much she'll be willing to tell you. Lot of our contracts are classified. And nobody talks about what goes on behind the scenes among the bidders."

"Can we at least give it a shot?"

"Sure. If you think it'll help . . ."

Davenport's voice faded away. Drew heard papers rustling in the background.

"Here's her number. Let me call her for you, break the ice. If she won't do it, I'll let you know. You're at your office?"

"Yeah. Thanks, Paul. I appreciate the help."

"You're welcome. Just come back to the poker game soon. We miss you."

"You miss my money."

"Yeah, mostly that. Talk to you soon."

Drew hung up the phone and turned to his computer terminal. He edited a Stanley Cup preview Sparky Anderson had left in his file the night before. Nice piece of work, and Drew didn't have to rewrite it much, though he wondered yet again if Sparky would ever learn the difference between "their" and "they're." Drew fixed the grammatical mistakes, inserted a comma or two, and tightened up the last few paragraphs where Sparky rambled a little. He was nearly done with the piece when his telephone rang.

"Sports. Gavin."

"Mr. Gavin? My name's Sylvia Smith. Paul Davenport asked me to call you?"

Drew had heard the word "auditor" and the name "Sylvia Smith," which rolled off the tongue like oatmeal, and he'd immediately filed her away in his brain as a dowdy older woman. But this voice was young and high-pitched and nervous.

"Thanks for calling. I'm trying to get some information on a contract over there at Sandia."

"Paul told me."

"Think you can help me?"

"I'm not sure. I'd need more information."

"Why don't we meet for lunch? I'll tell you what I know, and you can tell me what more I need to know."

She laughed. A quick, sharp sound. "I'll show you mine and you show me yours?"

"Something like that."

"All right. But I'm warning you: I may have to turn you down after I hear what you're interested in."

They made plans to meet midway between their two offices at El Patio, a Mexican place near the University of New Mexico. Sylvia knew the restaurant, and agreed with Drew that it would be noisy enough that no one would overhear their conversation.

"I'll wait for you outside," Drew said. "I'm a real big guy with dark hair."

"I'll find you," she said confidently, and hung up without giving Drew a description of herself. That made him a little uneasy. She might show up, look him over and decide no way was she talking to this mook. Or, she might not show up at all.

And then what?

EIGHTEEN

Sylvia Smith spotted him when she still was half a block away. A hulking man, standing outside the gate to the restaurant's fenced patio, a sheaf of papers dangling from his big paw. He wore jeans and sneakers and a striped polo shirt, and Sylvia thought he looked like an oversized kid, waiting around in the shade of the elms that lined the street, kicking at a pebble on the sidewalk.

So far, so good. She'd never talked to a reporter before, and she wasn't certain she wanted to do it now. But this guy looked all right. Big and bluff and normal.

He looked up as she approached, and she felt his eyes rake down her. He looked away quickly, trying not to stare, and Sylvia had to give him credit for that at least. Better than most men.

She ought to be used to it by now. She was twenty-six years old, and men's eyes had followed her since junior high, from the moment her tall, lean body blossomed in all their favorite places. Her hair was naturally blond, her eyes unnaturally green, and her lips had the sort of fullness that other women paid surgeons to inject.

Some women, so blessed, would use their looks to their advantage, but Sylvia tried to play it down. She wore serious clothes. She wore her hair pulled back. She wore very little make-up. Sometimes, she resorted to horn-rimmed glasses she didn't really need. Anything to keep the men's minds off her and on business.

It's hard enough for a woman to be taken seriously in the workaday world, but especially in the mystical circle of numbers crunchers. Most of her colleagues were Ancient Geeks, slide-rule junkies who were already old when she was born, and who never in their lives had a chance to interact with a woman who looked like Sylvia. They didn't know what to do with her in their midst.

Other men were worse. The leers. The nudging elbows. The hoots and grunts of the lower primates. Sylvia tried to ignore them as much as possible. She tried to act as if she looked just like everyone else.

The reporter's eyes widened when she tapped him on the shoulder and he turned to find her standing there in his shadow.

"Drew Gavin?"

"Um, yeah. Sylvia?"

"That's me."

He looked her over again, but he was polite about it, spending most of his time on her face.

"You're not what I was expecting," he said.

"No? What were you expecting?"

"A little old lady with her glasses hanging around her neck on a chain. Sitting behind one those big old adding machines with a crank."

His glance ran down her again and, she couldn't help it, she looked, too, as if she would suddenly see what men found so captivating. She stood with her head bowed, feeling her cheeks warm as the silence grew between them.

"Is that the way I sounded on the phone?"

"Not at all. I just, I don't know, I guess I got an impression in my head."

"You mean, like, a dent?"

He laughed, and she could look up again. He looked nice when he smiled.

"I've taken more than my share of shots to the head," he said. "Probably all kinds of dents up there."

A hostess greeted them and led them inside the restaurant, which was in an old pitched-roof house squeezed between other buildings. The place had a few paintings on the walls, but it was about the least atmospheric Mexican restaurant in town. What kept Sylvia coming back was the cold beer and the hot, hot chile.

They were seated at a table for two in a corner, which she took as a good sign. Less chance of being overheard. She didn't recognize anyone, but that didn't mean the guy at the next table wasn't a security type at Sandia. The labs were huge. Sometimes, it seemed half the city worked there.

"I'm still not sure I should be talking to you," she said. Her voice sounded quavery. She didn't like that. She cleared her throat. "I mean, talking to the newspaper."

He looked up from his menu and smiled at her. "Let's eat first, then talk business. You can tell me about yourself."

"For the record?"

"No. To make the meal more pleasant. Just for fun."

Sylvia was surprised to find that it *was* fun. Drew Gavin was a good listener. She hesitated at first, but soon she was telling him about growing up in Iowa and going off to school in Arizona and how she followed a friend to New Mexico and got a job at the labs. She'd been in Albuquerque for two years, but didn't feel as if she knew the city very well. She spent most of her time working, which had stifled her social life.

Drew raised an eyebrow when she got to that part of the story, as if he couldn't believe a nice-looking woman could feel lonely, and she hurriedly changed the subject.

He was a good talker, too, once she started asking him questions. He told her about being a football player, a sports editor, a hometown boy. She liked the way he looked her right in the eye when he spoke.

By the time they'd covered all the bases, her food was nearly gone and Drew had pushed his plate away. An hour had flown past. She'd forgotten how that felt, to be caught up in conversation with a man. It had been a while. She realized she'd missed it.

Drew rested his big hands on the tabletop, and Sylvia studied them. He wore no wedding ring, and his ring finger showed no telltale stripe in his suntan. She wondered if he'd ever been married and, if not, why not. He seemed to be what her mother would call "a good catch." Maybe he was like Sylvia, married to his job. His other hand was bruised and puffy around the knuckles. She wondered what had happened there, but she didn't ask.

Drew glanced around before he said, "Guess it's time to get down to business."

Sylvia sat up straight and tried to clear her head. She'd enjoyed the conversation so much, she'd allowed foolish notions to intrude. She reminded herself of the inherent danger of talking to this reporter, especially these days. Since the fiasco of the failed espionage prosecution against Los Alamos scientist Wen Ho Lee, security at the defense labs was tighter than ever. The feds searched furiously for anybody they could nail for leaking secrets. She needed to be on her toes.

He told her about Cerf Software and Mertek Industries and their competition to win a thirty-million-dollar software contract. She hadn't seen such a contract go out to bid, and she felt disappointed. She'd like to be able to help him.

"I'm sorry, Drew, but I don't know anything about this. I wish I did."

A cloud passed over his face for an instant, but he chased it away with a smile that was as tentative as a rainbow.

"Oops," he joshed, "Guess I've been wasting your time."

"No, I've been wasting yours. Unless it would help to give you some general information about how the contracts work, stuff like that."

The waitress dropped the check on the table as she flew past, a tray held high in her other hand. Drew scooped it up before Sylvia could reach for it, and stuck it in his shirt pocket.

"Anything would help," he said.

"Okay." She cleared her throat, wondering where to begin. The bidding process was complicated.

Drew seemed to read her mind. "I just need the big picture. Tell it to me like I'm eight years old."

She smiled. "I didn't bring my crayons."

"Damn. Well, do the best you can."

She took a deep breath. "Defense contracts work like other government contracts, up to a point. The department decides it needs something, and it puts out a request for bids. Companies draw up proposals that show how they could supply the need, whether it's a product or a service, and how much they would charge. The department opens the bids and awards the contract to the low bidder. You with me so far?"

He grinned. "Walking right alongside you."

"Okay, here's where it gets trickier. A lot of the contract process for Defense falls outside the laws for public records because the stuff's considered top-secret. But the bid request might be in public files. Depends on whether the proposal was generated inside or outside the lab."

Drew looked confused.

"Sometimes," she said, "Defense doesn't know it needs something until a company points it out. Take one of your software companies. They'll develop some new way to do research. Then they'll come to us with it, show us the military applications. The department then puts out a request for bids to see if anybody else can offer the same software cheaper. Still with me?"

"You've pulled a little ahead, but I can still see your tail lights."

She felt herself blush and quickly continued, "We've got proprietary information here. The company owns the software and doesn't want anyone else to know about it. But it has to tell Defense some details so a request for bids can be assembled. And Congress often has to approve an appropriation. A lot of information leaks out. So, if I'm another company, one that specializes in the same field, I'll try to come up with my own version of the software and beat the original guy to the punch."

Drew mulled this for a moment. "Doesn't seem fair, does it?"

"No, but that's the way the game is played. Companies go to great lengths to hide their secrets, and their competitors try to discover those secrets and duplicate them. There's a lot of industrial espionage going on out there. The government looks the other way because it's the ultimate beneficiary. It gets a new product at a lower price."

Drew ran a hand through his short hair.

"That sounds exactly like the situation between Cerf and Mertek. I wish I could find out which one of them had the idea first. Who's stealing from whom."

A yawn suddenly tore at his face. He covered his mouth with one hand, and the other arm shot out straight to stretch. He arched his back, and Sylvia could see the muscles in his shoulders moving underneath his soft shirt. Damn, she liked the way he looked, liked it even better now that she'd gotten to know him a little. She wanted to get to know him even better. One way to guarantee that would happen.

"I could look into it for you," she said. "See if I can at least get my hands on a copy of the bid request. That might give me some ideas. And if either company has already put in a preliminary proposal, I might be able to get hold of one."

"You could do that?"

"I could try."

He smiled broadly. "That would be great."

"Think it will help your friend? The one's who in jail?"

"To tell you the truth, I don't have the slightest idea. But maybe Curtis was getting close to something, so close that somebody had to set him up. Get him out of the picture."

"Why don't you ask him?"

"I will. But he might not have realized what he'd stumbled onto. Knowing Curtis, it would have to bite him on the butt to get his attention."

She laughed, and felt a bubble of excitement inside her chest. She could hardly wait to get back to the office and start plowing through documents.

She'd help this man, for all the wrong reasons. She'd help him because she was attracted to him. Because he was handsome. For all the superficial reasons people constantly judged and underestimated Sylvia herself. The hypocrisy of it nearly made her laugh out loud.

"I'll call you as soon as I have anything," she said.

"Oh, here," he said, handing her the sheaf of papers that had sat beside him on the floor through the meal. "These are copies of all the financial documents on Cerf that my friend had collected. Maybe you can make heads or tails of them. Better than I could anyway."

He set the papers on the table and she reached for them. Before she could pick them up, he rested his warm hand on top of hers. Their eyes met.

"Thank you."

Sylvia paused, enjoying the moment, then pulled her hand away.

"I'll call," she promised.

NINETEEN

Drew's long lunch threw his day out of whack. When he got back to the office, he found that copy had backed up in the pipeline, two of his sportswriters were on the verge of fisticuffs, and his desk was buried under a flurry of pink phone messages. And, of course, Bob Goodman wanted him in another meeting.

By the time he plowed through all the work and three more meetings, it was dusk. He said good-night to the Dwarves and stumbled out to the parking lot, so tired he could barely lift his feet.

His head was swimming. So much input all day long, so many decisions, so many mind-numbing meetings. He'd barely had a moment to think over what Sylvia Smith had told him.

He was playing a long shot, and he knew it. The chances that Scott Cerf was involved in the death of Fontanelle Harper at all were slim. That the murder might somehow be connected to the pending defense contract was just plain overreaching. But he didn't like coincidences, and he didn't have much else to chase.

Drew hoped Sylvia might shed some light on the progress of the contract process. That, at least, would indicate whether the timing of the cheerleader's death might be related to Cerf's business. But it probably was all wasted effort. Simpler answers usually are the right ones.

As he steered his Jeep out of the parking lot, he wondered whether he had some other motive in staying after Cerf. Maybe he resented (or coveted) Cerf's lifestyle. Money, fancy cars, babes on his arms. Maybe he was as guilty of sour grapes as Wally Mertz. Maybe—and this notion he found a little overwhelming—maybe he wanted Sylvia to pursue those contracts simply because it would give him a chance to see her again.

A magnetism existed between them, and he knew she'd recognized it, too. At lunch, he'd tried to keep busy with the menu and his food, but his eyes kept coming up to meet hers, and his gaze snagged there every time. Those green eyes were something to behold.

Thinking about the attraction made him feel guilty. He'd been a one-woman man since he'd hooked up with Teresa. Sometimes, other women would wander into his orbit, and he'd sense that gravitational pull, but he'd stifle it, too loyal to consider the alternative.

But now Teresa could very well be leaving him behind. And all the pledges and promises in the world won't necessarily keep a long-distance romance alive. If Teresa moved to L.A., he'd accompany her or he'd lose her. Too many temptations in California. And, clearly, there were women here in Albuquerque who could tempt him, too. Or at least distract him when he should be thinking about more urgent needs. Like getting Curtis out of jail.

Southbound traffic on Interstate 25 slowed to a crawl as it neared the Big I construction, giving Drew plenty of time to check out the towering cranes and the earth-movers rumbling around like giant Tonka toys. The sweeping new overpasses were painted "desert" colors—peach with a wide stripe of swimming-pool blue—and they always made Drew think of water slides. The Big I Amusement Park.

The renovation was a huge project, expected to cost nearly three-hundred-million dollars. The emotional price was harsh as well: Two years of traffic tie-ups and missed appointments and road rage. Drew was finally getting accustomed to it all, learning to relax into his stalled commute. It gave him time to think.

Right now, he should be thinking about Curtis White. Get Sylvia Smith out of his head and quit obsessing on Scott Cerf, and figure out a way to spring Curtis. So far, all he'd done was spin his wheels. He needed to go see Curtis again, pick his brain, see if it was even possible that Cerf had known Curtis was investigating his finances. See whether Curtis had stumbled onto the competition for the defense contract and Cerf's financial straits. He decided to go see him at the jail the next day, soon as he could get away from the office.

The tempo of the traffic picked up again as the clot of cars cleared the construction zone. Drew looked over his shoulder to change lanes, and saw an anonymous-looking black Ford make the same lane change. Something about the car made the back of his neck tingle.

He signaled for his exit onto Lead Avenue and watched in his mirrors as the dark car followed.

It's nothing, he told himself, just another weary commuter, headed the same direction. With the construction mess, intact freeway exits were scarce. Plenty of cars getting off behind us.

Lead was one-way downhill into downtown, and Drew

stayed in the middle lane, trying to time the stoplights so he hit them green. The Ford let some distance get between them, but it was still back there.

West of downtown, Drew turned onto a side street, headed for home. The black sedan followed.

Now he was getting nervous. Maybe messing around in Scott Cerf's business wasn't such a good idea. Somebody had been willing to kill Fontanelle Harper. If her death *was* linked to Cerf somehow, then that same person might be willing to kill a snooper.

He slowed as he reached his block. He thought about driving past his house, going to a police station or back to the office, but it seemed silly. What if it was nothing?

He turned into his driveway and cut the lights on the Jeep. Swiveled in his seat to watch the trailing car.

The sedan seemed to slow as it passed, but then it speeded up and disappeared down the street. Drew tried to get a look at the driver, but it was too dark. All he could tell was that the driver was a large man. Big round head silhouetted behind the window.

Could've been Otis Edgewater. But why would Edgewater be tailing him?

He sat in the Jeep a while longer, waiting to see whether the car came creeping around again, but there was nothing.

You're kidding yourself, he thought. Inventing surveillance cars and grand conspiracies. Turning into a fucking nut.

He climbed out of the Jeep and dragged himself indoors.

TWENTY

Otis Edgewater cursed. The jock had spotted him, no question. He gunned the engine and sped away from Drew Gavin's house.

He'd been fine, tailing Gavin home from work, until they reached that construction tie-up. Then he'd had no choice but to get right in behind the Jeep. He'd seen Gavin watching his mirrors, but he hadn't wanted to turn the cocksucker loose.

He wanted to watch the house for a while, see if Gavin had people coming and going, see if there was any indication that his fumbling around in Cerf's business was leading anywhere. But he couldn't do that now, not after Gavin made the tail. He'd be on alert all night now. Otis might as well go elsewhere.

Which was fine and dandy. He had business to attend, and he was looking forward to it.

He'd like to give this Gavin character his full attention, at least until the Fontanelle Harper investigation was concluded and Gavin's buddy took the fall. But Otis had a lot of irons in the fire right now, not the least of which was holding Scott Cerf's hand and telling him everything would be all right. Pussy.

At least Gavin didn't just wring his hands at the first sign of trouble, the way Cerf did. At least he went out and *tried* to do something to solve the problem. Big dumb jock, he couldn't help it that Otis stayed three steps ahead of him.

But Cerf was another story. Skinny little shit got the trembles every time he thought about somebody dying. Wanted to sit in his office, surrounded by his computers and his yes men, pretend nothing bad could happen in the whole wide world.

At least Cerf was bright enough to recognize his own weakness. Bright enough to hire retired Army Major Otis Edgewater, someone who understood strategy and tactics and command. Otis was exactly what Cerf needed.

They'd met at a conference on corporate security, and Cerf had acted like a needy woman, exerting all his charms to woo Otis into a position at Cerf Software. The lure couldn't have come at a better time. He was getting bored, working as an instructor at ExecuForce, the security firm that sponsored the conference, training lumbering bodyguards and soft executives how to take evasive action during a kidnapping attempt. Cerf participated enthusiastically at the conference, one eye always on Otis, who knew right away that Cerf wouldn't be any good if the shit ever hit the fan. He'd be too busy pissing his pants.

That's why he needed Otis. He needed someone to lead him through the corporate jungle. Someone who lived by the quick, harsh rules of predator and prey. Someone who could snuff out a life like blowing out a candle.

Otis had suggested such a fate for Gavin. Take him out. Problem solved. But Cerf had forbidden it, getting up on his high horse, ragging Otis about taking chances and attracting attention. As if killing a *journalist* was somehow different from killing anybody else. The only difference Otis could see is that he'd find killing Gavin more personally satisfying.

He was going along with it, at least for now. But if Gavin got much closer, Otis wouldn't let Cerf fuck things up. He'd take care of Gavin himself, quickly and quietly. And he felt certain that time was coming.

He smiled to himself as he steered the car onto a freeway ramp. Damn, he enjoyed his work.

"I'll be getting back to you real soon, Drew Gavin," he said to the windshield. "I'm looking forward to it. But right now, I've got things to do. Places to go. People to kill."

TWENTY ONE

Drew knew something was wrong as soon as he walked into the newsroom Tuesday morning. People were clustered around a trio of televisions that hung from the ceiling. They were like statues, silent and stony, all staring up at the yammering TVs.

He hurried across the newsroom toward them. Pete Jurgenson, a bearded assistant city editor, was near the back of the group.

"What's up, Pete?"

Several people shushed Drew, then turned back to the screen, where footage of a large adobe house was giving way to a sleek anchorwoman at a desk.

"Thank you for that report, Kevin," she said. "And that's the latest on this breaking news story. We'll bring you updates as we get more information on the apparent murder of Wally Mertz, founder and chief executive of Mertek Industries."

"Holy shit!"

Drew's co-workers shushed him again, but the newsbreak was over and the TV cut to some daytime talk show. Conversation fluttered among the assembled, but Drew was too stunned to say anything. Jurgenson held a remote above the heads of the others and clicked off the TVs.

"Okay, people, time to get moving," he shouted. "Burns, get to the cop shop and see what they've got. Dover, go to Mertz's house and get some color from the neighbors. Sheila, go to Mertek and see what they'll tell you there."

Three reporters hurried away, snatching up notebooks and purses and cell phones from their desks on their way to the door.

Drew reached out blindly and grasped Jurgenson's shoulder. Jurgenson was nearly a foot shorter than Drew and he wheeled on him, irritated.

"*What?*"

"I, um, I need to talk to you."

"Can it wait?"

Drew shook his head. He felt dizzy, off-balance, as if the world had been set askew.

"Well, it's gonna fucking *have* to wait for a few minutes," Jurgenson snapped. "This is a big story."

Drew let his hand drop and turned away. He trudged back over to his desk, sat down and ran his hands over his face.

Damn. Wally Mertz. Murdered less than twenty-four hours after Drew sat in his office, pumping him for information about Scott Cerf. The little Alley Oop lookalike wasn't going to be around to give Cerf his comeuppance.

Jurgenson appeared at his desk a few minutes later.

"You all right, Drew? You look pale."

"Mertz. What happened?"

"You know that guy?"

Drew nodded, and dropped his gaze to his desktop, bracing himself.

"Too bad. Somebody strangled him at his home. TV says he was in bed, lying on his back, his mouth stuffed full of computer disks. We're checking it out."

Drew slowly raised his head and looked Jurgenson in the eye.

"Just like Fontanelle Harper."

"The cheerleader?"

"Strangled. Something stuffed in her mouth."

"Jeez, that's right. I'd better mention that to Burns. See if the cops have made the connection. I mean, *if* there's a connection—"

"Oh, they're connected all right," Drew said grimly. "Through me."

"What?"

"I went to see Mertz yesterday, asking questions about the Harper murder."

"You talked to *Mertz*?" Jurgenson was goggle-eyed.

"Yesterday. Asked him about Scott Cerf."

"Jesus Christ on a bicycle. Why did you do that?"

"Curtis was looking into Cerf when he got busted. I decided to keep looking, to check out his business dealings. Mertz and Cerf are at each other's throats over a defense contract. The cheerleader's involved somehow. She's dead. Mertz gets involved with me. He's dead. Somebody connected to Cerf is killing them."

Jurgenson looked around the room, as if searching for a fire exit.

"Aw, Christ. I can't process all this. I don't know what the hell you're talking about, except that you're somehow mixed up in it. We're gonna have to tell Goodman."

"I know."

Jurgenson swallowed and glanced around again, tugging nervously at his beard.

"Guess you're probably gonna want me to go in there with

you," he said. "To see Goodman, I mean."

"No, I'll do it. You've got a story to go after."

Relief broke across Jurgenson's face like a wave against a rocky shore.

"Thanks, Drew. I'm pretty busy."

"I can see that. When's Elliott get in?"

"Our esteemed city editor will be arriving any minute now. That's why I need to get people on the story first. Elliott's gonna have a heart attack."

"Why?"

"Because of you."

Jurgenson smiled at Drew, a sad, pitying smile, the kind you'd give a condemned man, in case it's the last one he ever sees. Then he hurried back toward the city desk.

Drew grunted up from his desk and walked stiffly across the newsroom toward Goodman's office, wondering whether he should request a blindfold and a cigarette.

TWENTY TWO

Curtis White followed the fat-assed jailer to the visiting room, watching the way his big hamhocks wrestled with each other under his pants. Looked like two babies in a sack.

Curtis was learning that some of the guards were all right. They weren't looking for trouble, just regular guys trying to make it through the workday. A couple were sadistic pricks like you always see in the movies. But old Fat Ass here apparently had donated his personality to science. He said as little as possible and his black, oily face never so much as twitched. Men like that made Curtis nervous. No way to read them.

He followed Fat Ass down the last, short hall to the visiting room. The route was familiar by now. Curtis had lots of visitors. Goodman came by every day. Manuel Quintana and his assistants stopped by to ask more questions. Spiffy O'Neil and Sparky Anderson from sports. A couple of the cityside reporters. Even that little blonde from the news library who'd helped him with his research on Scott Cerf. People had been coming and going so, he'd hardly had time to worry about getting killed in jail.

All his visitors asking one question over and over: Who killed Fontanelle Harper? And he couldn't remember shit.

Now here was Drew again, sitting at the long table, waiting for him, somber and weary. Looked like he was brimming over with bad tidings.

"Hey, Curtis, how you doing?"

"I'm all right. The hell's wrong with you?"

Drew blew out his cheeks and shook his head. Looked like a big old horse.

"Lot of shit's going down, Curtis. You'd better have a seat."

"If you've got bad news, I might as well go back to the day-room. I can't take any more bad news. I was in a card game—"

"I don't know how bad it is. It's just news."

Curtis leaned his cuffed hands on the table and looked down into Drew's face.

"No, it's bad. I can tell." He sat in the chair across from Drew, his hands still resting on the table. "Hit me with it, man."

Drew sighed heavily. "Ever hear of a guy named Wally Mertz?"

"Didn't he pitch for the Tigers back in the '60s?"

"Different guy. He's local. Software company."

Curtis shook his head. "Naw, man, haven't met him."

"You won't be meeting him in the future. He's been killed."

Curtis frowned. "They gonna try to pin that murder on me, too?"

"No. He was killed last night. But here's the deal: Somebody strangled him and stuffed computer disks into his mouth."

"Computer disks?"

"He had a wide mouth."

"You know the man?"

"Met him yesterday."

"And now he's dead. Uh-oh."

"Exactly. I go see him, then someone kills him the same way someone killed Fontanelle. Of course, I had to tell Goodman the connection. He's been making a tasty dish of my ass all day."

Curtis didn't care about Goodman. He'd seized on the other detail.

"You're thinking the same killer did them both."

Drew nodded, his lips pressed together.

"But that's great, man! They catch the dude, tie 'em together and I'm sprung."

Drew nodded again. "Maybe. Too bad Wally Mertz had to die to prove it."

"Sorry, man. I can see you're shook up about this. But I didn't know the man. If it means getting me out of lockup, I'm down with it."

"It's probably going to take a while," Drew said. "But I think Wally Mertz is going to get you out of this mess. Eventually."

"They could say it's a copycat. That I was the original cat, and somebody just copied my method while I was in here."

"That's right. Which is why I don't think you'll get out right away. But you seem to be surviving okay so far. You still the big celebrity of the jail?"

"No, the new has worn off. Now, somebody strikes up a conversation, he either wants me to be his girlfriend or he wants to lead me to Jesus."

A smile cracked through Drew's grim expression. "Which one is worse?"

"Not sure. I didn't know so many of these fuckers were so religious. Guess it gives them something to do with the time. I even met this one brother who was a Jew, trying to get others to convert. Not every day you see a black Jew."

"Sammy Davis, Jr."

"Yeah, him. Name one other."

Drew smiled again and shook his head. "How you feeling otherwise? Still doped up?"

"No. Back to normal, except I still can't remember much about what happened that night."

Curtis felt frustration uncoil within him. He'd strained his brain, trying to recall what had happened at Fontanelle Harper's party, but very little had come.

"I remembered one thing. Fontanelle was in an argument with Raj Davis. In the kitchen, as the party was winding down. Remember, I told you they were dating? They fought about something, but I can't remember what. Mostly, I just get flashes, where I can see them up in each other's faces."

"You remember how it ended up?"

Curtis shook his head.

"No, man, I don't have anything else. Not yet anyway. I'd like to find out what happened to me, why I'm so fucking foggy. I'd kill the bastard who did this."

Drew made a shushing face. Curtis looked at Fat Ass filling up the door. His expression, naturally, hadn't changed. But Drew was right. Old Fat Ass probably memorized every word of their conversation.

Drew looked at his wristwatch as he said, "Let me ask you about something else. You know anything about Cerf Software trying to land a big contract at Sandia? Virtual reality stuff. Bombs."

Curtis felt his eyes widen. "I never heard about that."

"Wally Mertz was after the same contract. I think it's all connected."

"Shit, man, sounds like it. But how would a smart guy like Cerf think he could get away with something like that? You don't get to kill the competition."

"It's un-American," Drew said, the smile peeking out.

"Damn skippy it is. That's no way to do business."

Drew looked at his watch again. Man always in a hurry.

"I thought maybe you'd come across the defense stuff when you were checking out Cerf's finances."

"Not that I recall, man. But that's all kinda foggy, too. And I hadn't looked over all that stuff before this shit happened."

Drew pushed back his chair, ready to go. "I was hoping you'd asked about that contract when you were grilling people at that party."

Curtis shook his head. "It ain't gonna be that easy."

"You said it, partner."

They sat in silence for a moment. Drew looked like he was chewing on something.

"Hey, man, I was thinking about something before you got here," Curtis said. "Remember the first time we ever met?"

Drew grunted. "You were in trouble then, too."

"Those fuckers in the dorm were ready to throw me out the goddamned window. Would've broken my neck."

"Three floors up."

"That's right. And you come running down the hall, roaring like a fuckin' lion, and scattered 'em."

"They fought back, as I recall."

"Not for long. That one bastard, remember? You caught him under the chin and he went flat to the floor. Looked like somebody dropped an ironing board."

"And what were you doing? Checking to see if they'd wrinkled your clothes? As I remember, I had to fight all three of them by myself."

"Hey, I was in shock, man. That was a close call. I thought I was gonna land face-down on the sidewalk."

"And you wouldn't want anything to happen to your pretty face."

Curtis grinned and put a hand to his chin. "Man's gotta protect his goods."

Drew shifted in his chair, looked like he was trying to keep from smiling.

"I believe your 'goods' got you in that situation in the first place. Wasn't it something about a girlfriend?"

"I didn't know she was his girlfriend."

"Hell, she was the homecoming queen. You knew she was *somebody's* girlfriend. But that didn't stop you."

Curtis smiled, remembering. The homecoming queen. Big old blond with an ass like a ripe peach.

"Damn, she was fine," he said. "I think it was worth the trouble."

"Wasn't much trouble for you. I was the one who had to whip those guys."

"Bunch of dickheads. You would've ended up whipping them eventually anyway, just to keep peace around the dorm."

"So you were doing me a favor, setting me up three-on-one in a freaking hallway?"

"A man could look at it that way."

"A cross-eyed man. Besides, you at least got the home-coming queen. All I got out of that brawl was sore hands."

"Not true, man." Curtis grinned. "You also got my undy-ing gratitude."

Drew laughed. "Yeah, that makes all the difference.

That's the reason I can sleep at night."

Curtis sobered and glanced over at Fat Ass.

"Anyway, I was just thinking about that time in the dorm. How you pulled my shit out of the fire. And now here you are, trying to do it again."

"Doing a helluva job so far." Drew shook his head, looked disgusted.

"You're stirring the pot, man. That's gotta lead somewhere."

Fat Ass cleared his throat. Curtis looked over again. The guard was tapping the face of his wristwatch with a thick finger.

"Time to go," Drew said.

He stood up and Curtis followed, his angular body unfolding from the low chair. They awkwardly shook hands, the handcuffs getting in the way.

"I left some of those French cigarettes for you. At the front desk. They said they'd get them to you."

"Thanks, man. And thanks for looking into all this. You might get me outta here yet."

"Maybe." Melancholy settled over Drew's face. "Or I might just get some more people killed."

Curtis reached across the table and patted Drew on the shoulder. "You didn't kill nobody, man. You're trying to help."

Drew nodded, but said nothing. He trudged out the visitors' door, deep in his thoughts.

Curtis thinking: That's Drew for you. Feeling responsible for everything. Taking on the woes of the world. Man felt like it was his job to fix things, make them right again.

Drew had adopted Curtis that day long ago in the dorm. He'd been looking out for him ever since, helping him land his job with the *Gazette* and pulling his ass out of trouble on more than one occasion. Now here he was, trying to do it again, and the stakes were higher than ever.

Curtis had speculated in the past that Drew felt compelled to help people because he'd grown up without a lot of family. No momma, no brothers and sisters. It was like Drew reached out to the world, picked particular people and decided *they* were his family. And he'd do anything to protect those loved ones. You're in a jam, you want Drew on your side.

Fat Ass cleared his throat, a low rumble, interrupting Curtis' thoughts. Curtis looked over to see Fat Ass jerk his head toward the door. Time to go.

He followed the guard through two sets of doors before Fat Ass removed the handcuffs. Then it was back into the noise and menace of the dayroom. But Curtis felt different now, less scared. The copycat murder had given him a glimmer of hope. He might see freedom yet again.

And he'd probably owe it all to Drew Gavin.

TWENTY THREE

This time, when Drew showed up late at Tingley Coliseum for a Rattler game, he sat alone in the stands. Wasn't hard to find a seat away from the Jim Shortzes of the world. The small crowd freckled the bleachers. The squeak of sneakers on the parquet floor was louder than the fans.

Dutiful Henry sat at the scorer's table with the other sportswriters, watching the action on the court. Drew winced when he saw her. He still needed to talk to her. She probably thought he'd been checking up on her when he got ejected from the last game. Now here he was again. He hoped she wouldn't spot him.

He surveyed the fans clustered behind the Rattlers bench, but he couldn't see Cerf or Edgewater. Two seats were empty, about where they'd been sitting last time.

The Rattlers were up by four points over the Tucson Bandits midway through the first quarter. The players were sweated up good, blowing up and down the court.

Playing defense and complicated offenses apparently were foreign concepts in the WABL. Both teams ran the court and put the ball up quickly as possible, pushing the fast break at every opportunity. Defenders lagged and stumbled, probably too busy thinking about their stats to keep up. Scoring and rebounding are the numbers that speak in pro basketball. You worry about defense after you make it to the NBA.

It made for a fast-paced game, and the fans liked that. They wanted a highlight reel of slam dunks and fast breaks and hard fouls. But Drew saw the artlessness that hampered some players—the tangled feet, the quick shoves, the dives for loose balls going out of bounds. Always a step slow for the block or languid with the pick.

The referees seemed to recognize what kind of game the fans expected. They had the slowest whistles he'd ever seen. Players banged around under the goals, and the refs watched with blank expressions, like they were waiting for a frigging bus.

Some players took advantage of the situation. Drew watched Raj Davis drag down an offensive rebound, his elbows swinging, his heavily-muscled arms like scythes in the faces of the other team. The Bandits fell away, and Davis leaped straight up and slammed the ball home with both hands.

Davis spun away from the goal, a scowl creasing his face, and threw a shoulder into the Bandit center. It was a cheap shot, thrown when the center was off-guard, and it nearly knocked him off his feet. Davis' lips moved, talking trash.

Drew felt himself frowning. He hated that kind of play. These days, basketball's all tattoos and beefcake and flapping lips. Everybody treating the sport like a neighborhood pick-up game. Players strutting around, talking shit, picking fights. The Rodman Effect, ruining the sport.

Raj Davis slapped the ball away from a Bandit forward on the other end of the court, clearly fouling him, but there was no whistle. Davis snatched the ball up like he owned it and whirled away to dribble up court, crashing right into his own guard and knocking the smaller man to the ground. Then he loped up the court, still scowling, daring the other players to get near him.

It was like freaking "Rollerball," but some of the fans were on their feet. Just the game they wanted to see.

Davis looked angry the whole time, as if he were being forced to play the game against his will. Drew wondered whether that anger spilled over into his life off the court. Could he have killed Fontanelle Harper? Curtis said they'd been arguing. Maybe Raj Davis thought Curtis and Fontanelle were flirting too much, getting a little frisky. That sounded like Curtis. But would Davis be canny enough to set Curtis up for the murder? Murders sparked by jealousy typically don't have much planning to them.

It could be the other way around. Maybe real life was spilling onto the court. Maybe Raj Davis was angry *because* someone killed Fontanelle. He'd certainly seemed to be mourning her—in his macho, menacing way—at practice. Maybe now he was taking out his grief on the Bandits.

The referees whistled a timeout and the players dragged their asses back toward their benches. Some of the Rattlers exchanged high-fives with Davis, but he kept the scowl on his face. Bonner, the guard he'd floored, looked pissed.

Raj Davis would be a simple solution to Fontanelle Harper's death. The cops always suspect the boyfriend. But Drew couldn't see it. Fontanelle's murder seemed calculated to him, not the product of a jealous rage. And that implied that there was something behind the scenes, some motive he hadn't uncovered, that made her death seem like a reasonable answer to the killer's problem. What could Fontanelle have known or done to make killing her seem like a good idea? Drew didn't have the slightest proof of anything yet, but his gut still told him it was linked somehow to Scott Cerf.

Cerf hadn't seemed like a killer during Drew's brief encounters with him. He came off like a rich kid, a playboy, soft. Not a man who could strangle a thrashing woman. His talents seemed to lie in talking people out of their money or their pants, not in formulating deaths. It takes a cold mind to carefully craft a murder and pin it on somebody else. Drew's money was still on Otis Edgewater.

He was looking around the sparse crowd when he spotted Edgewater walking down the steps toward the reserved seats behind the Rattler bench. His big shoulders rolled as he walked and a smirk stretched his lined face. He stepped into the row and edged toward the empty seats. Spectators leaned backward, making room for his thick body to pass.

Edgewater settled into place, then reached up to pat his combover, make sure everything was lying down up there. With his hand over his head, his sleeve stretched tight, Edgewater's arm looked like a tree trunk.

Still no Cerf. Edgewater apparently was attending the game solo. Which, Drew thought, means there's an empty seat right there next to him. And it's got a much better view than where I'm sitting.

Drew hesitated only a moment, not wanting to think about it too much and change his mind. He stood and headed that way.

TWENTY FOUR

Otis Edgewater felt instant fury when he saw Gavin approaching. *Fucking idiot, coming here. This isn't the place. I'll come to you when I'm ready.*

Gavin grinned like a mule as he sidled past the knees of the ticket-buying suckers. Like he could pull off friendly after their last encounter. He squeezed into the vacant seat next to Otis. The two of them filled the seats and more. Otis could feel Gavin's arm pressing up against his own rock-hard shoulder. Not room enough to insert a dime between them.

"Hi there," Gavin said. "We need to talk."

"Don't think so, son. And I believe you're sitting in the wrong seat."

"Cerf won't mind, I'm sure. In fact, I wish he were here. I've got some questions for him, too."

Otis kept his face impassive, though his temper surged up within him.

"I thought I made it clear, son. We're not answering your questions."

"You don't have a choice. And I'm not your 'son.'"

Otis looked Gavin in the eye.

"Damned right you're not. You was my son, I would've taught you some manners when you were growing up. How to respect your elders."

"Age doesn't necessarily merit respect." The jock's jaw was twitching.

"All right. Let's make it 'respect your betters.' I'm guessing you were never in the military, *son*, or you would've learned to salute the better man."

Gavin said, "Take it easy," and half-turned in his seat, away from Otis, glancing around at their seatmates. Otis knew it was a form of surrender, the way a growling dog will turn tail and run if you stare him down. He almost smiled.

Look at him, he thought. Big, dumb jock. I could break his neck before he could even turn back around. A man doesn't take his eye off the enemy. Not unless he's a slinking, yellow dog.

"What do you hear from Wally Mertz?" Gavin said out of the side of his mouth.

Otis kept his face stony. That wasn't a name he expected to hear from Gavin. The sportswriter might know more than Otis had guessed.

"The fuck you talkin' about, son?"

"Mertz. He's dead. It's all over the news."

"Yeah? So?"

"So he's your partner's chief competitor. Somebody killed him. Somebody killed Fontanelle Harper the same way."

"I told you, we've got no comment on that girl. And I don't know anything about this guy Mertz."

"Looks funny to me."

"Maybe you ought to try focusing your eyes. Instead of waltzing in here, accusing me of something."

"Did I accuse you? We hadn't gotten to that point. Yet."

Otis hated this fucking jock. Hated all guys like him. Wiseass would-be tough guys, didn't know shit from Carter's

Little Liver Pills. Otis would like to pitch him down onto the court. Go down there and mop up the floor with his smug face. Give the fucking fans something to cheer about.

"I've had about enough of your lip, son. You'd better leave now."

The reporter's face flushed. Otis thinking: Here it comes.

"You gonna make me leave?"

Otis smiled at him. Heat spread through his arms, his legs. Christ, he'd like to pound the shit out this asshole. But not here, not now.

"I got something right here that'll do the trick," he said, and reached inside his blue blazer.

Gavin tensed beside him. Otis' smiled broadened. Dumbass thinks I'm going for a weapon.

He pulled a little walkie-talkie from his breast pocket and held it up to his lips.

"Security, this is Edgewater. I've got a problem down here."

"Ten-four. We're on our way."

He put the radio back in his pocket.

"You know, son, you *amuse* me," Otis said, smiling. "You blunder around, thinking you've got some idea of how the world works, but you really don't know shit.

"I used to see boys like you in the Army. They'd come into boot camp, big talkers who think they've got the world whipped, who try to run things. And some night after lights out, the other men in the unit, the *real* men, would wrap the guy up in his blanket and carry him out behind the barracks and kick the living shit out of him. After that, the asshole usually learned to keep his mouth shut."

"This isn't the Army," Gavin muttered.

"It ain't Disneyland either. This here's the real world.

People die. The rest of us carry on. The smart ones stay real quiet about it."

Otis heard heavy footsteps hammering toward them. He smiled at Gavin.

"Come see me again after you get smart," he said. "Somewhere more private. We'll have a quiet talk."

Gavin stood up to greet the two guards, who had their hands on their nightsticks. He said, "You can count on that talk. I'm looking forward to it."

Otis kept the smile on his face. "Be seeing you. Son."

The guards grabbed Gavin by either elbow and led him away to the exits.

Otis hushed the whispering of his seatmates with a quick, brutal glance, then turned his eyes toward the game. But his mind wasn't on the pituitary cases galloping up and down the court. He was thinking about Drew Gavin and the value of keeping quiet.

And whether Gavin needed to be silenced altogether.

TWENTY FIVE

Bob Goodman lay in wait when Drew arrived at the *Gazette* late Wednesday morning. The editor's bald head glowed like a stoplight. Before Drew could even reach his desk, Goodman crooked a finger at him and pointed toward his office.

Drew marched across the newsroom, conversations dying all around as people turned to look. Goodman closed the office door after they were inside—never a good sign—and Drew felt the staff watching through the glass wall. He sat with his back to them, facing the editor, who perched behind his cluttered desk, leaning forward on his elbows.

"I got a phone call from the publisher a few minutes ago," he said. "Somebody complained about you."

So far, not so bad. Newspapers are deluged daily with complaints from readers and flacks and politicos who feel wronged by the headlines.

"Seems you caused a stir last night at the Rattlers game," Goodman said. His mouth was set in a thin line. His face and bald pate shone so red, Drew wished for sunglasses.

"Bob, I—"

"Seems you were grilling Scott Cerf's security man about these murders."

"Not grilling—"

"And the two of you got into a shouting match in front of witnesses."

"We weren't exactly shouting—"

"This, after I explicitly told you to mind your own goddamned business."

Drew hung his head. Nothing he could say to squirm out of it. When Goodman said nothing further, he finally asked, "Who called?"

"Edgewater himself. Told the publisher you slandered him. What the hell were you thinking, Drew?"

"I think Cerf and Edgewater are involved in these deaths. First, the cheerleader, now Mertz, killed the same way—"

"We covered all this yesterday, damn it. You've got no proof. Maybe the murders are connected. But that's a job for the police, not some big lug who thinks he's a white knight. You're going to get us sued, Drew. You can't go around in public places, loudly accusing people of murder."

"I never actually accused him of anything. I was trying—"

"I don't want to hear it. You want to pin it on somebody other than Curtis. I don't blame you. Nobody's happy that he's in jail. But I'm not going to eat a lawsuit just so you can go around playing detective."

"I'm just a reporter, asking questions."

"That won't hold water. We've got reporters asking the right questions. We've got people scouring the city, trying to figure this damned thing out. But you're not one of them. You've been expressly warned to leave it alone. If Cerf's guy wants to sue for slander, this newspaper will cut you loose in a heartbeat. You can face the courtroom alone."

"You told Curtis the newspaper's behind him 'a hundred

percent,'" Drew said. "What happened to that?"

"We're behind Curtis. We're doing everything in our power to help him. But we're not supporting this bullshit you've been up to."

Drew cracked his knuckles, thinking it over.

"So, my job's on the line?"

Goodman leaned back in his chair and rubbed his face with his hands. Drew bet his blood pressure was through the roof.

"I'm not going to lie to you. You're on thin ice. The publisher's getting calls, and that's never good."

Drew cleared his throat, which felt thick and scratchy. His eyes felt hot. He didn't want to lose his job. The *Gazette* was his home, his colleagues were his family. But one member of that family was in jail, and he couldn't sit idly by.

"What do you want me to do, Bob?"

"I want you to keep out of it, like I've said about a million times now. I want you to sit at your desk, put out the sports section, and keep your head down. I've got a feeling this will be over soon. Curtis will be cleared. Things will get back to normal, or what passes for normal around here. And then maybe the publisher will forget you've been acting a fool."

Drew nodded and got to his feet. "I'll do my best."

Goodman picked up some papers on his desk. Drew was dismissed. He started to say something else, but thought better of it. Better to return to his desk, get to work and pretend, at least, like he was obeying orders.

Before he could get out the door, though, Goodman called, "Drew?"

"Yeah?"

"No shit. The ice is thin."

Drew nodded and tried to turn away.

"And the water's cold."

"I got it, Bob, I got it."

Drew slogged back to his desk. He felt like he was underwater already, like his coworkers were a school of gulping fish, all gawking at him, ready to flit away if he moved. As he reached his desk, the phone rang.

He took a deep breath before answering it.

"Drew? It's Sylvia Smith."

Sylvia. Exactly what he didn't need at the moment. "Hi. What's up?"

"I've got some information for you. Some ideas."

Drew's internal alarms clanged. He pictured himself skating out onto the thinnest of ice. But he said, "Lunch?"

"Sounds good. El Patio again?"

He looked at his watch. "Same time, same station."

"I'll see you there," she said, and hung up.

Drew looked around at the Dwarves, who were busy trying to act like they didn't want to hear every word Goodman had said in the closed-door meeting.

"I'm going to lunch," he said, and he left.

As the door of the employee's entrance closed behind him, he wondered if it was for the last time.

TWENTY SIX

Drew found Sylvia sitting at a corner table on the restaurant's patio, dappled by the shade of a locust tree. She looked different, flushed, a spark in her luminous eyes. She wore the same sort of conservative clothes as before, but her glowing blond hair was unpinned, and it draped onto her shoulders in a way that made him think of old movie stars. Veronica Lake. Lauren Bacall. She looked beautiful and desirable and breathtaking, the way a roller coaster is breathtaking.

Her hand was cool in his, but he dropped it like it was hot. Then he squeezed into his chair and exchanged pleasantries with her. He caught himself looking away while she talked, searching for the waitress, reading the menu, admiring the weather. Anything to avoid contact with those piercing green eyes.

After they ordered, she said, "I must look a fright. I was up all night, poring over those papers."

"All night? You didn't have to do that—"

"I wanted to. Once I get started on something, I can't turn it loose."

Drew sighed. "I know exactly what you mean."

"I got hold of some data on Cerf's bid for the virtual reality software. Had to cut some corners, but I don't think I left a paper trail. Between that stuff, and all the documents you brought me yesterday, I had a night's worth of reading to do."

Drew felt excitement welling within him. He tried to stifle it, tried to tell himself this was all going nowhere but the unemployment line.

"What did all this reading tell you?"

Sylvia smiled broadly. She had a great smile. He averted his eyes.

"Well," she said, "I think you're onto something."

Drew risked looking at her. She still beamed, but he could take it now.

"Cerf's got money troubles, just like you thought," she said. "I don't know where he's getting the money to fund the basketball league."

She couldn't stop smiling. He said, "And?"

"And he's in real trouble on the virtual reality contract. I got a look at his bid. It's complex stuff, but I could see for myself that Mertek has him beat."

"Think he knows that?"

"Maybe. Cerf Software was late on the most recent filing. Maybe they're dragging their feet, already aware they don't have a chance."

"Wally Mertz, before he died, told me Cerf would go under if he didn't get that contract."

The mention of Mertz finally wiped the smile off her face. "I heard about him getting killed. You think it's connected, don't you?"

"Yeah, I think so, though I don't know precisely how yet. I mean, why kill Mertz? Mertek's bid will still win. Just be somebody else running the company."

"Maybe he was the only one who understood how the software worked."

Drew shook his head. "Mertek's a big place. Lots of people must be involved in developing the software. No, I think it's because he talked to me."

He swallowed heavily. He'd thought all along that he was to blame for Mertz's death, but it still stung to come out and say it.

Sylvia saw the look on his face and began to console him, but he talked over her.

"The hell of it is I don't know what Mertz might've known that would be worth killing him. He told me a lot about Cerf, but I could've gotten that same information from other sources. He didn't tell me anything so, so *momentous* that it should cost a life."

The food arrived, and Sylvia busied herself with silverware and napkin until the waitress was out of earshot. Drew did the same, though he'd lost his appetite.

"Maybe," she said, "he knew a lot more than he revealed to you. The person who killed him knew it, too, and didn't want him telling you."

Drew shrugged and took a bite of his enchilada.

"If that's the case," she said, "then his death isn't your fault. He never even told you whatever it was that got him murdered. It was all just, I don't know, a misunderstanding."

"An accident."

"Sure, like an accident."

"Doesn't feel that way to me."

The spark returned to Sylvia's eyes, and she smiled slyly. "Maybe you'd feel better if you proved to be right about Cerf and the rest of it."

"Think you can help me do that?"

"I've got some ideas. First, we forget about the defense contract."

"What?"

"I know, it's interesting and all. And Wally Mertz is connected to Cerf through that contract. But we knew that already, and we've kind of hit the wall. Mertz is dead. We can't ask him what's going on behind the scenes."

"Okay, so we ignore the contract," he said dubiously. "Where do we look instead?"

"The Rattlers."

"Why?"

"Because we still haven't accounted for the money Cerf's pouring into that basketball league."

"Yeah, but we don't have all the information—"

"We've got a lot," she said quickly. "I went through all those financial documents twice, then got on the computer and did some more research on Cerf. I can't find any source for the millions he's put into basketball."

"But what does that *mean?*"

She pushed her plate aside. She'd hardly taken a bite, too eager to share her theories. Drew was surprised to find his plate was half-empty.

"It looks like Cerf took out loans to pay his share of the new league. He was late with a payment or two, late enough that somebody talked to the newspaper about it."

"I read those stories, too. But he paid up later, right?"

"Yeah, but where did those payments come from?"

Drew shrugged, exasperated.

"I'm an auditor, right? This is what I do, follow money trails. In my business, anytime somebody suddenly has money that can't be accounted for through normal channels, we suspect laundering.

"Say Cerf's come into a bunch of dirty money. He could

deposit it in various accounts connected to the Rattlers and the league, so nobody notices. The money is recorded as income from the ticket office or whatever, then he uses it to cover the payments on the loans. Dirty money becomes clean when the bank accepts payment. The money's freshly laundered."

"But that's just taking this mystery money and giving it away," he protested.

"Some of it. But there might be millions more concealed in the system, being cleaned up and stored away in overseas banks."

Drew shook his head. It just didn't make sense.

"And," she said, "the Rattlers eventually will start making money."

"Maybe."

"If they do, then every time the team sells a bag of popcorn, he's changed more dirty money into clean. And it goes right in his pocket."

"But where did this dirty money come from? Drugs?"

"Probably not." She hesitated and glanced around. "But he might be smuggling something else."

Drew found himself gripping the edge of the table. He forced his hands into his lap before asking, "Like what?"

She leaned toward him, keeping her voice low. He inhaled her sweet perfume.

"The virtual reality software."

Drew leaned closer, too. Their noses were only inches apart. He felt the magnetism between them again, and had to fight off the urge to kiss her.

"The stuff they're making for the defense contract? But they're still developing it, right? And their bid's still in—"

"If they know they're going to lose that bid, maybe they've turned elsewhere," she whispered. "Plenty of foreign nations would like to get their hands on that technology. Since the test ban treaties, these computer programs have been the secret to developing new weapons. Maybe Cerf saw another way to keep afloat."

Drew sat back and let a low whistle escape. Other diners turned to look, and Sylvia smiled and flushed.

"Holy shit," he whispered. "How could we prove something like that?"

She shook her head slightly, which made her sleek hair dance about her shoulders. "I don't know. That's the tricky part."

"Something to think about, isn't it?"

Sylvia smiled. "Just what you needed. More on your mind."

"No, this is good," he said. "It's a big help. Thank you."

"You're welcome. Wish I could do more for you."

He let that hang in the air a moment before saying, "You've done plenty. I appreciate it. Now I'd better let you get back to work."

Disappointment flashed across her face, then disappeared behind that blinding smile.

"Okay," she said, "but work's going to seem awfully dull after all this intrigue."

She reached down by her feet and picked up the fat sheaf of papers that sat beside her handbag. She passed them across to him.

"I made copies of everything," she said. "Hope you don't mind. Thought it might save steps in the future. If you think of something else, or want somebody to steer you through some of those documents, call me. I'd love to help some more."

Drew thanked her again. He paid the check and walked her out to the sidewalk. The magnetism kept pulling him toward her, and he had to steer away to keep some distance between them.

"I put my home number in that folder," she said. "In case you need to reach me after hours."

God, she kept throwing up these openings, these invitations. The temptation was strong, but he simply thanked her again.

She stepped toward him, close enough that he could feel the heat from her bosom, and grasped his arm. Then she stood on tiptoe and her lips brushed his cheek. To Drew, it was like getting punched in the jaw. He teetered, then caught himself as she stepped away.

"Bye," she said. "Call me."

Drew stood there, gaping, until she was halfway down the block. Then he snapped out of it and hurried to his car, casting quick glances back at her long, curvy form walking away.

Under his breath, he said, "Damn."

TWENTY SEVEN

Otis Edgewater watched from behind the wheel of the Ford as Gavin parted company with the good-looking blonde outside the restaurant. Otis didn't recognize the woman, hadn't turned her up when he was gathering intelligence on Gavin. The sportswriter had a girlfriend, a reporter named Vargas, but this blonde babe wasn't her.

His eyes flicked between Gavin and the woman as they went their separate ways along the shady sidewalk. He saw the sheaf of papers Gavin carried under his arm like a football. The jock hadn't had the papers when he went into the cafe, so the woman delivered them. Otis decided to follow the woman, see if he could find out more about her. But first, he'd watch Gavin for a minute. For kicks.

Gavin reached his Jeep and stopped dead on the sidewalk. He dropped his head and his lips moved, probably cursing. Otis felt a smile stretch his face. He knew what Gavin had found. A flat tire on the Jeep, something guaranteed to keep him busy for a while.

Slashing the tire's valve stem had been an unnecessary risk, kid stuff, but Otis couldn't help himself. It gave him an outlet for the impatience building up inside of him. Bought him a little time. He'd get to satisfy that urge soon, give Gavin what he deserved, but this would have to do for now.

Otis laughed as Gavin kicked the deflated tire, then he turned his attention back to his mirrors, checking on the blonde. She climbed into a Toyota parked at the curb and cranked up the engine. Otis started his motor, too, ready to follow her.

He glanced back at Gavin. The big jock's shoulders were slumped in resignation. Gavin set the papers in the Jeep and opened the back to get out a jack. Otis cackled and pulled away from the curb, dropping in behind the woman's car.

Who could she be? What was her connection, if any, to Gavin's investigation?

She didn't seem to be watching for a tail. Otis stopped right behind her at a red light, and saw she didn't bother to check her mirrors. He wrote her license plate number down in a little notebook he carried in his shirt pocket. One of the whizzes at Cerf Software could tap right into the Department of Motor Vehicles computers that listed all license plates. Otis could get the driver's name and address with a phone call to the geek.

But he continued to follow her south out of the university area. Maybe she'd lead him right to her house, save him that call. The fewer people at Cerf Software who knew about Gavin and the woman, the better. Otis tried to always think ahead.

For a few minutes, he thought she was headed toward the airport, which really got him wondering how far Gavin's investigation had reached. But she went east on Gibson Boulevard, bypassing the turnoff to the airport, her little blue car climbing the long rise past the runways and then hurrying downhill into the busy area around Lovelace Medical Center and the VA hospital and Kirtland Air Force Base.

Otis knew the area well. His retired military status gave him access to the post exchange at Kirtland, where he occasionally went for discount groceries and booze. He'd even visited an officer's club there with a retired Air Force guy he'd met at Cerf Software. Kirtland was a huge base, a city unto itself, separated from the rest of Albuquerque by tall wire fences.

An idea dawned, and he suddenly was sure where she was headed: Sandia National Laboratories shared the same sprawling chunk of real estate with Kirtland. The woman must be connected to the labs.

He followed her to the Wyoming Boulevard gate into the base, and watched her breeze past the guardhouse. He turned around before he reached the sentry.

So Gavin had himself an insider at Sandia. That changed things. It broadened the scope of Cerf's battlefront, and might require Otis to make what the military brass liked to call "surgical strikes."

Might be time for some surgery, he mused. Time to remove the cancer before it spread any further.

"Calling Dr. Edgewater," he said aloud. He laughed and slapped the steering wheel. "Dr. Edgewater, please report to the operating room. Your patient's dying."

TWENTY EIGHT

It was dark by the time Drew got home. He glanced around the neighborhood as he got out of the Jeep, but saw no mysterious cars tailing him. The old house smelled stale and musty as he let himself inside. He left the front door standing open while he sorted his mail and opened a beer.

God, he was exhausted. First, the emotional roller coaster of the threats from Goodman and the lunch with Sylvia Smith. Then the flat tire, which the garage guy had confirmed was an act of vandalism, just as Drew had suspected. Then back to the office for more meetings with Goodman and, oh yeah, putting out tomorrow's newspaper.

He fell into the big reclining chair that dominated the room and used the remote to flip through TV channels, but his mind was elsewhere. Thinking about what Sylvia had told him about Scott Cerf.

Cerf's business dealings looked fishier all the time, but how could Drew prove any connection with the murders? Mertz's death might be linked to the software contract, but how would a cheerleader fit into the equation? And what about Sylvia's theory about money laundering? Drew couldn't think of any way to confirm whether Cerf had been shopping his software to foreign governments. And, even if he could prove it, what good would that do Curtis?

He'd consumed half the beer before he noticed the red light blinking on the answering machine that sat on a scarred table beside his chair. He leaned over and pressed the "replay" button and his father's gravelly voice filled the room.

"Drew? You there? I need to talk to you. Right away."

The voice paused, waiting for Drew to pick up, and the machine spewed static until it clicked off a few seconds later.

Drew hauled the phone into his lap. He dialed the nursing home's number from memory and asked for his father's room.

"Hello?"

"Hey, Pop, it's me. I got your message. What's up?"

"Good to hear from you. I was getting worried."

Chuck grunted into the phone, and Drew could picture him trying to sit up in bed, dragging his paralyzed limbs into place.

"Worried about what, Pop? What's going on?"

"I got a phone call this afternoon. Some guy, said you were in trouble."

"Who was it?"

"He didn't give his name. He just said I'd better be looking after my son. That you were messing in stuff that was going to get you hurt. Then I couldn't reach you at the paper or at home. I've been fretting all afternoon."

Drew had been at his desk much of the afternoon, but he wasn't surprised his father hadn't been able to get through to him. The *Gazette* phone system was infamous for its inefficiencies, and the receptionists couldn't be bothered to track people down. You didn't pick up on the first ring, they assumed you were out of the building. Usually, though, they at least took a message.

"Sorry, Pop. If I'd known, I would've called you back sooner. This guy, did he say what it was about?"

"No, I've told you everything he said. But he managed to sound serious about it."

"What did you say?"

"I told him to kiss my hairy ass."

"Way to go, Pop. Don't let it upset you. Just some jerk trying to get to me."

Drew was steaming. Some son of a bitch—and he'd bet it was Otis Edgewater—playing phone pranks on his ailing father. That was too low for words.

"This has something to do with Curtis, doesn't it, son?"

"I think so. Sounds like somebody thinks I'm getting close to something."

"You better be careful. This man, he sounded like he meant what he said. When he said you'd be in trouble, I believed him."

"I'm not in any trouble. Nothing I can't handle anyway."

Okay, a little lie. No sense in telling Chuck about Goodman's threat to boot him out of his job, or the strange car following him in the night. The old man had enough on his mind already. And he had all day, every day, to lie in bed and worry.

"You talk to Curtis?"

"I saw him yesterday."

"How's he holding up?"

"He's doing okay. I hope we'll get him out of jail soon."

Chuck exhaled loudly into the phone. Drew knew phone conversations wore him out quickly. The damaged parts of his brain didn't like to talk on the phone, though he seemed to do fine face-to-face. Drew felt like running over there, keeping the old man company for a while. But he had too much on his mind. Chuck would read it on his face.

"I hope so, son," Chuck was saying. "I want this to be over. I didn't like the way that guy sounded. I don't want you getting hurt."

"Don't worry, Pop. I can take care of myself."

"Famous last words."

Drew chatted with him a little more, changing the subject, getting Chuck's thoughts on another track. But he felt hot inside.

He was getting pretty fucking tired of Otis Edgewater. He felt sure he was the one who called Chuck. And he probably ruined that tire as well. And Drew knew for certain that Edgewater had called the publisher, trying to get him in hot water.

The bastard was enjoying this. Taunting Drew, daring him to do something about it. And Drew couldn't say a thing, not without risking a slander suit. He wondered whether Edgewater was operating on his own, or whether Cerf was behind it. These chickenshit maneuvers—the phone calls, the tire—didn't seem to fit Edgewater. He was a man of action, more likely to try to beat the hell out of Drew than to pick at him this way. But what kind of man was Cerf?

Distracted, he managed to get his father off the phone and hung up. His thoughts roiled with Edgewater and Cerf and contracts and sabotage and Sylvia Smith.

He wondered whether Sylvia would know someone at Sandia who'd have information on Edgewater's military background. Or, whether the Department of Defense had any tips that Cerf was shopping his software around illegally. He thought about calling her at home, maybe getting her to do some checking for him.

But he didn't pick up the phone. She might take the call as a come-on, no matter the context, and God knows what would happen next. They were like two live wires dancing about, and she seemed ready to touch them together, see what sparks flew. Drew wasn't ready for that. He felt guilty even considering it. His feelings for Teresa were solid and strong. Why let Sylvia Smith chip away at them?

Guilt moved him to call the Los Angeles hotel where Teresa was staying. He should talk to her, see how people were treating her there. Reconnect with her, so the enticement of Sylvia Smith would seem foolish and sinful, like a rich dessert to a dieter.

He let the phone ring eight times, but there was no answer. Teresa was out, probably cruising around L.A., seeing the sights. Or being entertained by her potential new colleagues at the *Times*. Or dining with some handsome editor. Drew wondered what temptations she was facing, out there in the Land of Temptation, and whether she was handling them any better than he was.

He cradled the phone and grunted up out of his chair to get another beer. He needed to eat something. He needed to get some rest. He needed to stop worrying about Teresa and Curtis and Cerf and Sylvia and the rest of it.

But a beer would do for now.

TWENTY NINE

Drew woke up early Thursday with Sylvia Smith on his mind. Had he been dreaming about her? Were they erotic dreams? He couldn't remember, which left him feeling that he'd missed something.

He dragged himself out of bed and drank coffee and had a shower, all the while trying to push Sylvia from his mind. Teresa returned from Los Angeles this evening. He didn't need to meet her at the airport with "Sylvia Smith" written all over his face.

Maybe, he decided as he dressed, he kept thinking about Sylvia not because she was a blonde knockout who was clearly interested in him, but because he was overlooking something. Maybe Sylvia held an answer for him, if he could only think of the question.

She plagued his mind as he navigated the freeway snarls to the *Gazette*. Did her theory about Cerf and his defense software have some hole in it that Drew was missing? Had she put herself in danger in some way, and he'd missed the signal?

It came to him as he steered the Jeep around potholes on the way into the *Gazette* parking lot. The flat tire. If whoever had ruined that tire had been following him, there was a good chance that person had seen him with Sylvia. She might've just become a target.

As soon as he got settled at his desk, he dialed Sylvia's office phone. A secretary answered, and told him Sylvia wouldn't be there today.

"Do you know where she is?"

"She called in sick. That's all I know. I'd guess she's at home."

"I'll call her there. Thanks."

He had her home number. She'd put it in that sheaf of paperwork, which was still out in the Jeep. He lumbered out to the parking lot and retrieved the papers. As he carried them into the newsroom, he got an idea.

But first, he needed to call Sylvia, make sure she was all right. She hadn't seemed sick at lunch the day before.

He let her home phone ring ten times, but not even an answering machine picked up. Perhaps she'd gone to a doctor. Or maybe she was just in bed, avoiding calls. But it worried him. He and Sylvia were playing a risky game.

And now it was time to add some players. Drew saw Felicia Quattlebaum at her desk across the room, hunkered over the phone, her thick glasses glinting squares of reflected light. The file folder of Cerf paperwork just begged to be handed over to her.

That would be the smart thing to do. Give the paperwork to Quattlebaum, see if she could use it in her stories. Tell her about the questionable money trail and the defense contract and Sylvia's theories. He could give her all of that, but not Sylvia. Try to keep Sylvia out of it as much as possible.

He felt possessive of all the information, as if he were working on an exclusive he wanted to share with no one, not even his colleagues. But handing the papers over was the right thing to do. It would make Goodman happy, indicating that Drew was keeping clear of Scott Cerf and his people. And, it would sic Quattlebaum on Cerf and Edgewater. They wouldn't know what hit them.

He sighed and stood up, uncertain and hesitant, looking down at the stack of papers.

"Sorry, Curtis," he said under his breath. "I wanted to do this myself."

Then he picked up the file and carried it the length of the newsroom to Quattlebaum.

THIRTY

Drew was running late as he wheeled his Jeep into the concrete parking garage at Albuquerque International Sunport. He checked his watch again. Teresa's plane should be touching down about now. He found a parking spot and hustled through a tunnel that led from the garage to the airport.

Escalators carried him up two levels to the main concourse, where he hurried past newsstands and coffee kiosks and the token Mexican restaurant for the tourists. The airport was modern and clean, done up in pastel tiles and Southwestern touches such as carved ceiling beams and heavy leather chairs.

Drew, who'd seen it all a thousand times flying to cover football games around the West, weaved through gawking sightseers to gate B3, where Teresa's plane already had nuzzled up to the jetway.

He stood near a clump of other greeters, catching his breath and waiting for Teresa to emerge.

A smile stretched his face when he saw her hiking up the ramp, her carry-on slung over her shoulder. From a distance, she looked the same as usual—black clothes head to toe, short black hair pulled up into fluffy little spikes all over her head, purple lipstick, chewing gum. But as she got closer, Drew could see the changes. She'd gotten some sun driving around

Southern California in a convertible. Her eyes sparkled. She looked tanned and rested and too damned happy.

"Hiya, tiger," she said, throwing an arm around his neck and planting a kiss on his lips. "Been waiting long?"

"Just got here. I almost didn't get away from the office in time."

"Thanks for coming. Trying to get a cab in Albuquerque is like requesting human sacrifices anywhere else."

"No sacrifice necessary. The Jeep's in the parking garage."

He lifted the bag off her shoulder and swung it onto his own. She grinned at him.

"Miss me?" she asked as they strolled along the concourse.

"You bet. Things have been pretty crazy around here while you were gone."

"Tell me all about it."

"No. First, tell me about L.A. Did they offer you the job?"

She nodded, a smile still playing about her face. Drew tried to return the smile, but he felt as if he'd been gut-punched. The job was hers. She'd leave now, taking a piece of him with her out to Los Angeles. And there wasn't a damned thing he could do about it.

Teresa read his expression and her smile evaporated. She looked away, out the tall windows toward the mountains, which were doing their usual amazing color-shifting as the sun sank in the west.

"That's great," he choked out. "I'm happy for you."

She glanced over at him, but it was too late. No amount of congratulations and fake bonhomie would repair that instant when he let his disappointment show.

"Yeah, well, I know part of you probably wishes it had gone the other way. It raises a lot of questions."

He hung his head. "Sure as hell does."

They walked on in silence for a while. Drew felt as if some-one had pressed a "mute" button. He couldn't hear the tumult of travelers all around him, too focused on recovering from Teresa's news.

Teresa smacked her gum furiously, not looking at him, as they rode down the escalators.

"The money good?" he managed finally.

"Double what I'm making now."

"You'll need that much to live in L.A. It's expensive out there."

"Who said I was going?"

That pulled him up short. He nearly stumbled as the esca-lator reached the lower floor.

"Aren't you?"

"I haven't decided yet."

They stopped and faced each other, off to one side, out of the stream of foot traffic.

"What's to decide?" he said. "Sounds like a great opportunity."

"Mostly. I'm not crazy about some parts of it."

"Like what?"

"Like, I wouldn't be working in the city. I'd be out in the Valley, working in one of the bureaus, getting my 'seasoning.' Do I look like a Valley Girl to you?"

He fought back a laugh. "Not at all. I think you'd scare the Valley Girls."

"Exactly. Not my scene."

"But you'd work your way up. Nail a few front-page bylines, and you'll be covering the cop shop, the capitol, what-ever you want."

She squinted at him. "Sounds like you're trying to get rid of me, tiger."

Drew took a deep breath. His words came out in a rush: "Of course I don't want you to go. I want everything here to stay the same. But you can't pass this up. Not if you plan to ever leave here. Door like this doesn't open every day."

"It's not stepping through the door that scares me," she said somberly. "It's the slamming-shut-behind-me part that I'm worried about."

He reached out for her, ended up just resting a hand on her shoulder.

"Listen, Teresa, I had my shots at the big time. Years ago. Big papers calling me up, offering me jobs. I passed them up, and I often wonder what I missed."

She glanced away, looking for a break in the stream of pedestrians coming off the escalator.

"And you don't want me making the same mistake," she said.

"Was it a mistake? I don't know. I'm pretty happy with my life, the way things turned out. And I may get offers again someday, after I've mastered the whole sports editor gig. But you've got your chance to shine right now."

She thought it over while they walked out of the tunnel and into the dim recesses of the low-ceilinged parking garage. As they reached the Jeep, she said, "I thought you'd try to talk me out of it."

"I want to. I don't want you to go. But I'm trying not to be a selfish prick. I'm trying to think of what's best for you."

"Then how about this: I'll take the job and you go with me."

"That's what you want?"

"I was thinking about it on the plane. I think you'd like it out there."

"And what would I do for food and shelter?"

"You'd turn something up. You could stay with me."

"Like, move in together?"

She shrugged. "Wouldn't you like that?"

Drew had thought of that very thing several times lately, but the image he had in mind was the two of them sharing his father's house, fixing it up, making a home together. He wasn't ready to marry her, but living together was a possibility, a trial period of togetherness, to see how well it all clicked. But move *with* her? Abandon Pop and the *Gazette* and his hometown in favor of the untried and perhaps untrue in sunny California?

"I can't do it," he muttered. "Not now. Not with Pop sick and all. I can't leave."

Hurt welled in her eyes, but she looked away and cleared her throat.

"That was a pretty fast answer," she said. "Don't you even want to think it over?"

"I've *been* thinking it over. That's just the way it is. I can't change it."

Teresa hugged herself while she waited for Drew to unlock the Jeep. She studied the concrete floor, and he couldn't tell whether she was crying.

Damn it, he hadn't wanted to have this talk, not yet, not here. Why couldn't he have simply congratulated her and given her time to think? But maybe that was the problem. Maybe she'd been thinking about moving together the whole time she was gone, the same way he'd been obsessing on her potential departure. Maybe it all needed to come bursting out now, spontaneous and emotional and weird. Get it all out on the table, so she can decide whether to stay or go.

"Then I don't know what I'll do," she said to the floor.

He pulled her to his chest and wrapped his arms around her shoulders. He rested his chin on top of her head. Her hair smelled warm.

"Take it easy," he said. "You've got some time, right? Think it over a while."

"I told them I'd let them know in a day or two," she said into his chest. "They're pretty eager for me to get out there and get started."

He gave her a squeeze, then steered her into the passenger seat. Her eyes were red as she pulled her seat belt across her, and Drew wanted to kiss her, to climb in beside her and hold her tight. But he trudged around the Jeep and got behind the wheel and started the engine. She stared out the window while he navigated out of the open-sided garage. Twilight gray climbed the face of the mountains, chasing a rosy pink to the crest as the sun went down.

"A day or two," he thought, less than forty-eight hours to decide the plotline of their lives.

And the decision's all hers. If he persuaded her to stay, then regret and recrimination lay in his future. Someday, she'd be sorry she passed up the opportunity, and she'd blame him, even if she never said it out loud. He prayed she'd stay in Albuquerque, give them time to work out a future together. But he wouldn't try to sell her on it. He'd wait. Let her decide.

And if she took the job, then the next decision would be his. Follow her out there or stay behind alone. Could he live without Teresa? He had a feeling he was about to find out.

It wasn't far to her apartment near the university. He parked the Jeep and reached for her bag to carry it inside, but she took it from his hand as she popped open the car door.

"You want me to come in?" he asked.

She bit her lower lip and shook her head.

"Not right now, tiger. I've got too much on my mind. Let me sleep on it, on everything. We'll talk more tomorrow."

He didn't like this plan at all. He wanted to be handy while she made up her mind. But he nodded and leaned across the seat and kissed her before she got out of the Jeep.

The kiss tasted like good-bye.

THIRTY ONE

Otis Edgewater pulled his Ford to the curb a block away from where Gavin's dusty Jeep had stopped outside a run-down apartment building. Gavin leaned over and kissed the slender woman he'd picked up at the airport, confirming what Otis already suspected: She was his squeeze, Teresa Vargas, who covered the cop beat for the *Gazette*.

He liked being proved right. It made him feel in command.

Otis imagined himself in uniform, medals dripping off his chest, addressing a battalion of recruits. He said under his breath, "See, men, planning is the key. Research. Reconnaissance. Know what you're getting into before you get into it. Know your enemy, and where his weaknesses lie."

Otis had never been much of a public speaker. He was too intimidating. People stayed too busy staring at his muscles to hear what he said.

"One of the reasons I never made colonel," he muttered. "Fuckers didn't see that intimidation *is* command. They want you to talk pretty in the all-volunteer Army. Take it easy on the men. Handle the women with fuckin' kid gloves. Whole country's going soft."

He watched the Jeep pull away. He probably should follow, but thinking about the Army had pissed him off. Motherfuckers didn't understand about action and the waiting. They'd begun to think serving in the Army was *about* the waiting. Just sitting around a barracks stateside, putting in your time like fucking convicts, all the while praying that war doesn't break out in some distant land. Praying you don't have to get off your ass and go see some combat.

Otis had begun to think he liked civilian life better. Out here, he could at least make something happen when the pressure got to be too much. Or so he kept telling himself. But what had he been doing for the past few days? Watching and waiting. Researching, reconnoitering. He was tired of waiting. He craved action and movement and blood.

The Vargas woman still stood on the sidewalk in front of her apartment building, her bag slung over her back. She watched the Jeep until it was out of sight. Then she turned to the door, her shoulders slumped.

"What's the matter, darlin'?" Otis whispered. "That big old jock didn't want to come in? He too much of a wimp to give you a proper welcome-home?"

He watched as she unlocked the door and went inside.

"Yes, men," he said inside the car, loud enough to address a crowd, "You've got to know your enemy's weaknesses. And I'm thinkin' one of them just went in that apartment there."

He got out of the car and walked toward the apartment buildling. A few bedraggled elms leaned over the building, casting ragged shadows on its tan stucco walls. The light was fading fast. Otis thinking: I probably should wait until dark. But it feels good to move around after sitting in the car for hours.

He walked past the woman's door to the far end of the building, which was long and narrow with eight little porches facing the quiet street. An alley split the block at the far end of the apartments, and Otis turned into it, marching along with his big chest thrown out, his posture perfect. The alley was gray gravel and his boots crunched as he reached the back of the building.

Nothing back there but weeds and utility poles and evaporative coolers sucking up to the rear of the building. Each apartment had one large window and one small one cut into the otherwise bare back wall. Otis picked his way through litter and weeds, counting off windows to reach the girlfriend's apartment.

The small window was frosted glass, and drapes were pulled across the larger one. Otis stood to one side of the large window, peering in through an inch-wide gap between the drapes. He saw Gavin's girlfriend pass by, but it was just a flash of bare skin and black bra. He squatted down and tried to get a better view.

"Hey, man! What are you doing?"

Otis turned to see a stick figure of a man standing in the alley. The guy was young, probably a college student. His black hair was shaggy and he had a thin, scroungy beard. A bright tie-dyed T-shirt hung loose around his bony shoulders. Just the kind of little hippie Otis used to love to see coming into boot camp.

Otis stood and moved from the window. The guy's eyes went wide as he got a look at Otis' build. He edged away, his mouth opening and closing.

"I'm gonna call the cops!" he shouted, then he turned to run.

Otis sprinted to the alley before the hippie could take three steps. He grabbed his narrow shoulders and threw him to the ground.

The hippie yelped and rolled over on the gravel, trying to get to his feet. Otis fiercely kicked him twice in the ribs and the kid gasped and cried and rolled into a ball.

"Get up, you little cocksucker."

Otis grabbed a handful of the T-shirt and tried to yank the guy to his feet, but the shirt stretched and tore.

"Fuck."

He grabbed the hippie by the hair instead and pulled him

to his feet. The kid couldn't straighten up all the way, his arms clutched around his naked chest. Otis leaned over until his nose was inches away from his face.

"You never saw me here, son. Understand?"

The kid nodded, trying to swallow, tears springing from his eyes.

"Aw, shit." This kid was no good. Fucking coward. He wouldn't fight back. He'd promise anything, but he'd call the cops as soon as he caught his breath. Otis grabbed the hippie's shoulder and spun him around. The guy let go of his ribs long enough to throw up his hands, trying to keep his balance. Otis helping him out by seizing a handful of hair. Then he snaked his free hand under the kid's whiskery chin, grabbed hold and twisted sharply.

The hippie's neck gave with a satisfying snap. He made a gurgling sound, then went limp all over. Otis let him fall to the ground.

Shit, he thought, I'm not even breathing hard. Civilians are too damned easy to kill.

He glanced up and down the narrow alley, but no one was around. He turned on his heel and marched back to his car, brushing his hands together to get rid of the feel of the hippie's oily hair.

He was behind the wheel and cranking the engine before he looked around the empty street again. He felt vaguely dissatisfied, wishing the kid had put up more of a fight. He slipped the car into gear and let it crawl up the block.

Then he got an idea. No way in hell the cops would ever tie the death to him, but it wouldn't hurt to buy a little insurance. He steered the big sedan into the alley and let it creep forward until it bump-bumped over the hippie's body.

Let the cops figure that one out. It'll look like the little shit got too stoned and passed out in the alley. Oops, somebody ran over him with a car.

Otis smiled as he drove away.

THIRTY TWO

Drew was at home and halfway through his second beer before he thought again about Sylvia Smith. He'd tried to call her all day, never getting an answer, and he'd been worried about her before Teresa's return distracted him. He certainly wasn't getting anywhere fretting over Teresa. Might as well try to locate Sylvia.

He called her home number again, and this time she answered.

"Thank God," he said. "I've been trying to reach you all day."

"Drew? Is that you?"

"Sorry, I didn't even say hello. I'm just relieved to finally find you. Are you sick?"

"No, I'm fine," she said. Her voice sounded sleepy and warm. "I've been in bed all day. I was worn out from pulling that all-nighter. They don't come as easily as they did when I was in college."

"Ain't that the truth. So you just took the day off?"

She giggled. "Aren't government jobs wonderful? I unplugged the phone and curled up under the covers and slept all day. It's been blissful."

"Glad to hear it."

"You don't sound glad. Why were you so worried?"

"People have been turning up dead lately, remember? I was afraid something might've happened to you."

"You think I'm in danger?"

"You never know. You've been hanging out with the wrong crowd lately."

"Just you."

"That's who I meant."

She yawned into the phone. Drew could picture her stretching, a loose gown twisted around her body. It was a pretty picture.

"Maybe," she said, and her voice was suddenly hushed, "you should come over and keep me company. Then you wouldn't have to worry so much."

"Be your bodyguard, huh? While you finish your long nap?"

"I'm finished," she said. "I'm wide awake now. Just plugged in the phone and there you were. I didn't even have to get out of bed."

Drew swallowed. His imagination worked overtime, picturing himself sweeping into her home, straight to her bed, where she'd be waiting, all warm and whetted.

He shook his head. Jesus. Try not to get carried away here, boy. Think about Teresa, about her possibly moving away, all that's been plaguing you. Think about Curtis, mouldering in jail. Hell, think about baseball. But get your mind to move it along.

"Well, get up and make sure your doors are locked," he said. "Then I'll stop worrying."

A long pause.

"That's why you called?" she asked, and her voice had lost

its warmth now. "To tell me to lock my doors?"

"I just wanted to make sure you were all right. I called your office and they said you were sick—"

"I'm fine, Drew. Thanks for your concern."

Boy, he thought, I've got a way with women today. I open my mouth and the temperature drops. A decided chill in the air for May.

"Look, I'm sorry if I bothered you. I was just worried, that's all. And, I was wondering whether you had any more thoughts on this whole deal with Scott Cerf."

"I haven't given it a thought," she said, and there was an edge in her voice. "I've been asleep all day."

"Right. Sorry. I've just kind of reached a dead end. I thought you might have something else for me."

Drew thinking: She's got something for you all right, but you blew it. Too mixed-up over your feelings about Teresa to take the bait. Dumbass.

"I'll think about it," she said. "Maybe tomorrow I'll see if I can turn up anything else on the virtual reality stuff."

"That would be great. But be careful. Don't let anybody know you're snooping."

"Afraid something will happen to me?" Her tone said: As if you'd care . . .

"I think this whole thing's dangerous. Watch yourself."

She hung up without saying good-bye.

THIRTY THREE

Drew had been at his desk maybe ten minutes Friday morning when his telephone rang. He could tell from the single ring that the call came from inside the building. Probably Goodman with another ass-chewing. He sighed and answered the phone.

"Hey, Gavin, it's Felicia."

His eyes automatically went to the other end of the newsroom, where Felicia Quattlebaum sat at her desk, the phone to her ear under a dark waterfall of shoulder-length hair. She was facing his way, and waved when their eyes met. She was a tiny woman, looked like she could fit in Drew's hip pocket.

"I've got to talk to Goodman. Thought you might want to be in on it."

"I've spent enough time in Goodman's office lately," he said.

"Have it your way. But it's about Scott Cerf."

"I'll be right there."

Drew creaked to his feet and headed for Goodman's corner office. He saw Quattlebaum rise and walk that direction, too. He went faster, trying to catch up with her, maybe get a little more information, but she had the angle on him and was already through Goodman's door by the time he arrived.

"I asked Gavin to join us," Quattlebaum was saying as he entered. "Some of the stuff I'm looking into, I got from him."

Goodman rolled his eyes, but said nothing. Plenty of time for that later, Drew thought, after it became clear he still was meddling in the Fontanelle Harper investigation. He gave Quattlebaum a shushing look, but she missed her cue.

"Gavin told me that Cerf's finances look suspicious," she said. "Gave me a bunch of paperwork to look through. I think he's right. There's something wrong there."

Goodman cut his eyes to Drew, who could feel his face warming.

"This is stuff I got earlier, Bob," he said quickly. "Curtis had collected a lot of it before he got arrested. All this dates from before you told me to stay out of it."

"Which time?" Goodman said. "The first time I said it, or the last time? Or one of the thousand times in between?"

"I'm being a good boy now, Bob." Which was only a small lie. "But somebody's got to go after this guy. I thought Felicia could make use of the material."

He glanced over at her. She had a crooked grin on her face, amused by Drew's squirming.

"I sure can," she said. "I'll carry it with me when I go interview Cerf."

"*What?*"

"Yup. I'm interviewing him in a couple of hours."

"Damn," Drew said. "I didn't think he was talking to the press."

"He'll talk to me," she said smugly. "Guess you just have to know how to ask."

Drew frowned and muttered, "Guess so."

"I called Cerf Software's PR department this morning and

started badgering them for a face-to-face with their boss. Cerf got wind of it and called me back directly, offering to give me an hour today."

Goodman raised a thin hand to halt them. "Here's the pertinent question: Why are you here in my office?"

"I wanted you to know about the interview. It could be our breakthrough, and you might want to hold space for it on the front page. Plus, Cerf's a big advertiser. Might be trouble from the publisher."

Goodman's bald head began to glow. Drew knew the signals. If it had been him stirring Goodman up like this, he'd already be heading for the door. Make his escape before the editor exploded. But Quattlebaum just stared levelly at Goodman.

"You do your job," Goodman blustered. "I'll handle the publisher. He doesn't meddle in the newsroom unless he wants to fight me first."

Drew got a mental image of the tall, bald editor wrestling in the newsroom entrance with the little bow-tied publisher. He had to suppress a smile.

"Okay," Quattlebaum said. "I'll try to nail Cerf. These documents raise certain questions. Like, how's he affording the basketball league and that nightclub he's involved with? And what it means to his company to have Wally Mertz dead and out of the way."

"Don't forget the cheerleader," Drew said. "I still think her murder is connected in some way."

"Right," she said. "It'll be interesting to see his reaction. Might lead somewhere."

Drew sat up straighter. "Maybe I should go with you."

Felicia frowned, and he could see she didn't like the idea of him muscling in on her interview. Before she could answer, Goodman said, "No, Drew. That would be you messing around in this again. I thought I made myself clear on that count."

Drew held up his hands in surrender, and said, "I'll go sit quietly at my desk."

"Good decision," Goodman said flatly.

Felicia looked relieved that Goodman had nixed the idea. They're probably both right, Drew thought, I should stay away. She can handle the interview fine on her own, probably better than if she had me moping around in the background. But I sure would like to see the look on Cerf's face when she asks about the murder of Fontanelle Harper.

THIRTY FOUR

Scott Cerf sat behind his desk, trying not to fidget. He'd thought this interview would be a snap—especially when he learned the reporter was a woman—but it had been fifty minutes of hell so far, and he still had ten to go. No sense trying to cut it short; he'd promised an hour and he'd have to deliver. This little bitch would demand every minute.

Felicia Quattlebaum seemed immune to his charms, which meant he'd lost the main weapon in his arsenal. Without the cool smile and the quick wink doing their work, he was forced to fall back on evasion and denial, which only seemed to make the reporter more dogged.

They'd covered the numbers on Cerf Software, confirming what she already seemed to know, that the company wasn't doing so great. Hell, anybody who could read the stock report could tell that, but she seemed to think it was significant. She hit a couple of times on the pending defense contract, but he managed to steer her away, saying it was all top-secret. He couldn't tell precisely where she was heading, but he felt she was backing him into a corner, talking endlessly about money.

"I think our readers," she was saying, "would be interested in how you finance the Rattlers and the WABL. You had to go millions in debt. How will you cover those loans?"

He tried the smile again, but she didn't smile back. "I have my resources," he said. "I prefer that they not all be public."

"A man of mystery, eh?"

He gave her a casual shrug to cover up the fact that he felt like screaming.

"Nobody likes to have their income trotted out for public view. How would you like it, if the *Gazette* put your salary under your byline?"

She didn't blink behind her big glasses.

"The WABL is a private enterprise. We take no government funds. We don't have to reveal our finances to the public.

What's there to hide?"

Her pen poised over her pad, waiting for him to make a mistake. Cerf felt a drop of perspiration slide down his ribcage.

Otis had warned him against granting this interview. The old Army vet had been watching Drew Gavin, and he said Gavin might be getting close to uncovering secrets. And Gavin undoubtedly had shared his information with this woman. It smelled like a set-up.

Cerf had shouted down Otis' objections, reminding him of who was in charge around here. The big ape needed to be put in his place. Cerf needed to show Otis there were some things he could handle himself. Of course, once Otis had stormed away, Cerf had his own second thoughts about meeting the press. What if Otis was right? Before the reporter arrived, he'd assured himself he could dazzle her, that he could talk his way out of trouble. It had always worked for him before. But Felicia Quattlebaum refused to be dazzled, and he now felt desperation gripping his chest.

She looked at her wristwatch. Cerf's eyes moved to the clock on the wall. Seven more minutes, then he could beg off, tell her he's too busy to give her any more time.

He told her that revealing his sources of income could give his competitors an unfair advantage. The answer sounded hollow in his own ears. Worse, it gave her a new line of attack.

"Speaking of your competitors, Wally Mertz was murdered this week. What do you know about that?"

He smiled, but the expression felt weak, uncertain. "Only what I've read in the *Gazette*."

"I've talked to the cops," she said. "They can't find any good motive for somebody to kill Mertz. But his death might help you get that defense contract."

Cerf sat up straighter in his swivel chair. Now was the time to trot out the indignation, but he felt suddenly tired. He didn't know if he could pull it off.

"Are you accusing me of killing Wally Mertz?"

"I didn't accuse you of anything. I asked what you might know."

"And I told you I know nothing about it. I hope you're not planning to put such insinuations in your article. I'm afraid I'd have to take legal action."

"Don't threaten me with lawyers, Mr. Cerf," she said calmly. "I've heard it all before."

"I'm not threatening anything," he sputtered. "But I won't stand still for character assassination either. If you try to tie me to Mertz's death—"

"Who said I was?"

He pressed his lips together. Don't get riled, he told himself, just ride this thing out. Her time would be up soon, and she'd go away empty-handed. So far, he hadn't told her enough to fill a brief in the back of the Metro section.

When she saw he wouldn't answer, she said, "And then there's the death of Fontanelle Harper. Two deaths in a week, and both victims have connections with you."

"I barely knew Fontanelle," he said. "I knew Mertz, sure, went to college with him. But Fontanelle had never met him, as far as I know. Maybe it's a coincidence that they both were killed."

Felicia Quattlebaum had been scribbling in her notebook, but she paused to lift up her hands and count off on her fingers.

"They both knew you," she said. "They were killed the same way, just days apart. The killer even left a calling card of sorts—something stuffed in their mouths—at both murder scenes. I'd say there are lots of connections."

Cerf stared at her for a long time. She stared back, waiting, her pen ready.

"If that's all true," he said finally, "then I'm sure the police are looking into it."

"Have they questioned you?"

"No. I don't have anything to tell them, as you can see. Talking with the police, I'm afraid, would be just as much a waste of time as this interview."

A furrow appeared between her eyebrows, and her face reddened slightly. Good. He'd pissed her off. He was beginning to think she was immune to all emotion. It might be playing with fire to make her mad, but he had to do something.

"These deaths are tragic," he said. "No one disputes that. But they have nothing to do with me. How can I convince you of that?"

He already knew the answer. No way he could convince her of anything. But he only needed to keep her talking for three more minutes. Then he could show her the door, and she'd leave with nothing more than the suspicions she brought with her. She flipped over a page in her notebook, framing her next question, but he beat her to the punch.

"Do you enjoy your job, Ms. Quattlebaum?"

She shrugged.

"Must be a terrible way to live," he said. "Always expecting the worst of people."

She shook her head slightly, refusing to take the bait. "Sometimes, the worst is true."

"Is that why you came here today? You thought there was some greater truth hidden at Cerf Software? That I was some mad scientist, killing anybody who gets in my way?"

He chuckled merrily, but he knew it sounded false. Most women would melt at his smile, his manly laugh. The reporter wouldn't even thaw.

"If you're not involved in these killings, then you've got nothing to hide, right?"

"Everybody has *something* to hide," he said. "In this case, you're trying to get me to reveal trade secrets. Naturally, I don't want to help you do that. But to take those secrets and extrapolate some connection with these murders, that's just absurd."

"People get killed for all sorts of absurd reasons," she said.

Cerf stood, taking his time to rise to his full height.

"I can't imagine any reason that would cause a murder to make sense. Maybe you'll find that these people were killed for silly reasons, too. But I can guarantee you, none of those reasons have anything to do with me."

It was a good line, a walk-away line, and Cerf thought she'd see it as that and leave. But she just sat there in his guest chair, her notepad in her lap, waiting him out.

"Sorry, Ms. Quattlebaum, but I'm afraid our time is up. I've got a lot of work to do."

She sighed and closed her notebook, but she had to take one last shot. Just as he'd expected.

"It would take a lot of suspicion off you if you'd talk," she said. "Tell us how you're affording the Rattlers. Make it clear you don't stand to benefit from the death of Wally Mertz."

Cerf shook his head. His face felt tight.

"I've answered your questions as best I can," he said. "Go back to your newspaper and see what you can put together. But you won't be getting any more help from me."

Her eyes sparked. "You haven't given me any help. Not so far."

"Sorry you see it that way, but I simply can't give you any more time."

He stepped around the desk to show her to the door. She hesitated, then rose and followed him out. He held the door for her, noting that he was more than a foot taller than her. How could such a little woman cause him so much anxiety? What's that old saying, about dynamite coming in small packages? Felicia Quattlebaum looked ready to explode.

"I'll be in touch," she snarled.

Cerf watched her go, repressing the urge to whew in relief. Only when she'd left the reception area did he notice that Otis Edgewater lounged on a sofa against the wall. The man sat perfectly still, his huge muscles like stone, and he reminded Cerf of one of those lifelike statues you see in parks and in front of city halls. What would this one be called? "Gargantua in Repose?"

Cerf jerked his head toward his inner office, and Otis rocked to his feet and followed. By the time Otis closed the door, Cerf was at the tall windows, watching the little reporter stalk across the parking lot to her car, her head down against a steady wind. He imagined what she'd tell her editors when she got back to the *Gazette* empty-handed.

"How'd it go?" Otis asked.

Cerf turned to face him. He hoped his expression didn't give anything away, that Otis wouldn't notice how he was sweating. Otis had been right about granting the interview, but Cerf wouldn't admit it. He wouldn't give the big monster the satisfaction.

"Fine, fine," he said. "She's got nothing on us."

Otis dipped his head, checking out his shoes or stifling some wiseass remark. Cerf's attention was caught once again by the strands of gray hair striped over Otis' bald head. He wondered about the connection between testosterone and hair loss. Maybe Otis had used up all his male juices building muscles.

"Hope you're right, chief," Otis said after a moment. "We've got that meeting with Ling coming up next Thursday."

Cerf frowned, but said nothing. He felt the reporter's presence still in the room, as if anything he said to Otis might somehow end up on the front page of the *Gazette*.

"I talked to Kamal on the phone today," Otis said. "His people are still interested, but only if we don't approach their neighbors."

This news should've pleased Cerf. It meant his deals still were on track, despite all the turmoil on the home front. But he didn't want to talk about it now. He didn't want to think about where he was headed, and how much it might cost. He wanted Otis to leave. He wanted to be alone, to give himself time to come down off the post-interview anxiety.

"See?" he said. "It's just as I said. It will all be fine."

Otis studied him.

"I don't know, chief. I think some more folks are gonna have to die before everything's fine and dandy."

Cerf's stomach knotted. He turned back to the window. He stayed that way, silently facing the windswept parking lot, until he heard his office door shut. He turned and was glad to see Otis had gone. The man was becoming a liability; he knew too much about Cerf's business and he enjoyed his work too much.

"Yeah," he muttered. "Somebody else might have to die. And it might just be you, Otis."

THIRTY FIVE

Teresa wasn't sure Drew would still be at the newsroom, but she called anyway. He sounded glum when he answered the phone.

"Hi, tiger, what's the matter?"

"Aw, things aren't going so great here."

"Everybody missing deadline?"

"No, not *my* people. They're *all* right on time."

He said this last loud enough to be overheard, and Teresa smiled. Drew's management style was like that of a coach: coax and kid and communicate. Tweak people until they did what they knew they should.

"Then what's wrong?"

"Felicia got back from interviewing Scott Cerf a little while ago."

"And?"

"And she didn't get a thing. The guy was too smooth. Every time she felt she was getting close, he claimed his privacy was being violated and skipped away."

"That's too bad. You were hoping it would help Curtis, right?"

"Just hoping something would break. I feel like I'm in a small, windowless room and somebody's bricking up the door."

"Aw, c'mon, tiger. It'll be okay. These things take time."

"Meanwhile, Curtis is *doing* time."

"He'll be all right. He'll have them dancing a conga line around the jail before he's through. Mr. Party Animal."

"Yeah." He still sounded gloomy, and she changed the subject. Nothing like news to perk up a newshound.

"Did you hear about the excitement around here?"

"What?"

"One of my neighbors got killed. We've had the cops here all day."

"Really? Who was it?"

"Guy at the end of the building named Jon Peabody. I didn't know him except to say 'hi.' He was one of these throwback college kids. Big pothead. Thought he was a hippie."

"How'd he die?"

"Looks like a hit-and-run. Somebody found him in the alley this morning."

"Jeez."

"Yeah. People are always zooming off the street into that alley. Looks like he was standing there at the wrong time. Or sleeping one off outdoors."

"That's too bad. Lot of death around lately."

"That's why you need to be careful," she said. "You don't want to get any of that on you. Besides, I have plans for you."

He paused before he said, "You do?"

"Sure do. A celebration of life, so to speak. When are you getting out of that office?"

Another pause. "I could be at your place in fifteen minutes."

"That would be good. I've got something I want to show you."

"Make that twelve minutes."

"You better hurry," she said. "I might start without you."

"I'm running to my car now."

He hung up, leaving her with a smile on her face. She'd felt bad after the talk on the way home from the airport. Career pressure seemed ready to blow them apart, and she wasn't handling it well. She'd lain awake most of the night, worrying about it all, before finally falling to sleep around four. She'd awakened thinking about him, and he'd been on her mind all day.

Sure, she still was inclined toward taking the job and, sure, that meant big problems for her and Drew. But it seemed stupid to let the future (even if it was the very near future) wreck the present. She intended to remind him of all they had together—starting with great sex—and maybe he'd decide he couldn't live without her. It would be a lot easier to face a new job and a new city if he'd go with her.

She went to her bedroom and slipped out of her jeans and tank top. She wriggled out of her panties and unsnapped her black bra and let it fall to the carpet. She kicked all her clothes into the closet and closed the door. A full-length mirror hung on the closet door and she paused to study the reflection of her naked form. Still taut, still trim. She felt warm and wet and ready.

She slipped a short, slinky nightgown over her head and checked her appearance once more in the mirror. Adjusted her spaghetti straps. Smiled at herself to make sure she didn't have lipstick on her teeth.

Out of the bedroom and through the living room to the kitchen, where she poured two glasses of wine. Then back to living room to put on some music.

She picked a CD of Fats Domino's greatest hits and slipped it into the machine. Teresa couldn't abide a lot of the old music that Drew liked, all that rockabilly stuff. But he'd turned her on to Fats, and she played the disc all the time. Fats Domino's smooth, rolling vibe was like a slow grind. Perfect for what she had in mind.

Someone rapped on the door and she looked out through the peephole before opening it. Drew stood on the apartment's little porch, turned away from her, looking off to where the cops still worked the scene of that poor guy Jon's death.

Teresa opened the door. Drew turned toward her, and his eyes lit up at the sight of her in the little nightgown.

"You gonna come in, or you gonna stand out there, watching the cops?"

He looked her over from head to toe.

"You'd better get back inside," he said, "before you get arrested."

"Maybe you'd better come in and frisk me."

He slipped into the living room and closed the door behind him. He wrapped his big arms around her shoulders and she tipped her face up to be kissed. It was a long kiss, deep and hot, and his breathing sounded ragged. He wrapped his arms around her back and lifted, and she raised her legs and looped them around his waist.

Drew carried her toward the bedroom, never breaking the kiss. Teresa's heart felt large inside her chest and heat flooded her down below.

They fell onto the bed together and kissed some more. There was a brief moment of hilarity when he tried to take his jeans off over his big sneakers, but soon he was atop her, plunging and panting, and it felt oh so right to have him inside.

He held off for a long time, but then he groaned and shuddered all over, and she felt his hot wetness inside her. Oh, my.

She arched against him, digging her nails into his back, and made an embarrassing little squeal through clenched teeth. She squeezed him tight with her arms and legs, and felt his weight press down on her as he relaxed into the afterglow.

"My God," he said into her ear. "It's good to have you back."

"It's good to be had. I should go away more often. Makes you glad to see me."

Drew raised up on his elbows and looked down into her face. The crease between his eyebrows deepened.

"What is it, tiger?"

"You might be gone completely pretty soon. Then what?"

"Aw, don't ruin the mood. We'll work it out."

"Think so?"

"Sure. I can't just abandon sex this good."

A grin slipped onto his face and he rolled off her, lying flat on his back with his legs hanging off the edge of the bed. "That's all I am to you? A sex toy?"

"That makes you a lucky man."

"You got that right."

He raised up on an elbow and kissed her lips, her cheeks, her forehead. But when he stopped and looked at her again, that crease was back on his face and his eyes were sad.

"You can't leave it alone, can you, Drew?"

"Sorry. I just don't want to lose you."

She pulled his head down to rest against her breasts and ran her fingers through his damp hair.

"I feel the same way. I'm torn about this job offer. I don't know what to do."

"It's a career move," he said into her chest. "You've got to think about it in those terms."

"And what about us?"

"A separate issue." He raised up and their eyes met. "We'll make it work out."

"Think so?"

"Sure," he said, but his voice didn't sound confident. "One way or the other."

"I don't know, tiger. It's not just leaving you, though that's the biggest part of it. I like this town. I like my job at the *Gazette*, the people there. My family's all down in Las Cruces. If I go to California, you'll all be far away, everything will be different. It's an alien landscape out there."

"If you hate it, you could always come back. Goodman would hire you again in a second."

"Wouldn't that be like running home, my tail between my legs?"

Drew grinned. "Is that what that is between your legs? A tail?"

She laughed and reached down for him. He was limp in her hand, but not for long.

"You're the one with a tail," she said. "And it seems to be growing."

His smile turned lascivious.

"I think we'd better hide it somewhere."

THIRTY SIX

Saturday morning, Drew awoke at home, still feeling warm from his marathon evening with Teresa. He lay in bed a long time, thinking about her and California and the deaths that had consumed him of late.

He wondered how Curtis was doing in jail, and made plans to visit him later in the day. He thought about Felicia Quattlebaum and the way she'd described Cerf dancing just out of her reach the day before. And whether there was another way to find out what happened behind the scenes in Cerf's businesses.

Finally, his bladder would let him lie still no longer. He got up and went to the bathroom and brushed his teeth and put on his old flannel robe. He sat at the kitchen table with the Saturday *Gazette*, sipping coffee and scanning headlines.

Felicia Quattlebaum was on the front page with a story on Wally Mertz and the cops' theories on his murder. Drew noticed that she slipped in the murder of Fontanelle Harper, and got Romero to say there were similarities between the two strangulation deaths. She even had a couple of paragraphs toward the end that included Scott Cerf denying any knowledge of the murders. Drew wondered how she got that past Goodman. Though Cerf was accused of nothing in the story, the mere mention probably meant a troop of lawyers marching on the publisher's office.

Drew was midway through his second cup of coffee when he got an idea. He was deep inside the *Gazette's* front section, reading about an FBI investigation into some white-collar crime in Philadelphia, and the story reminded him of a contact he hadn't tried yet.

He abandoned the newspaper and went into the living room, where he sat in his La-Z-Boy while looking up a number and dialing the phone.

"Hello?"

"Is this Stu Kapinski, famous special agent for the FBI?"

"Who the hell is this? Gavin, is that you?"

"I'm surprised you recognized my voice. We haven't talked in months. Guess your sharp ears are why you're the *famous* special agent."

Kapinski was a short, stout guy with curly black hair who couldn't look like the standard-issue Feeb in a Suit no matter how hard he tried. Drew had known him since college and was fond of him, though Kapinski was as prickly as a porcupine.

"You know, Gavin, flattery will get you nowhere with me."

"No?"

"It just means you want something. And it must be something pretty important for you to call me at home on a Saturday."

"Why, Stu, I'm surprised at you. Always suspecting ulterior motives."

"Can it. I know when I'm being buttered up. What do you want?"

"Well, now that you mention it, I was looking for some information—"

"Aha! Just as I thought. Bye now."

"Wait, Stu. I just need a minute."

Kapinski grumbled, and Drew talked faster.

"You know of a guy named Scott Cerf?"

"Sure. 'Cerf the 'Net.' He's in all the computer magazines."

"You read computer magazines?"

"As I was saying, good-bye—"

"Come on, Stu. What do you know about this guy?"

"Nothing much. He's not on our radar screen, if you know what I mean."

"You're not investigating him?"

"Who's this I'm talking to? A newspaper guy? You know we never confirm or deny whether we're investigating anybody."

"A convenient out. But I'm guessing if he's not on your 'radar screen,' that means you've got nothing for me."

"I don't know." Kapinski hesitated. "I seem to recall something . . ."

"Come on, Stu. Give."

"What's in it for me?"

"How about a press box seat at the Lobo games? Get a great view of the games from way up high in the press box."

Drew knew Kapinski couldn't resist. The man was crazy for football. It was one reason they'd stayed friends over the years.

"Press box, huh?"

"Sure. We can get an extra seat at the games for another spotter. I know it's months away, but you'd like it."

"If you're messing with Scott Cerf, I don't want to be anywhere near you for months anyway," Kapinski said. "Too many people been dying lately."

"That's what I'm trying to find out about."

"Those murders on your front page today? They're strictly local. We don't care about them."

"Then what have you got?"

"This press box seat, it's free, right?"

"Come on. Quit dancing around it. Are you guys after Cerf or not?"

"Not us. But I hear he is being investigated."

"By whom? Treasury?"

"Nah. Try the Department of Defense. Those are the guys you want."

"I knew it! I figured somebody else was trailing the guy, trying to put something together. That's why he's so scared to talk to the newspaper."

"Might be nothing. Just something I heard on the grapevine."

"You know anybody over at DOD? Somebody who'd answer my questions?"

"My advice would be to stay away from those guys. They think civil liberties are for sissies."

"They don't scare me."

"Yeah, yeah, nothing scares the big, tough jock. Let me tell you: You mess around with Defense and, next thing you know, you've got a missile up your ass."

"I'll risk it. Thanks a lot, Stu. I appreciate the help. Call me in a couple of months and we'll set you up in the press box."

"Will do, assuming you live that long."

THIRTY SEVEN

An hour later Drew was at the office, looking for help. He didn't know any investigators inside the Department of Defense, wasn't even sure how to go looking for one. But one person at the *Gazette* knew it all: Bill Morrison, a rangy guy who specialized in covering the military.

Morrison usually kept everyone at the *Gazette* at arm's length, preferring to sit alone at his landfill of a desk, poring through the reams of paper generated by Kirtland Air Force Base and the national labs. Morrison had the toughest beat on the paper—dealing with scientists and military bureaucracy and Washington—and he handled it well. The fact that he was openly gay should've made his job even harder, especially with he-man military types who were busy not asking and not telling. But Morrison never complained. He just kept working.

Drew wasn't surprised to find Morrison at the newsroom on a Saturday. He sat with his loafers up on his desk, long legs crossed at the ankles. He had a thick folder full of paper in his lap, and he wore half-glasses as he read. Drew thinking: All that bureaucratese could make you go blind.

"Hey, Bill, got a minute?"

Morrison peered at him over his glasses.

"What's up?"

"I need a favor."

"You and everybody else I know."

"Mine might be easy."

Morrison let his feet drop to the floor. He leaned over and moved another stack of paper from a side chair and gestured for Drew to sit.

"What do you need?"

"I hear DOD is investigating a local guy, Scott Cerf. You know who he is?"

Morrison nodded, but his skeptical expression didn't change. "Why's he being investigated?"

"I'm not sure. His company is up for a big defense contract, so it might be linked to that."

Morrison pursed his lips, but said nothing.

"I've been looking at him in connection with these murders, including the one that landed Curtis in jail," Drew said. "Maybe DOD's sniffing around after that, too."

Morrison shook his head. "Doesn't sound like them. The contract, though, might have them investigating. Is it top-secret stuff his company's working on?"

"That's what I hear."

"Then that would make sense. Lot of investigation gets done on those contracts. Security clearances, stuff like that."

"Can you give me a name? Somebody over there who might be willing to talk about Cerf?"

Morrison picked up a pencil and let it slide back and forth between his long fingers while he thought it over.

"I don't know, Drew. I can't afford to burn any sources."

"I wouldn't burn anybody."

"Maybe not, but they don't know that. I've got relation-

ships to maintain. I let you go crashing around over there, saying I sent you, and pretty soon nobody's talking to me."

Drew didn't like that answer, but he understood it. A beat
reporter can't afford to unnecessarily piss off his sources, not if
ever wants more stories from them.

"Could you ask around about it?"

"I suppose. Sounds like there could be a story there."

"If Cerf's up to what I think, there's a whole series, maybe
a Pulitzer."

Morrison almost grinned before he caught himself.

"You sound like every crackpot who calls me up with the
latest government conspiracy," he said. "It's always a big, big
story, a prize-winner. They always mention the Pulitzer, but I
haven't won one yet."

Drew couldn't help but laugh. He'd taken such phone calls
himself.

"Okay, you got me. But there might be something there.
And it might help Curtis."

Morrison tossed the pencil back onto his desktop, where it
came to rest against another stack of government paper.

"I'll ask around," he said. "There's this one investigator I
know who might be willing to talk. But it would be strictly off
the record."

"That's okay, at least for now. I just need to know what
direction their investigation is taking, you know? Do you
know this guy well enough for that?"

Morrison blushed slightly, and grinned.

"I think so. I see him at the clubs occasionally."

It took Drew a second to realize which clubs Morrison
meant, and then he blurted, "You mean—"

Morrison nodded, didn't let him finish.

"He's a great dancer," he said, still grinning.

Drew laughed. "Then take him dancing. I'll buy the drinks."

Morrison reached for the phone, saying, "I'll hold you to that."

"Thanks, Bill."

Drew ambled away as Morrison began dialing the phone. I'm here anyway, he thought, might as well see if I can get some work done. But he winced as he reached the sports department. The only writer present was Henrietta Morehouse, and she glared at him as he approached.

"Hey, Henry. You're in early."

She looked away, toward the windows.

"Real busy," she said in her Oklahoma drawl. "Trying to do my job and Curtis' job, too."

Filthy Hogan's desk was closest to hers, and Drew walked around behind it and pulled out Filthy's chair so he could sit facing her. He brushed dunes of crumbs and dandruff out of the seat before he sat down.

"Look, Henry, I've been meaning to talk to you. We've both been so busy, I've hardly seen you."

"I saw you at the Rattlers' game. Twice."

"That's what I want to talk about. I thought you might've gotten the wrong idea, seeing me there."

"I don't know what you mean," she said curtly.

"I was afraid you'd think I was there checking up on you," he said. "Is that what you thought?"

Henry stared down at her cluttered desk, her mousy hair hanging like curtains on either side of her narrow face.

"Something like that," she muttered.

"That wasn't it at all. I was there trying to help Curtis."

She looked up at him, and some of the hurt lifted off her face.

"Help him how?"

Where to begin? he wondered. How to sum up all the wild-ass guesses about Cerf and the rest?

"I'm trying to find out who really killed that cheerleader," he said. "I think Cerf is involved somehow. He's the only connection I can find between her and Wally Mertz."

She squinted at him. "That's why you came to those games? To check on Cerf?"

"Yeah, and I was trying to get a feel for the team. Looks like a money-loser to me."

"Me, too. They play some pretty god-awful basketball. I don't know how Curtis stands it all the time."

"Beats jail."

She nodded somberly.

"What about you, Henry? You've been around the team. Seen anything suspicious?"

"I haven't noticed anything. But then I didn't know I was supposed to be looking. If you had talked to me—"

He held up his hands to stop her before she could get started.

"I know. I'm sorry. I should've told you what I was doing. But our schedules haven't matched up."

"Last time I saw you, Goodman had you in his office, raking you over the coals. Least that's how it looked."

"He's been doing that a lot lately. He wants me to stop poking my nose into this thing, but I just can't. Not as long as it might do Curtis some good."

She smiled shyly. "Might get your nose bitten off."

"I might at that. I keep running across Cerf's security guy,

Otis Edgewater. You know him?"

"I've seen him around. Spooky dude."

"Yeah, he keeps throwing me out of Rattlers games. Has he said anything to you?"

"He's ignored me. So far, at least."

"Probably better that way. But keep your ears open when you're around the team. You might pick up something I could use."

"Like what?"

"That's the problem. I don't know for sure."

Henry glanced at her computer screen, then back at him.

"I'm not going to be working the Rattlers for a few days," she said. "They've got some time off. Mid-season break."

"Oh. Well, don't worry about it then—"

"But there is one thing you should know."

"What's that?"

"The team's having another party."

"When?"

"Tonight."

Drew felt his eyebrows rise. "Is that so?"

"Yeah. They're celebrating the midpoint in the season, being over .500 and all. I heard some of the players talking about it."

Drew glanced over his shoulder toward Goodman's office. Nobody there.

"This party, you know where it's going to be?"

"It's at Cerf's nightclub. That new place, Snake-Eyes. Do you know it?"

"I haven't been there, but I've heard of it."

"I guess, after the way the last party went, Cerf wanted the team at a place where he could keep an eye on them."

"Cerf's going to be there?"

"That's what I hear. Does that mean you're going to be there, too?"

Drew smiled at her. "Maybe so."

"Should I go?"

"No, stay away from those guys. It's one thing covering the games. But don't go socializing with them. Somebody in that group plays rough."

Drew stood up, the talk over, but she reached out and grabbed his arm.

"Hey, boss," she said. "You be careful."

"Sure, Henry. Don't worry. I can handle myself."

She frowned at him. "That's probably what Curtis thought, too."

THIRTY EIGHT

Snake-Eyes was just off Montgomery Boulevard in Albuquerque's sprawling Northeast Heights, not far from the high-rise where Drew had lived before he moved back to Barelas. The nightclub floated in a sea of asphalt that flowed from a strip mall of small shops and discount stores. It was the only nightclub in the complex and it sat facing the street, its back turned on its neighbors.

The building was low and sleek, with tinted windows along two sides. It could've been an office building, except for its neon sign, which featured the club's name suspended below two dice, each showing a single glowing red dot.

Drew was surprised the club didn't use the Rattler logo as a way of doubling-up marketing power. Maybe insiders knew the connection already. Or, maybe the owners wanted to keep the endeavors separate, so people wouldn't know what sort of snakes worked behind the scenes.

He'd gone by his house after finishing work for the day, taking time to eat a quick bite and to change into khakis and a button-down-collar shirt. He gathered that Snake-Eyes was an upscale place, and he didn't want to stand out any more than necessary.

The place was hopping, though it was early evening and

Albuquerque clubs don't usually start rocking on Saturdays until late. Drew circled twice before he found a parking spot for the Jeep.

Inside, he could tell at a glance that Snake-Eyes wasn't his kind of joint. Angular Jetsons furniture and a gleaming, stainless-steel bar. No TVs tuned to sports broadcasts, just low-level jazz toodling under the buzz of fevered conversation. Men in suits and chunky gold jewelry. Expensive-looking women dressed to the nines. Desperate flirtation and macho aggression filling the air like a bad odor. Albuquerque's a casual town—there's only a handful of establishments where jeans and sneakers aren't welcome—but Drew felt underdressed and invisible.

He floated up to the bar and ordered a beer from a barmaid whose elaborate hairdo was sprayed into place with so many chemicals, looked like you could cut yourself on it. She gave him a Heineken and took his four dollars, but never looked him in the face.

He turned away and rested his elbows on the bar, surveying the crowd. He recognized no one, which seemed odd. He'd lived in the city so long, he could hardly go anywhere without seeing someone with whom he had at least a nodding acquaintance. But this was a different set, the young elite, and he guessed they didn't spend much time hanging around smelly gyms and sports arenas, the places where Drew felt at home.

He'd finished his beer by the time Carl Moss, the Rattlers coach, walked through the door. Moss was looking at his wristwatch, running late. Probably got lost on his way here, Drew figured. Moss was so dumb, it was a wonder he could find his way home at night.

Drew tracked him with his eyes and saw Moss push aside heavy maroon curtains that covered an archway at the far end of the bar. Laughter spilled out the door as the coach disappeared inside.

Ah. A private room. Drew had noticed the curtained doorway earlier, but had figured it hid an office. No bouncer guarded the doorway, and Drew left his empty bottle on the bar and strolled over as if he belonged back there.

He pushed the curtains aside and found a long, windowless room with horseshoe-shaped booths facing each other down opposite walls. At the far end, a solid-looking door was centered in the wall and a skinny white guy poured drinks behind a bar wedged into a corner.

Rattlers team members and various hangers-on filled the six booths, laughing and drinking and talking. No one seemed to notice him at first, but then conversation faded at the nearest booths and he could feel them staring. He plastered a big smile on his face and nodded to a couple of guys he recognized. They didn't smile back.

In the second booth sat Raj Davis, his big arms resting on the table, straining against the sleeves of a purple sport coat, looked like something The Joker would wear. Drew tried smiling at him, but Davis gave him back a stony stare. Others at the table, picking up Raj's vibe, stopped talking and looked at Drew.

Boy, he thought, I sure know how to put a damper on a party. No wonder I wasn't invited.

He walked on, party noise dying in his wake.

He found Scott Cerf, Otis Edgewater and Carl Moss in the booth nearest the small bar. The tabletop was littered with empty glasses. Moss sat next to Edgewater, and he was dwarfed by the larger man, whose scalp gleamed through the gaps in his combover. Edgewater was the first to notice Drew standing there like a big, gate-crashing mook. His eyes narrowed and his jaw jutted forward.

"The hell you doin' here, son?"

Edgewater spoke right over Cerf, who'd been holding forth about the team, and Cerf swiveled his head to look up at Drew.

"I heard there was a party," Drew said. "I didn't get an invitation, but I figured that was some kind of oversight."

Edgewater pushed against Moss, trying to get disentangled from the booth. Drew felt a surge of adrenaline, but he kept his eyes on Cerf.

"I know you guys wouldn't *intentionally* keep the media out," he said. "That would be bad PR."

Edgewater said through clenched teeth, "I'll show you some bad—"

"No, Otis," Cerf cut in quickly, raising a hand from the tabletop. "It's okay."

Edgewater stopped trying to get up, but Drew could see that his shoulders remained tensed, ready. Moss had gone pale and his head twitched around, looking for a polite way to exit.

"Join us," Cerf said to Drew. "Mr. Gavin, isn't it?"

Cerf flicked his eyes to the right and Moss bounced up off the bench, looking relieved, and said, "Here. Take my seat."

Drew sat next to Edgewater, who kept the scowl on his face.

"Want a drink?" Cerf asked.

"Sure. I'll have a beer."

Cerf raised an index finger toward the skinny bartender, who hustled over to the booth and took Drew's order and returned with the beer in record time.

"What brings you here, Mr. Gavin?" Cerf asked. He had a smile on his lean face, but it looked as if it took an effort to keep it in place.

"I'm interested in the Rattlers," Drew said. "Thought I'd get to know you all better. Particularly you."

The smile didn't waver, but Drew saw something cold rise behind Cerf's gray eyes.

"So this is just a social call?"

"What else would it be?"

"I thought perhaps you wanted to ask me some questions. Every time I turn around, there's someone from the *Gazette* with more questions. You're certainly persistent."

"Like a case of the clap," Edgewater said.

Drew ignored the security man. He stared at Cerf, searching for a crack in the man's cool exterior.

"I spent some time with one of your reporters yesterday," Cerf said. "A Ms. Quattlebaum? A very interesting woman. But, like you, she seems to harbor some sort of grudge against me."

Drew opened his mouth to protest, but Cerf cut him off.

"Maybe not against me in particular," he said, and his smile returned. "But, if you'll excuse the expression, you all seem like a bunch of conspiracy nuts."

"How's that?"

"You're looking for plots where none exist. I'm a businessman, Mr. Gavin, that's all. The *Gazette* seems to think there's something more to my dealings."

"Isn't there?"

Cerf shook his head slightly, still smiling. Drew felt like cuffing him, but he reminded himself that Edgewater was braced for action beside him. He needed to worm his way into

Cerf's confidence somehow, get the man to relax, to slip and say something he could use.

"I love what I do, Mr. Gavin. It's made me a rich man. And I love basketball. I played in high school, you know, was pretty good, too. It only seemed natural to invest some of my wealth into the Rattlers."

Raj Davis suddenly appeared at the booth, towering over them. The purple sports coat practically glowed in the room's dim light.

"This dude botherin' you, Mr. Cerf?" he asked.

Cerf looked up at Davis, and gave him that winning smile. "No, Raj. Everything's fine, but thanks for asking."

Davis looked from Cerf to Drew and back again. Then his eyes lit on Edgewater.

"I've got things under control here," Edgewater said tightly. "Go enjoy the party."

Raj Davis glared at Drew, who gave him back impassive. When Davis finally turned away, he said over his shoulder, "Call me if you need me."

Edgewater snorted as Davis walked away, and said under his breath, "The day I need help from a *basketball* player is the day I hang up my spurs."

"Now, Otis," Cerf said, "remember your manners. We're here to celebrate how well these men have been playing. Which reminds me: I'm supposed to give a speech about now. If you'll excuse me, Mr. Gavin."

Cerf rose to his feet and clinked two empty bottles together to get the room's attention. Drew glanced at Edgewater, who was watching his boss, smirking as Cerf cleared his throat and started telling the Rattlers what a fine job they'd done the first half of the season.

Drew tuned him out. He'd heard a million such speeches over the years. Real athletes didn't need pep talks; they got their rewards on the playing field. But owners and coaches always felt it necessary to praise them.

He looked around the room while Cerf talked. The players seemed appropriately bored, anxious to get back to their drinking and jawing.

Cerf wrapped up his speech by telling the team he had somewhere to be, but that they should stay and enjoy themselves. They gave him a nice round of applause, and he waved and smiled.

When Cerf looked down at him again, Drew said, "You're leaving? I wanted to talk some more."

"Sorry, Mr. Gavin, but I've got a young lady waiting for me. Some things are more important than press relations."

He smiled as he added, "Otis here can look after you. Make sure he has a good time, Otis."

"Sure, chief," Edgewater drawled. "Whatever you say."

Drew didn't like the sound of that, and he liked it even less when he and Edgewater were joined at the table by Raj Davis. He felt hemmed in between Edgewater and Davis, the meat in a oversized sandwich, and he kept his mouth shut for a change.

"So," Edgewater said, the smile on his face again, "you're still trying to get that other reporter off the hook."

Drew didn't want to talk about Curtis. Anything he said about Curtis and Fontanelle and the murder would likely set off the grieving Raj Davis.

"Just trying to find out what happened that night," he said finally.

"The cops know what happened," Davis muttered. "That

asshole killed Fontanelle."

Drew's shoulders tensed, but he said calmly, "I don't believe that. Curtis wouldn't kill anybody, especially a woman."

"Women die just as easy as men," Edgewater said. "They just look better doing it."

Drew kept his eyes on Davis. Edgewater had his orders from Cerf: Be hospitable. He'd march to that tune. If trouble came, it would be from Davis.

"Your buddy's lucky he's still in jail," Raj said. "If he was out, I'd track him down myself."

"Yeah? And do what?"

Raj didn't hesitate. "Give him the same thing he gave Fontanelle."

"Raj," Edgewater said. His voice had an edge to it. Davis broke the eyelock with Drew and glanced over at him. Some unspoken message seemed to pass between them.

"Mr. Cerf said to be nice to this here journalist," Edgewater said. "He's a guest here."

"Yeah? Who invited him?"

Edgewater loosed a mirthless cackle. "You got a way of hitting the nail right on the head, son. I like that. Nobody invited him. But that don't mean we have to sit around here all night, comparing to see who's got the biggest balls. Let's have another round of beers."

Raj Davis' mouth spread in a smile, showing bright teeth. It looked like such an unaccustomed expression, Drew was afraid his face would crack. Davis rose and went to the bar.

"You'll have to excuse Raj," Edgewater said. "He's been upset."

Drew didn't like Edgewater's tone. It seemed unnatural for him to suddenly act friendly after all that had passed between them. But Drew said only, "He took Fontanelle's death hard?"

"We all did. She was a crackerjack, that girl."

"You knew her well?"

Edgewater's face hardened, but he kept a grin on his face. Looked like it was a struggle.

"No more questions, son. You're here as our guest. Don't make me regret being polite."

"But—"

"No, really. You're gonna ruin the party for the others. I wouldn't take too kindly to that."

Davis returned to the booth, holding three longneck Buds in one huge hand. He passed beers to the other two men and sat down, not looking at Drew.

Drew took a slug of the weak-assed beer and thought, what the hell am I doing here? I'm not going to get any help from these goons. Cerf was the one I wanted. I should've left when he did.

He was so caught up in his thoughts, he missed what Edgewater was saying and had to ask him to repeat himself.

"I said, where you from, son?"

"Right here in Albuquerque."

"A hometown boy, huh?"

"That's right."

"Always lived here?"

"Yeah. Why?"

"Just wondering. Your worldview seems a little narrow, if you know what I mean. I'm not sure you know how to see the big picture."

"That's my problem?"

"Man stays in one place all his life, little ole town like this, he can lose track of what's really important."

"Yeah? Like what?"

Edgewater shrugged. "Ain't for me to say. But it might explain some things about you."

Drew felt himself bristle, but he reined it in. The man was just needling him, looking for something that would make him rile. Drew drained half of his beer.

"Raj here, now he's a big-city boy. Ain't that right? New York City."

Davis gave a barely perceptible nod. Didn't look as if he was paying much attention.

"I imagine he sees things completely different from you. Probably different from me, too. New Yorkers have a reputation for going after what they want and not letting anything stand in their way. Right, Raj?"

"Sure." Davis' expression didn't change. "Man's gotta look out for himself."

"That's exactly right," Edgewater said. "And I'll bet you can see the big picture, can't you?"

"Sure."

"See, that's important. You've got to look beyond your own little problems, see the big picture. I remember when I was stationed at Fort Hood, there was this one old boy—"

Drew felt his attention waver. He didn't want to sit here, swilling beer and listening to Edgewater's Army stories. He'd come to the nightclub with the notion that he could shake things up, get some information that would help Curtis. Nudge these guys until somebody spilled something. But he clearly was getting nowhere. Edgewater didn't look like he wanted to fight anymore. He'd bore Drew to death instead.

A wave of dizziness washed over him and he blinked his eyes and shook his head. What the hell? Edgewater still spouted. He could see his lips moving, but his voice was lost in a roaring inside Drew's ears.

He felt suddenly tired, too. Couldn't be the beers. He hadn't had enough to get drunk. But something definitely was wrong. His head swam and he had trouble focusing.

"I, uh—" he said aloud, interrupting Edgewater. "I think I'd better go. I'm not feeling so great."

Drew tried to stand, but Davis didn't move. He was trapped in the booth between the two big men.

"You sick, man?" Davis said it as if he was concerned, but his white teeth gleamed in his dark face.

"I don't know. Maybe."

"Shit, man, don't be puking on my clothes." Davis stood so Drew could slide out of the booth.

Drew teetered to his feet, feeling wobbly. He reached out to catch his balance, got a handful of Davis' jacket.

His vision went fuzzy, and he felt himself falling, falling, for what seem like a long time. Before he could hit the floor, everything went black.

THIRTY NINE

Drew opened his eyes to a white so bright it instantly made his head hurt. He quickly shut his eyes, flinching against the pain in his head, his chest, his shoulder, his right hand.

The darkness behind his eyelids was comforting for a moment, then dizziness rippled through him and he felt queasy. He blinked his eyes open again, trying to find a steadying point, but all was white.

He didn't know where he was. He didn't know how he'd gotten here. He remembered nothing from the night before, only a blackness that had swallowed him whole. Compared to the painful dazzle that filled his vision now, the darkness seemed friendly and comfortable. He missed it.

Then movement broke the unbearable brightness and a pale face swam into view. An old face, a woman's. She wore startling stop signs of rouge on her wrinkled cheeks. She went out of focus, and he blinked some more, trying to keep her there, trying to keep the brightness from blinding him again.

"He's coming around," she said to someone beyond his field of vision.

Then the old woman disappeared and her place was taken by a black man in dark clothing. Drew's vision swam, but he concentrated and managed to pull the man into focus enough that he could see he wore an Albuquerque Police Department uniform.

"Mr. Gavin?" the cop said.

"Where am I?"

"In the hospital. How you feeling?"

Drew worked his dry lips together until he was able to bring up the words: "Like shit."

A smile flashed in the cop's dark face. "I'm not surprised. Somebody worked you over pretty good."

Drew wanted a drink of water. He wanted to close his eyes and go back to sleep. But he managed to say, "What happened?"

"A security guard found you in a parking lot," the cop answered. "You were out cold, looked like somebody had stomped you. Do you know who did it?"

Drew shook his head, which caused a new wave of dizziness to crash over him. He closed his eyes, searching for his equilibrium, then opened them again. The cop still stood there, his face lined with concern.

"I don't know," Drew croaked. "I was at a party—"

"At the nightclub? Snake-Eyes?"

Then a memory, an inkling, tiptoed through Drew's brain. Raj Davis. Otis Edgewater. The Rattlers. He told the cop what little he could remember about the party.

"Then what happened?"

"No idea. I must've blacked out."

"I guess somebody worked you over after you were unconscious," the cop said. "Looks like you were kicked in the ribs several times. Got a couple of broken fingers."

That explained the pain snatching at Drew's body. But the pounding in his head felt like something else.

"I think I was drugged."

"You take drugs?" the cop asked.

Drew shook his head and the world shifted. He needed to stop doing that.

The cop looked away, over toward the nurse, Drew guessed, and asked, "Have you taken his blood? Doing a toxicology check?"

Drew didn't hear the answer. He felt himself drifting away, back to that warm, black place that had welcomed him before. He closed his eyes and let the darkness take him.

FORTY

Chuck Gavin sat beside Drew's bed at University Hospital, a blanket over his legs and his good hand tapping on the arm of the wheelchair. He'd been there for two hours now, since shortly after Teresa Vargas called and told him what had happened to his son. Those shitheads at the nursing home hadn't wanted to drive him to the hospital for this vigil, but Chuck had made them see the error in their thinking.

Christ, he hated to get loud like that, but those folks don't understand about an emergency. His boy was injured, and Chuck would by God be by his side.

Now that he was here, though, he had to admit he couldn't do much to help. Drew remained asleep, as still and pale as a corpse, and Chuck just sat there, watching him. He needed to take a leak, but he didn't want to take his eyes off Drew for a second. Besides, he'd have to call a nurse to assist him, which would prove correct all those warnings they'd handed him at the nursing home. Fuck 'em, he thought, I'll make a puddle and sit in it before I let them be right.

His eyes roamed Drew's sleeping face. Drew looked a lot like his dad—the same square jaw and creased browline—but what Chuck saw were the features he inherited from his mother. The high cheekbones. The full lips. Drew was all that remained of Ellie in this world. And he was about all Chuck had left, too. The things Chuck cared about—his job, football, physical activity—all had been taken from him by the stroke. But the thing he cared about most was Drew. Raising Drew alone had been Chuck's true life work. He'd put everything he had into shaping and molding the motherless boy into an honorable man. Then he'd turned that man out into the world to make his own way. Sometimes, like now, the world spat him right back, all beat to hell.

Chuck wanted to be there to pick up the pieces. Sometimes, his confined life seemed not worth living. He often thought about death, about moving on, reuniting with Ellie after all these years. But Drew's visits gave Chuck reason to stick around. He wanted to help his son however he could. He wanted to see how it all turned out.

His thoughts slipped again to California, toward the possibility that Drew could move away. He'd stewed over that a lot the past few days, wondering how he'd manage with his son so far away. At the nursing home, the only thing Chuck had too much of was time to think.

Then Drew moved, shifting in the white sheets, and pain flitted across his face. Chuck reached out with his good hand and touched his forearm.

"Son? You awake?"

Drew's eyelids fluttered and it took him a while to focus. Chuck fitted a big, crooked smile on his face. He knew that with one side of his face paralyzed his smile was a frightening sight to most people, but it was the best he had to offer.

"Hey, Pop." Drew's voice sounded raspy.

"Morning, son. This the way you spend your Sundays? Just sleeping all damned day?"

"Is that what it was? Sleep? I thought I'd died."

"Naw, you got a lotta life left in you yet. Though you look like somebody tried to kick it out of you."

"Bad, huh?"

"You've had worse. I remember that one time, when you busted your ankle in that game against BYU—"

"Hey, Pop? Not now, okay?"

"All right. What you need is some water."

Chuck inched his wheelchair around so he could reach the water glass that old bat of a nurse had left on the bedside table. He handed it to Drew, who drained it.

Drew smacked his lips and passed the glass back to Chuck. "Good," he said. "So thirsty."

Pouring another glassful was one of those jobs that seems simple until you try to do it with only one hand, with the weight of your paralyzed side pulling you in the wrong direction, but Chuck managed and handed the glass to Drew again.

He sipped slower this time, blinking and looking around.

"Where the hell are we?" he asked.

"University Hospital. You've been here since about two o'clock this morning. Somebody found you all beat up in a parking lot."

A light fired in Drew's eyes, which pleased Chuck. The boy was coming around. For a while, Chuck had worried about brain damage. Who knew how many kicks to the head he'd taken?

Drew was naked from the waist up, his chest wrapped tightly in bandages and tape to hold broken ribs in place. His shoulder sported a bruise the size and color of an eggplant. The first two fingers of his right hand were in metal splints. It was the same hand that had been bruised when Chuck saw him on Sunday. Now the whole thing was swathed in gauze and tape with his splinted fingers sticking out.

Drew lifted the hand and studied the splints for a moment, looked like he was trying to figure out what they meant.

"I think somebody stomped on your hand after you were down," Chuck said. "Those fingers are broken. You got a couple of broken ribs, too."

"Shit. What else?"

"Just scrapes and bruises. Like I said, you'll live."

Drew drank some more water, but his eyes kept straying to the broken fingers, as if checking whether the splints were still there.

"What the hell happened, son? You remember anything?"

Drew sighed and let his head drop back against his pillow, his eyes closed. Chuck thought he might've passed out again, and wondered whether he should summon one of those pushy nurses, but then Drew batted his eyes open.

"Not much, Pop. I was at a party at this nightclub. With people from that basketball team?"

"The Rattlers?"

Drew nodded, then cringed, as if moving his head made it hurt.

"Isn't that where Curtis got into trouble? At one of their parties?"

He didn't nod this time—he'd learned his lesson—but he pressed his lips together, looked like he was awaiting a scolding.

"Well, goddamn, Drew, what were you thinking?"

"That I could help Curtis."

"By getting the shit kicked out of you? You could've been killed."

Drew let that settle over him for a moment, then said, "I think they drugged me, Pop. I think it's the same thing that happened with Curtis. Remember, I told you how he was all messed up when I found him at that cheerleader's apartment?"

"So you went to their party and let them drug you, too?"

"I had a beer or two, and then I felt all dizzy—"

"Those bastards. Any idea who did it?"

Drew managed to grin though the pain.

"I got all kinds of ideas, Pop. That's why I was there. I think one of those assholes killed that girl and set Curtis up. I've been trying to prove it."

"And now you're in the hospital and can't prove shit."

"True." Drew took another sip of water. Watching him drink made Chuck need to piss even worse. "But maybe the cops will listen to me now. Maybe they'll believe Curtis got drugged."

"Yeah, and maybe bluebirds will fly out of my ass. All you've managed is to get yourself hurt."

"How did you even know I was in here?"

"Your girlfriend called. I guess the hospital or the cops called the paper, looking for someone who knew you, and she got wind of it. She was here when I got here, but she had to leave a little while ago. She'll be back."

"Is she okay?"

"Worried sick, but she doesn't know you as well as I do. You always bounce back well from injuries."

"I think it gets harder as you get older."

"You got that right. I keep hoping somebody'll knock some sense into you, but that doesn't seem to work. They break your ribs instead."

"And my fingers."

"You're going to have trouble typing for a while."

"That's okay. Way things are going, they're about ready to fire me at the *Gazette*."

Chuck shook his head. "When you going to learn to stay out of trouble, son?"

"It wasn't my idea to get the shit kicked out of me," Drew protested. "I was just trying to help Curtis."

"Well, I hope he appreciates it."

"Pop, this is Curtis we're talking about."

Drew laughed, but quick pain took his breath away and he clutched at his ribs.

"You all right?"

"It only hurts when I laugh."

"Bullshit."

"Yeah, but I've always wanted to say that."

Chuck frowned at him. The big lug's beat all to hell, and he's making jokes. Chuck guessed that was a good sign, that the boy was getting his senses back, but he'd feel a lot better if Drew wasn't in here at all, if he'd stayed out of Curtis' troubles. He started to say so, but he caught himself. What the hell, the boy's hurt, he's *hospitalized*. Chuck could give him a break for once.

"When they gonna let me out of here?" Drew asked.

"They haven't said. Soon, I'm guessing. You ain't hurt that bad."

Chuck thinking: He'd be better off if they kept him in the hospital for a while. At least, in here, he couldn't get into more trouble. But again, he held his tongue. He reached out and rested his hand on Drew's forearm, felt the warmth emanating from his son.

"I'm glad you're going to be okay. I was worried."

"Aw, hell, Pop. You know me. Not going to let a little physical abuse get me down."

Chuck studied him, checking his eyes, which were looking sleepy again.

"You'd better get some rest, son. Your body's trying to heal."

"Yeah, I'm real tired. Maybe I'll take a little nap."

"Do me a favor, though, before you conk out again. Push that button over there to call the nurse. I need to take a piss, and I'll need help to get out of this wheelchair."

Drew smiled, his eyelids drooping. "Gonna get them to help you aim, too?"

"Just push the goddamned button."

FORTY ONE

Drew awoke sometime later to a telephone ringing. It took him a second to orient himself in the white hospital room. Chuck was gone, and he was alone. He wrestled around in the bed, pain stabbing his chest, until he could reach the phone.

"Yeah?"

"Drew? That you, man?"

"Hey, Curtis. You calling from jail?"

"Where else?"

"How'd you know to find me here?"

"Goodman came by for his daily visit, told me what happened. You gonna live?"

"I'm still considering my options."

"Dyin' be less painful, huh?"

"Something like that. How you doing? I've been meaning to come see you."

"But you've been busy. . . ."

"Yeah. Trying to find out who killed Fontanelle."

"Sounds like you about got yourself killed, man."

"I'm all right. Coupla busted ribs. Nothing I haven't had before."

"Goodman said they stomped your fingers, too."

"I'll never play the violin again."

"Thank God for that."

"Listen, Curtis, I think they drugged me. Same thing as happened to you. I was out cold when I got this beating."

"Might be better that way."

"Waking up wasn't much fun."

"You were partying with the Rattlers when this happened?"

"Yeah. Cerf. Raj Davis. That Edgewater guy."

"Know which one kicked your ass?"

"Not yet. But I plan to find out."

"Right. Soon as you can sit up again."

"I'm close to something, Curtis. That's why they took me out. One of those guys is behind these killings."

"You're lucky you're not choked to death with something stuffed in your mouth. What would it be for a sportswriter? Your notebook? A jockstrap?"

"Thanks for that mental image."

"Hey, man, speaking of mental, I remembered something else from my party with the team. Raj and Fontanelle, they were arguing, right? I told you that. Well, I was thinking about that and I think they made up. You know, kinda slowed to a simmer. I was talking to them, trying to keep them from fighting anymore."

"Raj cooled off? That's hard to imagine. Man looks like he's got a mad on all the time."

"Got that right. But hear the rest of it. People are waiting to use this phone."

Drew held the receiver tighter to his ear.

"I started asking them questions, man. If they knew anything about Cerf and how he was paying for the team, shit like that. And Fontanelle, she got real sly. Made some crack about how she knows plenty about Cerf. And Raj got all pissed again. Told her to shut up."

"Really?"

"Yeah, man. That's the last thing I remember."

"Hmm. Maybe Raj has some connection to Cerf that I don't know about."

"Maybe, man, but don't sound like you're in any shape to go find out. That Raj Davis is a mean motherfucker. You best keep your distance."

Someone rapped once on the door of Drew's hospital room, then the wide door silently swung open.

"Somebody's here, Curtis."

"That's okay, man. I gotta go anyway. Get better."

Drew thanked him and hung up as Lieutenant Steve Romero hulked through the door. The homicide detective's square jaw was set and his eyes were weary.

"I hear they're about to let you out of here," he said gruffly. "Thought I'd better come talk to you before you start flitting around the city again, trying to get yourself killed."

"I'm getting out?"

"They're doing the paperwork. But you can't leave until I'm done with you."

"You going to stop me from leaving? Arrest me?"

"I'll just keep anybody from helping you out of that bed. You look too banged up to make it on your own."

Drew tried grinning at him. He didn't mind talking to Romero. He finally felt like he had something to tell him. But he had to tease him with it first.

"Homicide's interested in a simple assault-and-battery?"

"We get interested when the victim is some newspaper guy, going around playing the Lone Ranger. Mucking up the investigation of not one, but two, murders."

"You think the same person killed Fontanelle Harper and Mertz?"

"What's that the cops always say on TV? 'I'm asking the questions here.'"

"Ask away."

"You've got no memory of how you ended up in that parking lot in such piss-poor condition?"

"Not much. I was drinking with some guys from the Rattlers. Guess I blacked out."

"Rohypnol," Romero said flatly.

"What?"

"Rohypnol. Roofies. That's what they found in your bloodstream."

"Roofies? That date-rape drug?"

"That's the one. You were out cold when they were breaking your bones?"

"Yeah. Lucky me, huh? I was just talking to Curtis White on the phone. I think someone slipped him the same drug the night Fontanelle Harper was killed."

"We're checking that out."

As usual, Romero was miles ahead. His mind worked that way. Drew's favorite moments of the recent murder trials had been watching Romero on the stand, outpacing smartass defense attorneys, anticipating every question.

"But they took Curtis' blood the night he was arrested," Drew said. "Shouldn't they have the results by now? Mine took hours, not days."

Romero sighed and his mouth compressed into a thin line.

"That's because you're already here in the hospital. His sample went through the jail system. The jail farms out the tests to private labs. We're lucky to get them in weeks. I've put an 'expedite' on his."

"Thanks. I'm sure it's the same thing. The blackout. The memory loss."

"Even if the tests come back positive, it doesn't mean your amigo will be sprung. The evidence against him is pretty strong."

"But—"

Romero raised a wide hand to halt him.

"I'm not here to talk about Curtis White. I wanted to see who you were sitting with at the party, whether you remembered anything."

Drew told him the few bare facts he remembered. Romero didn't bother to make notes, but he watched Drew closely with unblinking eyes. It felt as if the cop's brain was tape-recording everything he said.

"Cerf had already left before you blacked out?" Romero asked. "You saw him go?"

"Yeah. But that doesn't mean he didn't tell somebody—"

Romero silenced him with a sour look. He didn't want theories.

"I talked to several of the players already," he said. "They say you got too drunk and wandered off. Disappeared. Nobody saw you getting stomped. They don't know a thing."

"Or they've been told not to say anything."

Romero shrugged his wide shoulders under his guayabera shirt. "For now, that's the same thing. One of them did offer a possible explanation, though."

"What's that?"

"That big guy, Raj Davis? Fontanelle's boyfriend? He said maybe you drifted out to the parking lot, drunk, and somebody mugged you."

"Mugged? In Albuquerque? How often does that happen?"

"More than you might expect. Besides, Raj is from the Bronx. He thinks that way."

"A city boy, huh? You get his autograph while you were hearing all about his hometown?"

"Funny," Romero said. "I gotta go. You remember anything else, call me."

"You going to keep an open mind about Curtis? I'd like to see him get bailed out. He's not doing so well in jail."

"That's the thing about jail. 'Not doing so well?' That's the whole idea."

"Yeah, but he's innocent."

Romero grunted and turned toward the door. He paused, remembering something, and looked back over his shoulder.

"Gavin? After you get out of here, go home. Rest. Let us handle this. You might live longer."

"Sure, Lieutenant," Drew said brightly.

Romero muttered something under his breath, sounded like "fucking reporters," and disappeared down the hall.

FORTY TWO

Teresa Vargas swung her Toyota Tercel into a parking lot off Lomas Boulevard and zipped up and down the lanes, looking for an empty spot outside University Hospital. She guessed the hospital had a loading zone for picking up and dropping off patients, but she couldn't go look for it now. She already was late, and Drew was in a hurry to get home.

He'd sounded alert enough on the phone, but she figured he'd need days of recovery before he could even dress himself. She'd take him home, put him to bed, then make sure he didn't go pestering Scott Cerf and the Albuquerque Rattlers anymore.

She wondered whether she should tell him her news. Even all busted up, he'd probably try to run out and stir things up once he heard what she'd learned. She toyed with the idea of keeping her secret, making him wait until she had the story in the paper. But he probably could use some encouraging news.

She found a parking slot and turned off the engine, then used the rear-view mirror to check her magenta lipstick. Her nails were the same color, the polish freshly applied while she sat up all night, unable to sleep. She used her glowing fingertips now to moosh the flesh around her eyes. The sleepless nights were having their effect on her face. She looked like the Insomniac from Hell. She'd smeared makeup over the dark circles under her eyes before she left her apartment—one reason she was running late—and now they looked like dark circles with makeup smeared on them. She sighed and got out of the car and hurried across the hot asphalt, her boots thumping out at a beat.

By the time she made her way through the labyrinthine halls to Drew's room, he was sitting up in a wheelchair, fully dressed, ready to go. His shirt was filthy and wrinkled, and his short hair was matted from hours on a pillow, but he smiled when he saw her and his eyes were clear.

"Hiya, tiger. Ready to go home?"

"I've never been more ready for anything. I hate being in the hospital."

"The food?"

"What food? They gave me broth. But it's not that. I can't stand the way these places smell. It's like Lysol and rubbing alcohol and germs all mixed together."

"Don't forget the aroma of that yummy broth."

"That, too."

She leaned over and kissed him on the forehead.

"How you feeling?"

"Pretty good. Stiff, you know, achy. But I'll live. And I'd rather recuperate at home."

"We'll have you there in no time."

She checked to make sure he had his possessions and his paperwork, then wheeled him out of the room and off toward the parking lot.

Outdoors, the sky was chamber-of-commerce blue, and Drew tilted his face to the sun.

"Sunshine feels good," he said.

"Well, enjoy it on the ride home because I'm planning to

lock you in your bedroom for the next few days."

"I need to go get my Jeep. It's still parked outside that nightclub."

"A fine place for it. You don't have a car, maybe you'll stay home and heal like a good boy."

"I don't like to just leave it—"

"No. That's the way it's going to be. We'll go get the Jeep in a day or two, after I see whether you're a good patient."

"Aw, come on, Teresa. I've been cooped up—"

"Nope. Now stop complaining or I won't tell you my big news."

Drew sobered, and she knew he was thinking about Los Angeles.

"What news?"

"Somebody else got killed."

"Jesus. Who?"

"Guy named Stan Fields. He was a private eye here in town. They found him in his office Tuesday morning. His neck had been broken."

"Not strangled? Nothing stuffed in his mouth?"

"No. Just a quick snap-o of the neck."

"Then why are you telling me this?"

"Because Stan Fields was the head of a little company called Fields Investigations."

"So?"

"And Fields Investigations' top client was the late Wally Mertz."

"Holy shit."

"That's right, tiger. One of the homicide cops working the case told me Fields had worked almost exclusively for Mertek the past several months."

Drew tried to whistle, but his chapped lips didn't make much of a sound.

"Fields got killed while I was in L.A. I went down to the office today, catching up, and saw that Burns had only done a brief on the murder. So I started digging around, thinking there might be some kind of hard-boiled news story there. You know, 'Private Eye's Mysterious Slaying.' But then I hear the cops are looking into the Mertz connection."

Teresa strained against the wheelchair—he was a heavy load—as they reached the end of the sidewalk and the wheels got stuck against a curb. Drew got it free by pushing against the wheels with his hands, his splinted fingers sticking out awkwardly.

"Next time you're in the hospital," she said, "remind me to recruit an orderly to wheel you out to the car."

"I should walk."

"No, sit tight. We're almost there."

She could tell Drew was distracted by what she'd told him, but they spoke no more while she wrestled him out of the wheelchair and into the passenger seat of the little car. He was stiff all over, and the tight bandages around his chest restricted his movements, but she managed to get him inside with only minor howling.

Then Teresa returned the wheelchair to the hospital lobby. She didn't like leaving him alone in the car, not when he'd so recently been unconscious, but she didn't have a choice. A wheelchair wasn't like a shopping cart; you didn't just leave it in the parking lot. After she hiked back to the car, she found him sitting up very straight in the passenger seat, a big grin on his face.

"What?" she said as she got behind the wheel.

"I've been thinking."

"I've warned you against that, tiger."

"If Fields was working for Mertz, maybe he was investigating Cerf. They're in this competition for that defense contract, right? Maybe Mertz was snooping on Cerf's research team. He seemed awfully sure about having the upper hand."

She cranked up the engine, letting him wait for it.

"And maybe," she said, "they found something that Cerf wanted to hide."

"That would explain a lot. I wonder if there's some way to nail it down. . . ."

"Uh-uh. You're going home to bed, remember? You'll have to leave it to me to get the story on Fields."

"Yeah, but—"

"No buts. Home. Bed. Period."

"Okay. Can I at least make phone calls from bed?"

"We'll see. I don't want you messing up my story."

"*Your* story? I'm the one who got beat up trying to track all this down."

"Yeah, and you were getting nowhere fast."

"Thanks."

"And now you're out of the picture. How would you sports guys say it? You're on 'injured reserve.' If I need you to help, I'll bring you off the bench."

"Why'd you have to put it that way? I always hated sitting on the bench."

"Get used to it. You're wounded and it's time to convalesce. I'm gonna be Florence Nightmare until you get better."

"Yikes. I can't even go get my Jeep?"

"I'd hate to have to handcuff you to your bed."

"You'd love it."

"In your dreams, tiger."

FORTY THREE

Sylvia Smith sat at the dressing table in her bedroom on Monday, the evening sun slanting through the windows. She wore the same stern blue business suit she'd worn to work and her blond hair was pinned in a tight bun. She dabbed on a discreet amount of lipstick, then studied herself in the mirror. The usual lovely face looked back at her. Perfect skin. Big green eyes. She sat up straight and noted the way the suit clung to her curves. She could be a blonde bombshell if she wanted. If she'd just let herself go, roll out the artillery. If she could find someone to light her fuse. . . .

She'd tried to turn it on a little with Drew Gavin, see if he felt the attraction between them. Let her hair down. Kissed his cheek. Made a fool of herself.

That was the problem with building walls around herself, keeping people at arm's length, treating life like business. She was lonely. Still settling into a new city, still trying to find her niche. Along comes a big lug like Drew Gavin, who pays a little attention to her, and she behaves like a schoolgirl. All he wanted was information, help for his jailed friend, and she'd mistaken that need from something more.

A mistake she wouldn't make again. Back to taking care of business. Doing her job. Keeping the sex appeal to a minimum so others wouldn't be distracted from their own work. It might be lonely behind those walls, but at least she could keep her self-respect, and not surrender to her hormones, her whims.

She picked up the lipstick and reached across to the mirror, holding her body very still and upright. And she drew a big mustache on her reflected image.

The telephone rang. She sighed and stood up, leaving the mustache behind, and went to a bedside table where the phone squatted.

"Hello?"

"Hi, Sylvia. It's Drew Gavin."

Imagine that. She made sure her breathing was under control before she said, "What do *you* want?"

"Still mad at me?"

"I'm not mad at you. I haven't given you a thought all day. I hadn't heard from you, so I figured you'd gotten what you wanted from me."

"I've been in the hospital."

"You sick?"

"No, somebody tap-danced on my chest. I'm back home now."

"I'm sorry. I didn't know—"

"I'm okay, but I'm hot on the trail of something. I could use your help again."

She bit her lower lip before she said, "What is it?"

"A private eye named Stan Fields was killed the other day. He'd been working for Wally Mertz."

Her breath caught in her throat. "Doing what?"

"We're not sure, but I'll bet it has something to do with Scott Cerf and that defense contract."

"Oh, my."

"I also hear the Department of Defense may be investigating Cerf. For something related to all this? We don't know. But it would seem likely."

"A DOD investigation? I didn't run across that when I was researching Cerf."

"Maybe it's all top-secret or something. Anyway, what I was wondering is: Do these DOD investigators know about the dead private eye? Have they linked his death to the work he was doing for Mertz?"

"I don't know how I'd find out something like that. I'm already worried that I left a paper trail at the lab. If somebody finds out I've been snooping—"

"No, no. I don't want you to snoop anymore. What I'm thinking is that we ought to let DOD know about the connection between Fields and Mertz. The local cops are looking into it, but the more people stirring things up, the better."

She thought it over, turning slowly, the phone cord stretching around her hips.

"You want me to leak it to the investigators? Make sure they're onto it?"

"Is there some way you could do that? Without exposing yourself?"

"Sure. The right e-mail dropped in the right box. You could probably do it yourself."

"I thought it might work better coming from inside the lab. They'll be suspicious if a newspaper reporter coughs up the information."

"Okay. I can do it first thing in the morning."

"I really appreciate it, Sylvia. I'm kind of laid up here, and all I can do is call people up and bug them."

"You're stuck in bed? Do you need anything?"

"No, thanks. Somebody's looking after me."

"Oh. Okay. I'll call you tomorrow and let you know how it goes."

"Thanks again. You're a sweetheart."

She hung up, thinking: Yeah, I'm a sweetheart. Lot of good it does me.

Sylvia peeled off the suit jacket and draped it over a hanger in her neat closet. She kicked off her black pumps and stood in her stocking feet, wiggling her toes, trying to decide between jeans or a fluffy bathrobe.

The doorbell rang, and she muttered, "Now what?" and went to answer it.

She peered through the peephole to find a large, older man waiting outside the door. He was well-dressed in a blue blazer and a white shirt, and he had a broad, fleshy face. His hair was gray and thin, with strands carefully combed across his bald scalp. He sensed her watching, and smiled. Sylvia didn't recognize him, though his military bearing made her think he could be from Kirtland. Maybe he was DOD. She should demand identification, but he didn't look dangerous. The big smile looked sincere. He reminded her of her father.

She opened the door.

FORTY FOUR

The cab driver didn't make a sound while Drew slowly creaked out of the back seat, and Drew gave him an extra-large tip for his patience. Then the taxi wheeled away, leaving him standing near his Jeep, stiff and gasping.

The tape wrapped around his torso compressed the lower part of his lungs, making him feel short of breath all the time. He'd worn a loose football jersey over it, along with the usual jeans and sneakers. He looked like any other citizen, out and about on a sunny Tuesday morning, until he tried to walk. Then he was like the Frankenstein monster lumbering across the parking lot.

It was easier to get into the Jeep than it had been to fit into the taxi. He could remain more straight up-and-down, and he could hold onto the steering wheel for balance. Drew took this as a good sign. He felt even better when he keyed the ignition and the engine cranked right up.

With the Jeep's stiff suspension, he felt every teeth-rattling bump and pothole as he drove to the *Gazette*. By the time he parked outside the employee entrance, he felt as if he'd been mugged all over again. His ribs ached and his fingers hurt and he still felt dizzy occasionally. In perfect shape, really, for a day at the office. He'd get a lot of sympathy. Maybe, once he saw how banged up he was, Goodman wouldn't fire him.

Drew was the first to arrive in the sports department. He kept his back very straight as he eased into his swivel chair. He caught his breath while his computer booted up, then picked up the phone while scanning the wire service budgets for the top stories of the day.

A secretary answered at Sylvia Smith's office, and told him she hadn't seen Sylvia yet today. He thanked her and hung up, wondering if that meant Sylvia was off doing his secret-agent work. He'd been having second thoughts about getting her further involved, but it might be too late.

He called Teresa, though he wasn't looking forward to telling her that he'd escaped her clutches and was at the office. She answered sleepy and slurry, and he apologized for waking her and told her he'd call later and quickly hung up. Teresa got little sleep, and he felt bad for robbing her of a minute of sweet slumber.

He might even be back home before she realized he'd sneaked off. If she was sleeping in, she must not be expected at the office until midday or later. Maybe he could get some work done, then scoot on back home. Truth to tell, he wasn't feeling so great. He'd taken some mild painkillers, but all they'd done was upset his stomach. He still hurt all over. And, he was quickly learning, he couldn't type worth a damn with his splinted fingers sticking up in the way.

Filthy Hogan shambled in, and Drew imagined that he trailed a cloud of dust, like Charlie Brown's pal Pigpen. Filthy stopped when he spotted Drew through his smudged glasses.

"The hell are you doing here?"

"Just getting a little work done."

"Well, that's stupid. You should be in bed."

"Thank you, Dr. Filthy, for your opinion, but I'm fine."

"You look like shit."

"Thanks again."

"No, really, go home. I can't work looking at you all day. Be like having Death sitting at the next desk."

"You never look up from your computer anyway."

Filthy grumbled and sat down at his desk. He'd brought his lunch in a wrinkled, greasy sack and he smooshed it into a crowded desk drawer. Drew got a whiff of the lunch—which he guessed was barbecued sweatsocks—and flinched. He already felt queasy; he didn't need Filthy's lunch aroma fogging up the place.

While Filthy settled in, Drew picked up the phone, thinking he'd call Morrison, see if he'd learned anything from his DOD investigator. But Spiffy O'Neil strutted in the door, and made a beeline for Drew's desk.

"What are you doing here, my boy?"

"Just getting a little work done."

"But you should be in bed! Maybe still in the hospital."

"I'm fine."

"You look like shit."

"That's what Filthy was just saying."

"Well, I'd hate to agree with Mr. Hogan on anything, but I must say shit was the first thing that came to mind when I saw you."

"Thanks."

"You should go home."

"Leave me alone."

Spiffy turned toward his desk. He huffed and slammed drawers and squeaked his chair and generally made as much noise as possible without actually screaming.

Drew hung up the phone and sighed. This wasn't going so well.

Then Henry came blowing in. She didn't even wait to clear the door before she started talking.

"Drew, what the heck are you doing here? I saw your Jeep out there and I nearly had a heart attack. Are you kidding me? You should be in bed."

"So I hear."

"Well? What are you doing here?"

He sighed wearily. "A little work."

"You look like shit."

"That does it." Drew teetered to his feet. "Mr. Looks-Like-Shit is going home."

"To bed," Spiffy sputtered.

"Maybe. But home anyway. I'll take a laptop with me, check in later from there, see what kind of manure you're trying to spring on the unsuspecting public."

"Don't worry about us," Filthy said. "We'll get the paper out."

"You just rest," Henry added. "Get well."

Drew couldn't help but feel grateful for their concern, though he was as annoyed as hell. He turned back to them as he reached the door.

"Tell Goodman I'm at home if he needs me."

"Shut up," Filthy said. "Go to bed."

Drew pushed through the door, the laptop computer under his arm. The swinging door whapped his bruised shoulder, and he grumbled all the way to the Jeep.

FORTY FIVE

Otis Edgewater had been busy around the clock, and his eyes were scratchy and his muscles were tired. Reminded him of when he was a kid, on patrol in the Vietnamese jungles: weary but alert, riding a wave of adrenaline, jazzed to make something happen. No more waiting. Just the slam-bang heart rush that comes with action.

The thought of what was to come gave him a warm tingle deep in his belly. He blinked and swallowed against the feeling. Not yet. But soon. Very soon.

He used the speed dial on his cellular phone to call Cerf. He didn't like using the phone, out here where any Radio Shack geek could be listening in, but he'd keep it brief.

"Howdy, chief, it's me."

"I've been waiting to hear from you." Cerf sounded wary. "That message you left was pretty cryptic."

"Nothing cryptic about it, chief. It's time to dance."

"Dance?"

"I'm following Gavin right now. Looks like he's headed for home."

"I don't know about this, Otis. Are you sure it's necessary?"

"What did that guy at Sandia tell you?"

"Yes, I know. But we can't be sure Gavin and friends

have gotten anywhere."

Otis squeezed the steering wheel in his powerful hands. Cerf was distracting, interfering with the anticipation. The little pussy better not mess this up.

"We need to find out what they know," he said. "I'm going to Gavin's. You can come or not, either way, but I'm not gonna let that asshole screw this thing up."

Cerf said nothing for a long time, but Otis could hear him breathing into the phone. Idiot.

Otis told him Gavin's address, and said he'd be there in three minutes.

"By the time you get there, it might all be over. You'd better hurry."

"Otis—"

He clicked off the phone and slipped it back into his jacket pocket. He was worried about Cerf. The boy didn't have the guts for this kind of mission. He put a nice face on the company, and he no doubt could sell Frigidaires to Eskimos, but he wasn't tough, mentally or physically. He relied on Otis for that. Without Otis, Cerf would have nothing but a company on the skids. Albuquerque's Most Eligible Bachelor wouldn't be worth piss.

Without Otis, Cerf would've had no way to smuggle his software overseas. Otis had contacts all over the world, fellow warriors he'd met during his travels with the Army. Men who spoke his language. Men who understood strategic advantages.

Otis got word to them about the virtual reality software that could help them design new bombs. Cerf's people broke the program down into interlocking sections, each more advanced than the previous, so Otis could market the pieces to various generals and politicians in countries like Pakistan and Korea and Iran. It was Otis who'd cut the deals and funneled the money through offshore banks. And, soon, it would be Otis who made the biggest deal of 'em all, selling the entire software package to Baghdad for a cool ten million dollars.

And what had Cerf done? He'd kept his R&D people busy developing the software. He'd found a way to launder millions of dollars through his suckass basketball team and his new nightclub. But he'd kept himself distanced from the mechanics of the operation. Otis had done all the dirty work.

Now it was time for Cerf to take a more active role. Otis didn't like the way things had been going lately—he took all the risks while Cerf sat in his office, wringing his hands. If things went south, Cerf might roll over for the authorities. Give them Otis to get himself a better deal. Otis wanted his boss directly involved, so maybe Cerf would recognize they were in this thing together. Make him show some fucking backbone.

They were so close. Otis would get them through it, if he had to take out a dozen people in the process. And if there was a way to eliminate Cerf, too, he might just take the chance. He could walk away with a big chunk of fuck-you money and go set up some other enterprise, one with even less waiting around. Plenty of action out there around the world, if a man is mercenary enough to go hunt for it.

But first things first. He needed to get the DOD off their backs so they could finish what they started. And the best way to slow up the investigation would be to eliminate some more witnesses.

He'd already taken care of Mertz and that private eye, who'd come closest to uncovering the overseas deals. Now it was Gavin's turn. Otis sure was looking forward to it. Gavin would put up a fight, the way that little fucker Mertz had. That should make it more interesting.

Otis wouldn't leave a calling card this time. That copycat business with Mertz, stuffing the disks in his mouth, may have backfired. It had seemed like a good idea at the time, a way to cover his tracks. Instead, it attracted more attention to Cerf. Gave Gavin and his newshawks more ammunition. Otis wouldn't make that mistake again. He'd take out Gavin, but he'd do it quietly. And the same went for anyone else who got in his way.

The company sedan bumped over a pothole near Gavin's house and Otis heard a thump in the trunk, a muffled moan. Tired as he was, as taut as he felt, he couldn't help but smile.

FORTY SIX

Drew was coming out of the bathroom, awkwardly zipping his jeans with his left hand, when he heard noises in the kitchen. A footfall, a rustle of clothing.

Had Nurse Ratchett come back to check on him? "Teresa? Is that you?"

No answer.

He walked through the small living room and rounded the corner into the kitchen. Otis Edgewater stood just inside the back door. In his left hand, he held a thin strip of metal. In his right, pointed at the floor, was a pistol. Drew recognized the model right away. It was an Army-issue Colt .45. His father had one just like it, stored away somewhere. He wished it were in his hand right now.

"Howdy, son," Edgewater said. The metal strip clattered to the floor as the barrel of the gun snaked upward to point at Drew. "You look like shit."

"That's what people keep telling me."

"Looks like somebody knocked you out, then stomped on you. Maybe squished those fingers under the heel of his shoe."

Drew tried to take a deep breath and was rewarded with a stab in the ribs.

"Good guess," he managed. "That's the way I figure it, too."

"Too bad. What's the world coming to? Violence everywhere."

Edgewater smiled at him, his eyes cold and fierce.

"Just the way you like it," Drew said.

Edgewater shrugged his shoulders, but his aim never strayed. "Conflict makes life interesting, son. Fight or flight, that's the human condition. Everything else is waiting."

"So we've got ourselves a conflict."

"Looks that way. Why don't you just sit down at the table here?"

Drew tensed, glanced around. No way he could run for it. He couldn't outrun a bullet, even when he wasn't wrapped up like a freaking mummy. Edgewater could take his time, and still put three or four bullets in him before Drew could make it to the front door. The back door was closer, but he'd have to go through Mr. Universe here to reach it, and he sure as hell wasn't up to that. But he had a feeling, if he sat down at that table, he'd never get up from it again. He needed to be on his feet.

"Want some coffee?" he asked.

"No, I don't fancy having scalding water thrown at me, if that's what you mean. Just sit your ass down."

Drew tried to take a steadying breath, but the constricting tape and the aching ribs thwarted him. He stepped forward and grasped the back of one of the old chrome diner chairs. He pulled it out from the table, making room to sit. Edgewater came closer, reaching for the chair directly across the table from him.

Drew snatched his heavy chair up off the floor and spun,

swinging its shiny legs through the air. Edgewater threw up his arms to ward off the blow, and one of the legs cracked him across the wrist and sent the Colt flying. The pistol banged against the front of the stove, then skittered across the floor.

Drew very badly wanted that gun, but he had Edgewater at a momentary disadvantage, and he swung the chair back the other direction, trying for his head this time. Edgewater snatched at the chair and got hold of a leg with one hand. He twisted it free of Drew's grasp and tossed it aside.

"All right, son." Edgewater smiled. "If that's the way you want it."

He grabbed the kitchen table and threw it over, sending newspapers and dishes flying. Drew's eyes were caught by his father's glass salt shaker smashing, a quick puff of white against the dingy wall.

Then Edgewater charged him. He came in low, trying to catch Drew in the ribs with his shoulder. Drew instinctively threw out his hands, the same way he'd handle a blocker on the football field, catching Edgewater's shoulders and pushing one direction while sidestepping to the other. His splinted fingers shot pain up his arm as he dodged aside. Edgewater threw out an arm and managed to catch Drew across the abdomen, knocking the wind out of him.

He couldn't take another shot like that. The broken ribs were as sharp as knives. If Edgewater dislodged one, it could pierce a lung. He covered his ribs with his right elbow, holding his injured fingers up out of the way, near his face.

Edgewater closed on him, swinging for his ribs again, but Drew deflected the blow with his elbow. He brought up his left and popped Edgewater hard on the ear. The man grunted and shook his head, but he kept coming. Drew threw two more lefts, connecting with one square on Edgewater's cheekbone, but it did no good. Edgewater absorbed the blows and waded in, smashing into Drew chest-to-chest. His thick arms went around Drew's middle, and he snapped them shut, squeezing, lifting him onto his toes. Edgewater drove him backward until they slammed into a corner of the kitchen.

Pain made Drew's head swim, and the lights dimmed for a moment. The bear hug would send him under in seconds. He leaned into Edgewater's embrace and turned his head to one side, reaching. Then he sank his teeth into one of his cauliflower ears.

Edgewater bellowed and backed away. His hand went up to his ear and came away bloody. He looked at his hand, then up at Drew. The smile spread across his face.

"Now, son, that ain't fightin' fair."

Drew wanted to answer, but he couldn't really breathe yet. He couldn't run; Edgewater had him cornered. He couldn't hold the man off, not with only one good hand.

He tried kicking, but Edgewater dodged it and charged again, this time leading with a left hook that caught Drew directly on the broken ribs. His hands dropped to cover, and a right uppercut caught him on the jaw. His teeth clacked together and a white light flashed in his eyes as his head snapped back into the wall.

And then nothing.

FORTY SEVEN

Drew awakened to a hard slap across his cheek. He blinked his eyes, his brain nibbling away at the edges of the darkness. A slap came back the other way, turned the other cheek, and he tried to lean his head back out of range.

Pain jolted him, head to toe, concentrating around his ribs and his chin and his tongue, which he apparently had bitten. He spat a couple of times while he tried to tell down from up. Edgewater swam into his vision, leaning over at him, sneering into his face.

Drew tried to take a swing at him, but his arms wouldn't move. He yanked at them, felt cord tighten around his wrists.

"Yeah, they're tied, son. You're right where we want you."

Drew strained at the binds, which didn't budge. He gave up and focused instead on seeing clearly. The kitchen was wrecked, the table still uprooted onto its side, chairs scattered, half the drawers hanging open. His chair sat squarely in the middle of the room.

"Had to take the cord off that old toaster," Edgewater said. "Don't people keep *rope* in their houses anymore? Can't ever tell when you might need some rope."

Drew pictured the heavy black cord that had connected the toaster to the wall for years, always in the way, a little too long for the toaster's place on the countertop. The cord was grimy, coated in years of grease spatters and counter crud. It felt oily against his wrists and that gave him hope.

The light shifted in the kitchen, and Drew looked past Edgewater to see Scott Cerf standing outside the kitchen door, peering in through the glass. Cerf looked furtive, glancing around, his shoulders hunched.

Edgewater crossed the room to open the door.

"Howdy, chief. You're just in time."

Cerf slipped inside, looking back over his shoulder into the yard.

"What's wrong?" Edgewater said. "Somebody see you?"

"I don't think so. I was careful."

Cerf looked around the kitchen before his wide eyes settled on Drew. "My God, Otis. What have you done?"

"Nothing yet. I was waiting for you. Gavin took a little nap, but he was just waking up."

Drew strained at the cord around his wrists, pulling slowly, feeling a little give there.

Cerf stepped closer, leaned over to look into Drew's eyes.

"He looks like shit," he said.

"That's what I told him. But he tried to put up a fight anyway. Sumbitch bit me on the ear!"

He turned so Cerf could inspect the wounded ear. Drew noticed for the first time that Edgewater held a paper towel he'd used to dab at the bleeding. Somehow, that made him feel better.

Cerf made a face at the display, but said nothing. He seemed jittery, and that made Drew nervous, too. He'd hoped briefly that having Cerf here might inhibit Edgewater, might rein him in a little. But he could see from the way Cerf jumped whenever Edgewater spoke that the bodyguard really was in charge.

Edgewater stepped past Cerf to stand over Drew. Then he casually reached out and thumbed Drew in the eye.

"Shit!" Drew jerked his head back, his eye squinched shut against the trauma. Felt like the thumb had gone clean through to the back of his skull.

Edgewater waited until Drew finished squirming before he said, "Do I have your attention, son? Now, this is the way it's gonna be. We're gonna ask you some questions. You're gonna answer 'em. We understand each other?"

Drew nodded, blinking the injured eye rapidly, trying to see.

Cerf stood behind Edgewater, his mouth agape, and the bodyguard turned and grasped him by the sleeve.

"Step on up here, chief. This guy can't hurt you. You've got questions for him. Ask away."

Cerf wore a twill blazer over jeans and an open-collared shirt. He tugged at the blazer's cuffs, pulling himself together. His eyes went cagey as he looked down at Drew, and he suddenly seemed dangerous.

"You've been messing in my affairs," he said calmly. "You've made yourself a pest. And now it's come to this."

Drew said nothing. He'd wait for the questions, and answer as evasively as he could. Maybe he could buy some time.

☆ ☆ ☆ ☆ ☆

Otis Edgewater strode across the kitchen and retrieved the pistol from where it had fallen to the floor. He tucked the gun in his waistband, then leaned his hips against a countertop and crossed his big arms over his chest. His ear had stopped bleeding, more or less. The knuckles on his right hand ached from the contact with Gavin's bony jaw, but he felt warm inside, steady and in control.

He watched Cerf question the sportswriter. The boss was being wily about it, coming in at angles, trying to learn how much Gavin knew without giving anything else away.

"Look," Gavin said, "I've just been trying to find out who killed Fontanelle Harper. I don't know anything about the rest of this stuff."

"If that's true, then why have someone pull my contract application at Sandia? You think I wouldn't hear about that? I've got friends inside the lab."

Gavin looked wary.

"I didn't know how it might be connected," he said. "But you framed my friend for her death. I figured you must have something to hide."

"*I* framed your friend? I didn't have shit to do with that. Believe me, it didn't hurt my feelings any that Fontanelle turned up dead. She had begun to be problem. But we didn't kill her. Right, Otis?"

Edgewater paused a second, grinning, before he said, "Right, chief."

Cerf turned back to Gavin and said, "I didn't even know your Mr. White was looking into my finances until Otis told me the next day, after your buddy had already been arrested."

"Then who killed her?"

"Who cares? Maybe your friend did it. That's not the point."

"Then what is the fucking point?"

Otis was across the kitchen in an instant, his open hand

slashing across Gavin's face. The force of the blow turned Gavin's head halfway around.

"Remember, son, no lip. Just answer the questions."

Scott Cerf flinched at the smack Otis' hand made against Gavin's cheek, but he quickly steadied himself.

God, he hated this. He felt as if he'd been led into a dark and scary place, one from which there was no escape. And leading him ever deeper, holding tightly to his hand, was Otis Edgewater.

Otis stepped past him to return to his post against the kitchen counter. Cerf's nostrils flared at his aroma, a body odor equal parts sweat and adrenaline and domination. The scent made him quake inside.

But he needed answers from Gavin, and he needed them now. He'd steel himself until this interrogation ended. Then he'd find an excuse to depart—quickly—and let Otis finish what he'd started. No need to witness that. He could go back to the office, have a drink, work the phone, and try to pretend that Otis wasn't out roaming the city like a hungry wolf.

Drew tasted blood in his mouth. He spat on the floor, narrowly missing Edgewater's shiny combat boot as the man turned away. Then Cerf stepped back up into the batter's box and said, "You went to see Wally Mertz."

Drew nodded.

"What did you tell him?"

Drew squinted at him, then settled on a new tactic.

"Aren't you more concerned about what *he* told *me*? Isn't

that why you had him murdered? He'd stumbled onto something, hadn't he? Him and that private eye who was killed. What are you trying to hide?"

Cerf leaned into Drew's face and said, "Do I need Otis to get your attention again? I'm asking the questions."

His breath smelled like peppermint. Drew strained against the cord around his wrists. God, he'd like to get his hands around Cerf's neck.

"Let me put it to you as a statement," Drew said. "You've been working on that virtual reality software for the Department of Defense. But you're not going to win the contract. Mertek has it sewn up. So you need another way to make money, to keep your company afloat, to pay for your expensive hobbies, like the Rattlers."

Cerf straightened up and looked down his nose at Drew.

"The Rattlers are not—"

"Yeah, yeah. I know. They're not just a hobby. They're also a way of laundering money. We've already figured that out, too."

Cerf's eyebrows rose slightly, but he gave nothing else away. The man had remarkable control, as long as Edgewater was watching.

"You're selling that software to the highest bidders, then laundering the money through the team. Aren't you?"

Drew was going out on a limb here. He'd either impress Cerf with how much he'd learned, or make the software magnate laugh at just how far off-base he'd wandered.

Cerf didn't laugh. He looked back over his shoulder at Edgewater, and they exchanged a look. Drew suddenly knew he was right.

"Who'd you sell it to?"

Cerf looked like he'd swallowed a chicken bone. He turned his back on Drew and walked away to peer out the kitchen window into the back yard. Edgewater took the move as a signal. He stepped up to Drew and cuffed him a hard one to the ear.

As Drew recovered, Edgewater said, "For a writer, you're not too clear on how sentences work, are you? I said no more questions."

Drew blinked back tears that had washed into his eyes and tried to hold Edgewater's gaze.

"You're a military man," he said, his voice barely above a whisper. "How can you commit treason? You sell those secrets, you're as bad as any spy."

Edgewater slapped him again, but not as hard. He was distracted now, and the blow was a mere reflex.

"You don't know shit, do you, son? It's like I told that fucker Mertz: This country needs an enemy. Otherwise, we get weak and lazy. We don't have one anymore, not since the Russians went belly up. All we've got left is a bunch of Third World countries, so goddamned backward they don't even count. Lots of them little countries think they could do more with nuclear weapons if they got hold of Mr. Cerf's software package. And they're willing to pay for it. Most of 'em are too damned dumb to work the software, but they want to outbid their rivals—"

Cerf turned away from the window and shouted, "Otis!"

"Yeah, chief?"

"You're saying more than necessary here. We don't need to give Mr. Gavin a stockholder's report. We just need to find out who he's told. Don't let him bait you."

Edgewater scowled and cuffed Drew again, but Drew saw

this one coming and ducked away so the contact was light. He needed to quit taking those hard shots to head. He needed to think. If he could get them to turn on one another . . .

"So?" Cerf said, taking Edgewater's place directly in front of Drew. "Who knows about this?"

"Which part of it?"

Edgewater growled under his breath, but he didn't step up for another swing.

"Any of it."

"You think I'll start naming my friends and co-workers so you can go after them, too?"

"I think you'd better start right now. Otherwise, Otis gets another crack at you."

Drew felt the muscle in his jaw throb. He cut his eyes to Edgewater, who was smiling.

"Bring him on then," Drew said. "Because that's all I'm saying."

Edgewater's big hand curled into a fist, and he took a step toward Drew, but then he stopped.

"No, son. I don't think I'm gonna hit you anymore. You're making me tired. I've got something better."

He turned and went out the back door. Cerf looked uneasy at his bodyguard's sudden absence. He backed away from Drew a couple of steps.

Drew heard a car door or trunk lid slam outside. He kept his eyes steady on Cerf, trying to stare him down, while his hands stayed busy with the cord behind his back, pulling at it, stretching it.

Then Otis Edgewater came back inside, his fleshy face red from exertion. He had a long bundle draped over his shoulder, wrapped in a green Army blanket. He bent over to set the parcel down, and Drew saw that it was a body inside the blanket.

Edgewater squatted and smiled up at Drew as he unwrapped the blanket, revealing Sylvia Smith, still beautiful as ever, though her clothes were in disarray and her stockinged feet were shoeless and her loose blond hair was stuck to her cheek. She was unconscious, but Drew couldn't see any marks on her. Her chest rose and fell with her breathing.

"Jesus Christ."

"Look, it's your friend," Edgewater said. "She's a good-looking thing, ain't she? But she's sleeping pretty hard right now. Wouldn't take much to kill her."

He clamped a wide hand over her mouth and nose, shutting off her air. One leg kicked and her head reflexively turned to the side.

Drew shouted in alarm and struggled, trying to get to his feet.

Edgewater pulled his hand away, and Sylvia took a deep, shuddering breath. Her eyelids twitched, but didn't open.

"Now, son, I believe you've got some more questions to answer."

FORTY EIGHT

Drew tugged and twisted against the cord around his wrists while Otis Edgewater crouched over Sylvia on the floor. He couldn't go at the knots, not behind his back, not with two fingers splinted like stiff rabbit ears. His only hope was that the old cord was greasy enough to slip free.

Edgewater pulled the pistol from his waistband and rested the muzzle against Sylvia's temple.

"Go to it, chief," he said, grinning.

Cerf cleared his throat. He locked eyes with Drew, who got the feeling he was trying to ignore what was going on beside him on the floor.

"Who have you told about the software? About selling it overseas? I'm guessing Miss Smith here—" He pointed down at Sylvia without taking his eyes off Drew. "—knows all about it since she was spying for you. Who else?"

Drew said nothing. He pulled against the cord, felt one of the knots pop against his wrist as the end of the cord worked loose. He needed a little more time . . .

Edgewater thumbed back the hammer of the big pistol. The click sounded like a loud crack in the close kitchen. Drew started talking.

"You just don't get it, do you? I'm a *newspaperman*. If I

know about it, then everybody does. It's public. Say I mentioned the software deals to one, two other reporters, an editor. That's all it would take. Reporters ask questions, which gets other people asking questions. Somebody calls up the DOD, say, and asks whether they're investigating you—"

Cerf winced.

"—and the DOD will neither confirm nor deny, because that's what they do. But they'll immediately start such an investigation, if they haven't already. And their investigators will talk to people, who'll talk to other people. Pretty soon, it's all over Washington, and your business goes down the crapper. Once the word gets out, it spreads. That's what news does."

Cerf towered over Drew, but he was distracted now, lost in thought. Drew pulled against the cord again, his arms trembling with the effort.

Edgewater uncocked the pistol and stood. "What do you think, chief?"

Cerf took a second to look at him, still sorting things out in his head. Then he said, "I think it's time for us to get out of town."

Edgewater nodded and walked into the living room, all business. Drew figured he was checking the street, seeing whether a couple of loud shots would attract attention. Time was running out. He'd dragged Sylvia into this mess, and now they both could die. Getting free was their only hope. He strained against the cord some more, felt it give, and one hand was free. He caught himself before he brought the hand up. Cerf didn't seem to notice. The loose hand was his right, the one with the splints, but if he could just get the cord loose from the chair, his other hand would be free—

Edgewater came back into the kitchen, carrying a pillow from the sofa. It was an old, saggy pillow, one that had floated around the living room furniture since Drew was a boy. He knelt over Sylvia Smith and put the pillow over her lovely face. His other hand still held the pistol, and Drew caught his breath, expecting him to shoot through the pillow. But Edgewater just pressed the pillow tighter to her face. Her legs kicked slightly.

"This'll only take a minute, chief," he said, smiling up at Cerf.

Cerf looked pale, unsteady on his feet, but he didn't move away.

"*Everybody* knows!" Drew shouted. "It won't do any good to kill us."

"Won't do any harm either," Cerf muttered. He still watched Edgewater and the squirming Sylvia, as if suddenly fascinated by the violence. Her legs gave a final kick and she stopped moving.

Drew felt hot rage well up within him, overpowering frustration and fear and loss. A roar rose up from deep in his lungs and he yanked hard with his left arm. The cord cut into his wrist, felt like it was slicing off his hand, but it came free from the chair. He was on his feet in a flash. The long black cord dangled from his wrist as he elbowed Cerf out of the way. He dived at Edgewater.

Edgewater sprang backward as Drew came hurtling over Sylvia's still form, and they went rolling and tumbling to the floor. They came to a hard stop against the kitchen cabinets, Drew on the bottom, his left hand free to grab Edgewater's wrist before he could bring the big pistol around. He tried to lock his elbow, tried to keep Edgewater from bending his arm, but the gun moved slowly, inexorably, toward Drew's head. Edgewater leaned over him, his face flushed, the strands of his combover standing up, loose and wild. He put all his strength into that arm, pushing down, only an inch away from lining the barrel up with Drew's forehead.

Drew's other arm was pinned between them, folded so that the splinted fingers were under his chin. As Edgewater shifted his weight, Drew pulled the hand free and stuck his chrome index finger into Edgewater's eye.

He howled and rolled away, clapping a hand over the injured eye. Drew felt like saying, "See there! That's how it feels!" But he couldn't get enough air into his lungs to waste any on talking. He pitched forward across the floor and snatched Edgewater's ankle as the security man attempted to stand. Edgewater still had one hand over his eye and the pistol in the other, but he threw both hands out to try to catch himself as he crashed to the floor.

Drew scrambled after him. He crawled up Edgewater's broad back and grabbed at his gun hand. He stuck an elbow in the back of his neck and pressed down as he tried to wrest the gun away from the fallen man.

He heard a noise behind him. Cerf. He couldn't look away, couldn't get distracted now. He gambled that Cerf, given the chance, would race out the door rather than join the dogpile. He pushed down harder on Edgewater's neck, his weight squishing the air from the strongman's lungs. The kitchen door slammed behind him.

Edgewater must've heard it, too, because he bellowed and lurched upward, throwing Drew off. They got to their feet, but Drew clung to the gun hand, pulling back Edgewater's fingers, nearly there.

The gun came free and clattered to the floor. Edgewater swung wildly with his other hand and caught Drew above the ear, knocking him dizzy. He backpedaled across the kitchen, stumbling and straining for breath. Sylvia still lay off to one side and he moved away from her. Maybe she still could survive this, if he did.

The pistol was right at Edgewater's feet, but he abandoned it in favor of a direct assault, barreling straight at Drew, fists swinging. Drew took a shot to the gut and one to the chest before he could get his arms up. The broken ribs felt like bayonets plunged into his chest.

He backed up some more, nearly tripping over the leg of an overturned chair, and managed to block the next three punches with his forearms. No jabbing for Edgewater; he put everything he had into every punch. The shots on the forearms made Drew feel like he was catching cannonballs.

But he had a chance now that the gun was out of the way. He threw two quick lefts at Edgewater's head, which absorbed them with the barest of movement. Edgewater closed, throwing hooks at Drew's ribcage, still going for his weak spot. Drew blocked most of them, but a one-two got through, and his knees wobbled and the air went out of him.

He couldn't find any way to hurt Otis Edgewater. The man was one big, hard muscle. Even his head, with its dancing strands of hair, seemed impervious to punishment. But there was one place where no amount of weightlifting made a difference . . .

Drew brought his knee up sharply, caught Edgewater in the balls. His pale eyes went wide and a gust of foul air blew out of his mouth.

Drew didn't hesitate. He popped Edgewater in the nose, and blood exploded. He felt the hot spatter hit his own cheeks as he closed in, windmilling at Edgewater's head with his left arm, connecting again and again, the black electric cord lashing through the air.

Edgewater stumbled backward, his arms loose at his sides, his eyes wide and surprised. The leg of the fallen chair caught the back of his calf, and he lost his balance. The chair skated off in one direction while Edgewater fell heavily in the other.

Drew huffed over to him, red pain streaking through his body. Edgewater was face down on the floor, but he wasn't out. He shifted, got one big hand under him to push to his feet. Drew howled, and kicked at Edgewater's face, once, twice.

Edgewater tried to dodge away, and the second kick came in wrong. Drew's toe went under the man's chin, caught him squarely in the windpipe. His mouth flew open and he flopped over onto his back. One hand clawed at his neck as he gasped, trying to get air.

Drew stood and watched, his breath coming hard, while Otis Edgewater slowly suffocated. His body stopped writhing. The wide, pale eyes stared up at the ceiling.

Drew clutched his arms to his ribcage. The pain was excruciating, but he still was breathing; his lungs didn't make the bubbling rale that would come if one was punctured. He looked around the sun-streaked kitchen. The wrecked furniture. The broken glass. The blood-spattered floor. He felt light-headed, but he stumbled over to where Sylvia still lay on the blanket.

He knelt beside her, though bending made his ribcage feel white-hot, and pulled the old pillow away from her face. He pressed his fingers against the side of her neck. He fumbled for her hand, clutched her wrist, but there was no pulse there, either.

Tears sprang from his eyes, and he nearly toppled over onto her. A sob tore from his throat and he sat back on his heels, shuddering against the pain inside.

He sat that way for several minutes, long enough for his breathing to return to normal. Then he wiped at his eyes and slowly got to his feet. Time to call the cops.

FORTY NINE

The coroner's people took away the bodies of Otis
Edgewater and Sylvia Smith while Drew was being inter-
viewed by Lt. Steve Romero. Every time Drew saw the chalk
outlines where they'd lain, he wondered whether he could
continue to live in his father's house, whether Sylvia's ghost
would haunt him forever. He'd moved back to Barelas after a
man had died at his old apartment. Could he stay here now,
knowing that Sylvia Smith had been killed in his kitchen?
That it was all his fault she'd gotten involved? That he'd been
unable to save her?

His breath came short and his throat tightened. He looked
down at his feet, hoping no one would see him cry. But his
head snapped up when he heard Teresa's voice.

"Drew?" she called from the doorway. "Are you all right?"

Her voice sounded tentative, and Drew leaned sideways to
see around Romero. She was peering past a uniformed cop,
her notebook raised in her hand.

"I'm okay," he said, but Romero already was turning
around.

"What's she doing in here? This is a *crime* scene."

The cop snagged Teresa by the arm and dragged her back
outside.

"I'm here as a journalist!" she shouted, but Romero just shook his head.

When he turned back, Drew said, "She's my girlfriend."

"Well, is she a journalist, or is she your girlfriend?"

Drew let that one sink in. "That's the question right now. Which is she going to put first?"

"What the hell are you talking about?"

"You don't want to know. Can I have a painkiller now?"

"Not until I'm done with you. You're already not making a lot of sense. Dope you up, and we'll never get to the bottom of this."

"I've told you everything that happened."

"Yeah, that you killed a man with your bare hands."

"More with my foot, really," Drew said ruefully.

"So you said. And this is all the result of some diabolical plot by this guy Scott Cerf you keep raving about."

"The dead guy is Cerf's chief of security. I told you that. He smothered Sylvia before I could stop him."

"Then you broke free and killed him."

"It was me or him."

"That's what they all say."

"Come on, lieutenant. You know me. I wouldn't make up this stuff."

"Only because it's a crazy story, one that no one would admit to dreaming up."

"Find Cerf. Ask him."

"We're trying to find him. I put out an APB. He's not at home."

"You find him, and you'll see I'm telling the truth."

Drew rubbed at his wrist, where the old electric cord had left a deep groove. Evidence techs still squatted around the kitchen, taking photos and gathering fibers. They'd bagged the toaster and the cord earlier, along with the pillow Edgewater had used to kill Sylvia, and taken them away. Drew knew he never wanted to see those items again.

One of the uniforms came through the back door and weaved between the techs to reach Romero. He whispered into the lieutenant's ear.

"Shit," Romero said. The uniformed cop scurried away.

"That was news about Cerf now. Seems his corporate jet left town an hour ago."

"Headed where?"

"The flight plan says Cancun, but it could be anywhere. Those jets have a range of hundreds of miles."

"So he's running."

"No, he decided to take a vacation."

"I'm telling you, he's behind the whole thing. All these deaths. He sent Edgewater out to kill Mertz and Fields because they were onto him. They killed Sylvia because someone tipped them that she was researching that contract. I was next, and it's pure luck that I'm here to tell you about it."

"What about the cheerleader? Edgewater kill her, too?"

"I don't know. I still don't see how she fits."

Drew rolled his injured tongue around in his mouth. It felt fat and sore, and all this talking wasn't helping.

Romero sighed and said, "Looks to me like you want to blame the man you just killed for every murder that's happened around here lately. Why not the cheerleader, too?"

"Come on, lieutenant. You know me. I'm telling the truth."

Romero's hawk-like expression softened a little and he

reached out and rested a big hand on Drew's sore shoulder.

"I'm not saying I don't believe you. But this story, it's a lot to choke down. And so far, all I've got is your version. Let's go through it again."

"Not again, lieutenant. I need medical attention. I need to go to bed."

"Again."

Drew sighed and said, "I was coming out of the bathroom when I found Edgewater in my kitchen. . ."

FIFTY

Teresa Vargas waited impatiently while the emergency room doctors X-rayed Drew's chest and massaged the broken ribs back into place and put new tape around his torso. They gave him some codeine first, but Drew's face twisted in agony while the doctors poked and prodded. It made Teresa's heart hurt to see him in pain.

She stood outside his ER cubicle, peeking through the curtains. Drew sat on a hard table, surrounded by doctors and nurses and monitors and trays of instruments and other medical doodads. His big feet dangled, and she thought about what one of the uniforms had told her outside his house: That Drew had kicked Otis Edgewater to death, that one of those dangling sneakers had caught the big man in the throat and killed him. She wondered how Drew felt about that and how the death of that woman, right there in his kitchen, would affect him.

She wondered about the woman, too. The cop had told her that the victim was a real beauty, that it was a damned shame that she had been smothered. What had she meant to Drew, Teresa wondered, and how had she ended up dead at his home?

Her cell phone chirped, and she said, "Dammit," as she dug through her purse to find it.

"Vargas here."

"Where the hell are you?" It was Goodman.

"At the hospital. The doctors are still working him over."

"I need both of you back here right now."

"He's hurt, Bob. I'll get him there as soon as I can. But the doctors haven't turned him loose yet."

"Can you talk to him? Find out more about what happened?"

"*You* want to come down here and tell these doctors to get out of the way? I'm doing the best I can, Bob."

She heard Goodman take a deep breath. "Sorry. But we're looking at deadline here. Morrison and Quattlebaum are working the phones, but we need to talk to Drew."

"You want me to see if I can put him on the phone?"

"No, I want him in person. Everybody's got questions for him. Best thing would be for us all to sit down in the same room. If they admit him to the hospital, we'll fall back on using the phone. But we need to talk to him as soon as possible, one way or the other."

"I'll get him there as quick as I can."

She clicked off the phone and stabbed it back into her open purse. The *Gazette* probably was the last place Drew wanted to be right now, but she'd get him there somehow. She knew Goodman had assigned her this duty because of their relationship. If anyone could extract Drew from the doctors' clutches and get him to tell all, it would be his girlfriend. But it wasn't a job she'd enjoy. Drew needed to go to bed. He needed time to recover. But the newspaper came first; it always did.

Then the doctors burst out of the cubicle and raced down the hall to their next emergency. Teresa glanced around, saw the nurses weren't paying any attention, and slipped through the curtains.

"Tiger? How you feeling?"

"I feel like I could sleep for a year."

Teresa cringed. She didn't want to tell him about Goodman, but she didn't see how she had any choice.

"No sleep for you yet," she said. "Goodman wants you at the paper. They need you to finish the story."

Drew grimaced, then ran a hand over his face. "Aw, Christ."

"I know, I know. You're tired of talking about it. But they want to get the story right. They need you there."

He stared at the floor for a minute, thinking it over. Then he nodded.

"Can you get me out of here?" he said. "They didn't say I could leave."

She smiled. "Don't worry, tiger. We'll make our escape."

Teresa helped him down off the table. He flinched when his feet took his weight, and one hand clutched at his ribs.

"Are you okay to walk?" she asked. "Should I steal a wheelchair?"

"I'm okay. Let's just get the hell out of here."

Teresa poked her head out through the curtain and checked the hall. The emergency room staff bustled about, but nobody seemed to be looking their way. She took Drew's arm and led him down a back hall and outside into the cooling night.

Drew said little while Teresa roared through traffic, and she worried about him. After all he'd been through today, shouldn't she be taking him home, putting him to bed? Did the *Gazette* *always* have to come first? And what did that say about her?

Fifteen minutes later, they arrived at the newsroom. Teresa held the door open while Drew limped inside. The place was the usual buzzing beehive, but silence fell over the room as she and Drew made their way to the city desk.

Bill Morrison and Felicia Quattlebaum were huddled over a computer, working over a story on the screen. Felicia looked up as they approached and said, "God, am I glad to see you."

"Are you all right?" Morrison asked.

"Alive and kicking," Drew said. Then he managed to grin. "More or less."

Goodman came racing out of his office. He pulled up short when he got a look at Drew—the lump on his chin, his sweat-matted hair, his bloodshot eyes.

"You look like—"

"Like shit," Drew interrupted. "I know. I've heard it before."

"Are you up to talking about what happened?"

"Yeah, just let me sit down somewhere."

Goodman escorted Drew to the conference room with Morrison, Quattlebaum and Teresa on their heels. Felicia Quattlebaum was the first to speak up after they were all seated around the long table.

"Well, Drew, you were right about Cerf. That much is clear now. Bill talked to the guys at DOD and they're investigating whether Cerf sold that software overseas."

"Oh, he sold it all right. Otis Edgewater said as much before I killed him."

No one said anything for a moment. Teresa looked around the table, marveling. She'd never seen these people shocked before. Then Goodman cleared his throat and said, "Jesus, Drew. Was that a confession to a homicide?"

"Self-defense. The cops are going to call it that way, though it was touch-and-go for a while. I thought Lieutenant Romero was going to throw me in jail with Curtis until he could get everything sorted out."

"But he let you go," Goodman said.

"Only because I needed a hospital. He won't be satisfied with my version of events until he talks to Scott Cerf."

"And Cerf's on the run," Morrison said. "We got that much from the cop shop."

"That's right," Teresa said. "I heard the same thing."

Drew nodded. "It's going to be hard to pin anything down until they catch up to him. It's all pretty murky. But I'm certain that Edgewater killed Wally Mertz and that private eye, Fields. They'd found out about the illegal software deals. He had to silence them."

"And then he tried to silence you, too," Felicia said. "You and that woman—" she checked her notes. "—Sylvia Smith."

"That's right." The muscle in Drew's jaw twitched. "He succeeded with Sylvia. I almost got free in time to save her, but I was too late."

Drew's eyes filled and he coughed a couple of times.

Poor baby. Teresa wanted to take him into her arms. Comfort him. But that wouldn't look right, not here in the newsroom. Not with a deadline looming.

Goodman looked up at the clock on the wall and said, "Morrison and Quattlebaum can fill in the blanks on the software stuff. Tell us what happened today, blow by blow. We don't have much time."

Drew massaged his face, then looked around the table. He took a deep breath and told them about finding Edgewater in his kitchen, fighting with him, waking up tied to a chair.

Felicia Quattlebaum and Bill Morrison furiously took notes and peppered him with questions. How long were you tied up? How long were you unconscious? How did you get free? How did Sylvia Smith end up at the scene?

"Edgewater drugged her," he said. "Probably Rohypnol, the same thing I got nailed with the other night. She was unconscious the whole time."

"That reminds me," Teresa said. "I talked to one of my sources today, and they finally have the lab results back on Curtis. They found Rohypnol in his bloodstream."

"I knew it," Drew said. "The symptoms were the same. That ought to help get him out of jail—"

"Drew," Goodman interrupted. "Not now. That's a different story. We're running out of time here."

"But the cheerleader's death is what started all this."

"Think Edgewater killed her, too?" Quattlebaum asked. Teresa loved watching Felicia work. She always got right to the point.

Drew shook his head. "Better downplay that connection. I think he probably killed her and set up Curtis to take the fall, but I don't have any proof. And I can't figure how she fits into the whole software deal."

Goodman said, "Drew—"

"Right, right. Just tell my story. Let other people write it."

Goodman smiled, but sweat beaded on his shiny forehead. "We've got an hour until deadline."

"Don't worry, Bob," Quattlebaum said confidently. "We'll make it."

She turned back to Drew. "I've got another piece of the puzzle. Remember you were told that Wally Mertz had been out of town a lot lately? I talked to his receptionist, a woman named Cassandra—"

"Nose ring?" Drew said.

"That's the one. She told me Mertz had been traveling all over the Middle East in the past few months. I think he was over there trying to find out about Cerf's smuggling deals. Probably trying to confirm what the private eye was hearing locally."

"Sounds right," he said.

"And—" Felicia drew the word out, letting it build. "Guess who we found in Wally Mertz's appointment book. Fontanelle Harper."

"What? When?"

"Appointment would've been last week. But they were both too dead to show up."

"I'll be damned," Drew said. "Fontanelle didn't miss a trick. She'd found out about Cerf's deals somehow and planned to sell the information to Mertz."

"That's the way it looks to me, too," Felicia said.

Goodman cleared his throat.

"Right, right," Felicia said. "We're running out of time. Tell us about Cerf showing up at your house. I want to nail his skinny ass to the wall."

Drew laughed, and Teresa felt relieved. It was the first sign that he'd recover, that everything would be fine eventually. She looked around at the others. Felicia's eyes shiny behind her thick glasses. Goodman beaming and glowing. Bill Morrison with his pen poised over his notebook, not missing a thing.

And she thought about Los Angeles. Could she leave these people behind? Could she abandon Drew after all he'd been through? The interview continued, but Teresa didn't hear much of it.

FIFTY ONE

Drew woke up late Wednesday, feeling as if someone had poured concrete through his veins during the night. He lay flat on his back, his eyes closed against the sun slanting through the bedroom curtains. He slowly flexed muscles and joints, trying to assess the damage. The verdict: He was in a world of hurt.

His ribs ached and his jaw throbbed and his arms were covered in bruises. His left fist was painfully swollen. His tongue hurt. Hell, even his teeth hurt.

He turned his aching head on the pillow far enough to see the clock—11:43—and a note Teresa had left propped against it: "Gone to the newsroom. Call me when you come to. Hope you're feeling better." Signed, "T."

Drew didn't get many handwritten notes from her. They communicated by phone or through internal e-mail at the office. He liked the way her bold handwriting looked against the paper. Be nice to get more of those notes. Maybe if they lived under the same roof . . .

He blinked his eyes and tried to steer his thoughts away from Teresa and loss and the Los Angeles freaking *Times*. Better to examine what had happened the day before, and see whether there was a way to tie up the loose ends.

Drew needed to resolve it all, so maybe, just maybe, he could live with himself. Sylvia Smith's pale, beautiful corpse would be in his mind for a long time to come. If Scott Cerf could be made to pay, perhaps it would diminish the grief and guilt he felt.

The more he thought about it, the more he kept coming back to Fontanelle Harper. Her death started a chain reaction of murder. But why? How did she know anything about Cerf and Edgewater and the defense contracts? A cheerleader, for Christ's sakes.

Fontanelle had told Curtis she knew something about Cerf, but Raj Davis had shut her up before she could say more. From what Curtis had said, the Rattlers party had dwindled by the time that conversation occurred. Edgewater had already departed. Who was there who would care whether Fontanelle blabbed about Cerf? Why did Raj shut her up?

The way she was killed meant something, too. The uniform around her neck, the pompon stuffed in her mouth. Was that a warning to others, not to talk? Or was it an act of rage? And why dope Curtis and put him in the bed with her? Was that an act of jealousy?

Drew turned it over and over in his mind, and one thing kept coming to the surface—the hard reptilian profile of Raj Davis. The basketball player kept showing up as Drew investigated Cerf. Facing Drew down at practice. Sitting with him and Edgewater at the party at Snake-Eyes.

A flash of memory—not much more than a snapshot—flitted through his mind. Raj Davis right up in his face, his arm around his shoulders, smiling. Drew didn't think Davis often smiled, but he remembered this moment clearly. His big, white teeth. The whiskey on his breath. His purple coat.

That sport coat. He was wearing it at Snake-Eyes, the night of the party. The night Drew was drugged. And then he remembered more. Raj Davis' arm around his shoulders as his head reeled. Raj leading him out the saloon's back door. It wasn't Edgewater who drugged him and kicked the shit out of him. It was Raj Davis.

Anger flowed through Drew's body, pushing away the aches and pains, clearing his head. He sat up and balanced there while the world whirled for a second. Then he put his feet on the floor.

FIFTY TWO

A call to the office turned up Raj Davis' home address. Henry found it in Curtis' Rolodex and read it into the phone.

"Why do you need his address?" she asked. "And what are you doing out of bed?"

"Gotta go, Henry." Drew hung up, tucked the slip of paper with the address into his pocket, and limped out the door.

He still hurt all over, despite the painkillers he'd taken. But he had adrenaline on his side now. He might look like hell, unwashed and unshaven, bruised and battered. But inside, he was stoked.

Raj Davis lived in a condo in the Northeast Heights, miles away, but the long drive did nothing to erode Drew's anticipation. He'd been looking for connections throughout this mess, trying to find the ways people were tied up in each other's lives. Raj Davis, he now believed, was the knot in the middle, the link between Fontanelle and Edgewater and Cerf and Mertz. And he was by God going to get some answers from him.

The condo complex was a collection of Tuscan-style buildings, rough tan stucco and red tile roofs. Drew sailed the Jeep across a small plaza to Number Forty-two and parked nose-in to the sidewalk, directly in front of Davis' door.

He banged on the door several times, feeling a little frantic at the thought that Davis might not be home.

Raj Davis opened the oversized door, then filled it with his hard-muscled body. His bare chest was covered with a film of gleaming sweat. He wore only a pair of gym shorts and a heavy gold chain around his neck, and his breath was coming hard. Drew guessed he'd been working out and thought: Great, this guy's all pumped up and I can barely stand here without screaming.

Davis scowled down at him. "What do *you* want?"

"Need to talk to you."

"Not interested." Davis reached for the door, ready to slam it shut.

"You seen the paper this morning? Seen the news?"

Davis hesitated, looked confused.

"Your boss is in a world of trouble," Drew said. "And that guy Edgewater? He's dead. Big headline on the front page."

Raj Davis' eyes widened. Clearly, he knew nothing about yesterday's events.

"People should read the newspaper," Drew said. "Fewer surprises that way."

Davis cut his eyes to one side, thinking, then said, "Sounds like you'd better come in."

He stepped aside, and Drew passed within inches of him to get indoors. He could feel the heat from Davis' body, could smell his musky sweat. When he'd left the house, Drew was ready to pounce on this guy, force him to talk. But now that he was here, Raj Davis seemed bigger, stronger. Maybe Drew should've called the cops. Maybe he should've stayed in bed.

The foyer emptied into a large living room that seemed

scantily furnished. A long sofa sat in the center of the room, facing a chrome cabinet that held a wide-screen TV and a state-of-the-art Sanyo sound system. A weight bench sat near the far wall, still glistening from Davis' perspiration. A few posters, including one of a high-flying Michael Jordan, were tacked to the bare white walls. The typical dwelling, Drew thought, of a minor-league ballplayer. Few furnishings. Money invested in stereos and other crap that could be packed easily and moved as soon as another team, another league, called with an offer.

An open kitchen branched off the living room to his right, and Drew spied a pot of coffee in there. It smelled good, but there wasn't much chance Raj Davis would offer him a cup. He found a straight-back chair against the wall, tugged it over to face the sofa and eased himself down on it.

Raj Davis casually flung himself onto the sofa, stretched out along its full length, and said, "What's wrong with you, motherfucker? Looks like somebody busted you up."

Drew wasn't sure how he wanted to reveal things to Davis. He wanted to surprise him, trip him up, but he was starting in the wrong place. After what he had to say next, he expected Davis to clam up, or show him the door. And if the man wanted him to leave, how much choice would Drew have?

"Got into a fight yesterday," he said. "With Edgewater."

Raj Davis eyed him coolly. "And that's how Otis wound up dead?"

Drew nodded.

"So you killed Otis, so what? Somebody was gonna do it sooner or later. That old redneck was lucky to stick around this long."

"I can wait quietly while you finish mourning."

"Fuck you, man. I barely knew the man. What do I care he's dead?"

Drew shrugged. Even that minor movement caused a fanfare of pain to blare through his shoulders and chest. He tried not to let it show on his face.

"Edgewater told me some things before he died. Some of them involved you."

Raj Davis' eyes narrowed. He waited.

Drew took a breath and made the plunge. "For instance, he said he didn't kill your girlfriend. I thought he was behind it, but somebody else killed Fontanelle."

Raj Davis shifted on the sofa, looking suddenly uncomfortable. His long, brown legs were crossed at the ankles, and his bare feet looked enormous. Drew thinking: The man's awfully vulnerable, stretched out like that. Guess he's got no worries about me jumping him. Guess I look too beat-up to pose a threat. And I guess he'd be right about that.

"So? Out with it, motherfucker. Who you think killed her?"

Drew hesitated, wondering how fast he could get to his feet if Raj Davis suddenly lunged at him. Probably not quick enough, but it was too late to back down now.

"I think you did it."

Davis' eyes widened briefly, then his face creased into the familiar scowl.

"You got a lotta balls, coming into a man's home, accusing him of murder."

"I don't hear you denying it."

"I don't have to deny shit. You're blowing smoke."

Davis sat up and put his feet on the floor. Drew didn't like that. He creaked up from the chair and wandered around the room, putting some distance between them, keeping his eyes open for any kind of weapon.

"Rohypnol is a funny drug," he said. "It blacks you out and you don't remember anything at first. But then memories start to come back. Little flashes. That's how come people get prosecuted, using it for date rape. The victims start remembering."

"The hell you talking about?"

"Curtis White's been getting some memories back from the night Fontanelle was killed. He says most everybody had gone from that party. That you and Fontanelle had an argument. That you looked mad enough to kill her."

Raj Davis grunted. "That fucker would say anything to get outta jail. Nobody's gonna listen to him."

"Yeah, but the cops are listening to *me*, and I told them what Edgewater said about you."

Edgewater, of course, had said nothing about Raj Davis. Drew *was* blowing smoke. But it had its effect. Davis shifted on the couch. He cracked his knuckles, his hard gaze following Drew around the room.

"Yeah? What did he say?"

Drew had to be careful now. He'd pieced together a lot, but much of it was guesswork. If he said the wrong thing, Davis would know he was lying and they'd never get anywhere. But would he ease into it if he really had the goods on Davis? No, he'd lead with the best stuff. If he was going to win with this bluff, he needed to show his best cards first.

"He said he told you to slip the roofies to Curtis. He wanted you to work him over, find out how much he knew. Same way you worked me over outside Snake-Eyes."

Raj Davis had a funny reaction, and at first Drew thought

he'd blown it by bluffing too big, too soon. Davis nearly smiled, his lips spreading wide, almost showing his teeth before he caught himself and pasted the scowl back on his face.

"So what if Otis gave me some roofies?" Davis said. "That don't prove shit."

"The cops found Rohypnol in Curtis' bloodstream."

"That don't prove I gave it to him. And it sure as hell don't mean I killed Fontanelle."

"You were mad at her, you were jealous. Curtis remembers that much. I think you got angry 'cause she was flirting with him. And then he mentioned Cerf, and she started mouthing off, and that was it. You let your anger take over, and you killed her while Curtis was unconscious."

Raj Davis' face grew sullen.

"That still don't prove a thing. And Otis is dead anyway, so he can't say shit to the cops."

Drew took a breath. Time to head for deeper water.

"Yeah, but Cerf's still out there," he said. "And once the cops nail him, he'll spill everything. You can bet you'll go down with him."

Davis' mouth turned down at the corners, and he shook his head. "Don't think so, motherfucker. Cerf's got nothing on me."

Time for more guesswork. "No, but you know plenty about him, don't you?"

"What's that supposed to mean?"

"Here you are, big strapping guy from the Bronx, out here in Albuquerque, middle of nowhere. You're ready to move up to the NBA. You've got the tools, right? You've got the ability."

"Damned straight I do." Davis' elbows rested on his knees,

and he flexed his overdeveloped arms at the thought of the Big Show.

"But your career's not going the way you planned. Which is how you ended up playing for the Rattlers."

"Why don't you get to the fuckin' point?"

"So maybe you're thinking the NBA isn't the way to cash out, that maybe you've missed your shot."

"It's never too late—"

"Maybe not, but what if you see a way to make a lot of money here? Screw the NBA. Get yours while you can."

"I don't know what—"

"And then you got some help. I think you found out that Cerf and Edgewater were making some funny deals under the table. Something to do with military software?"

Davis tried to look confused, as if he'd never heard of such a thing, but Drew saw something click in his dark eyes.

"I bet Fontanelle was the one who found out about it. What was she doing? Over at Cerf's house, playing a little footsie with the team owner? Cerf seems to have a thing for cheerleaders. She overheard him talking to Edgewater, or maybe talking on the phone, and she put two and two together. Fontanelle was a smart girl, right? She'd see a way to make Cerf pay off."

Raj Davis slowly got to his feet and looked down at Drew.

"If she's so smart, how come she's dead?"

Only six feet separated them, and Drew backed away a little. Casually, trying not to look like he was retreating. If Raj Davis suddenly came at him, he wanted some room to work. Though, in his condition, he probably ought to be looking for a soft spot to fall down.

"She's dead because she trusted the wrong guy," he said.

"She thought you'd come in on it with her, milk Cerf for some hush money. But you saw your opportunities going the other way, didn't you? Take her out of the picture, and you'd be doing Scott Cerf a big favor. You could become his new pet, ready to catch whatever crumbs fell as he raked in the bread from his illegal deals."

Davis looked away, then back again. "That's what you think, huh?"

Drew hoped he was right, or at least right about enough that Davis would recognize he was caught. "There's more. But that's the gist of it."

Raj Davis took a step toward him. Their eyes locked.

"And you told this to the cops?"

"Most of it."

"So how come you're here instead of them? Cops want me, they know where to find me."

"Maybe they're on their way. I don't know. Guess they're not in a big hurry. But I am. Curtis White is my friend. He's in jail because of you. I want him released."

Davis came another step closer. Drew wanted to back away some more, but the weight bench was close behind him and he didn't want to fall over it. He wanted, in fact, to be heading the other direction. It was a long way to the front door. And Raj Davis towered in the way.

"I don't give a rat's ass about your friend," Davis said. "And I didn't kill nobody."

Drew rolled his shoulders, sending pain down both arms. What the hell was he doing here? He'd let his emotions carry him away, zooming across town to confront Davis. But now the adrenaline was subsiding, leaving only the chill of fear. If he was right, if Raj was a killer, what were the chances that he'd let Drew walk out of here alive?

He cleared his throat—suddenly felt like something was stuck in there—and coughed into his battered fist. He didn't know where he wanted to take this conversation next, but he knew he needed to keep talking. Once he ran out of things to say, it could get physical. And he wasn't ready for that.

"You don't have to admit it," he said. "The police will find a way to prove it."

"They can't prove shit."

Drew took a step to the side, measuring the distance to the front door. It looked like miles. Then he got an idea.

"Here's the problem," he said. "You killed Fontanelle, so what? Bitch was running around on you, trying to enlist you in a blackmail scheme. She probably had it coming, right?"

An image flashed through his mind: Fontanelle Harper spread out on the bed, the uniform knotted around her neck, the pompon stuffed in her mouth. Nobody deserved to die that way.

Raj Davis just glared at him, waiting.

"But your friend Otis, he played it smart. He set you up."

One of Davis' eyebrows crawled up his forehead, but he said nothing.

"Remember that guy Wally Mertz? Otis killed him, and set it up to look just like Fontanelle's death. Guy was strangled, computer disks stuffed in his mouth. Otis was protecting himself, see? The cops think the same person killed Fontanelle and Mertz. That means you've got double trouble. They'll want to charge you with both murders."

Raj Davis' scowl deepened, looked like his face was folding into itself.

"The cops link you to Fontanelle's murder, and the rest will be easy. I tried to tell them that Edgewater killed Mertz, but he's beyond prosecution now. They're looking for a scapegoat, someone they can use to tie it all up in a tidy package. You're it."

Davis' hands clenched into fists beside his thighs. This is it, Drew thought, time to fight. But Davis opened his hands, shook his shoulders loose, trying to relax. He let a big smile spread across his face. The smile reminded Drew of that night at Snake-Eyes, Davis giving him the big grin while he led him outside to stomp on him. He felt the heat rise in him again, but he forced it down. Better to walk away. Live to tell his story to the police.

"I'm it, huh? The cops, that's the way they see it?"

Drew nodded and took another step sideways. He was clear of the sofa now, had a straight line to the front door. But he didn't think Davis would let him just sprint away. He needed a diversion, a distraction, something that would buy him the minute or so he needed to run for the Jeep.

"I'd expect them any time, if I were you," he said and took another step.

"Where the fuck you think you're going?" Davis said, stepping sideways to cut him off. "You think we're done here?"

Drew swallowed heavily. "I'm done. I've said what I came to say."

"Thought you could get me to confess or something?"

Drew shook his head. "Maybe I just wanted to see your face when I laid it out for you. But you've heard it all now. What happens next is up to you."

Davis took a step forward, crowding him.

"No, motherfucker, it's up to you. You're the big man here, right? You come into my home, accusing me of all kinds of shit. Killing Fontanelle. Fucking you up after you were doped.

You told all this shit to the cops, trying to sic 'em on me."

Drew clung to that. "They'll probably be here any minute. You've got choices, Raj. You can run. You can talk to them, try to ride it out. You can take your chances in court."

Davis glowered. "Maybe I ought to just kill you right here. If I'm this badass murderer like you say, why would I let you live? You're the main witness against me."

Drew squared his shoulders.

"You can try it," he said. "But you'd better bring your lunch. Killing me's going to be an all-day job. I'm no cheerleader. And I'm not drugged this time."

Raj Davis eyed him, measuring him.

"You all beat up already, man. How much of a fight could you put up?"

Drew made his voice cold. "You want to find out, let's go."

He kept his hands at his sides, waiting. Davis' eyes narrowed as he studied him, but then he stepped back and shook his head.

"Fuck it, man. Be my luck, the cops would show up just as I was finishing with you."

"Good decision."

"Get outta my goddamned house."

Drew nodded and started toward the door. He passed Davis, who remained planted in place, watching him, his brain clearly working overtime. The hair crawled on the back of Drew's neck once the taller man was behind him, but he kept walking, his back straight, his shoulders square. Just a few more steps, and he'd be out the door.

The sunshine outside was blinding, and Drew squinted against it as he closed Davis' door and limped the eight feet or so over to the Jeep. A yuppie-looking couple walked past his car and an old woman teetered on a walker across the way. Good, he thought, witnesses. I've made my escape, and now I have these nice witnesses watching me drive away. He took a breath and let it out in a huff. He'd entered the Rattler's den and come out alive.

He climbed behind the wheel and started the Jeep. He sat there for a moment, feeling the tension drain from his shoulders, his neck. Raj Davis' door remained shut, and Drew wondered what the basketball player was thinking, who he was calling, what he was doing behind that closed door.

Then the door flung open and Davis, still shirtless, stepped outside. His eyes met Drew's as he came out into the sunshine. Drew saw the determined glower on his face, the big veins on his bulging arms, and the black pistol dangling in one hand.

Drew lunged sideways, throwing himself down on the passenger seat, as Raj Davis brought the gun up and fired. The Jeep's windshield exploded, raining glass everywhere. Another blast sent a bullet whistling past Drew's shoulder.

He grasped the gearshift lever and threw the Jeep into "drive." Then he fumbled with his foot, found the accelerator, and slammed it to the floor.

The Jeep's fat tires screamed as the car climbed the curb. Drew stayed down, not trying to steer, not trying to aim. He let the Jeep do the work, plunging forward as another shot rang out. Then there was a loud thump, a shriek, and the Jeep crashed into the building.

Drew's head and shoulder hit the dashboard. He lay there a minute, dazed, not moving until he heard excited voices outside. He'd sent the Jeep hurtling forward blindly. For all he knew, Raj Davis had dodged the car and was waiting for him to sit up so he could send another bullet flying his way.

The voices came closer. Drew cautiously raised up and peeked over the dash. What he saw made his stomach roil.

Raj Davis was pinned between the Jeep and the condo. The car had staggered over the sidewalk and slammed into the wall beside the door, crushing Davis' torso. His eyes were round and unseeing. His mouth hung open, scarlet blood dripping from his chin.

Faces appeared at the side window of the Jeep, the yuppie couple peering inside, their eyes wide and their faces pale. They stepped out of the way as Drew opened his door.

He fell out onto the pavement.

FIFTY THREE

More cops. Another silent ambulance carrying away another corpse. Lt. Steve Romero standing over Drew, asking his pointed questions. TV cameras. More questions.

Drew sleepwalked through it all, too shaken to object, even when Romero made noises about locking him up for his second killing in as many days.

But there were the witnesses. They'd seen Raj Davis shoot before the Jeep creamed him, and they were only too willing to talk. Romero listened to them, and he listened to Drew's theories about Raj killing Fontanelle. And around sunset, he turned Drew loose.

Cops milled around the entrance to the condo. Drew ducked under the yellow "Crime Scene" tape and walked outside into the cooling air. He stood motionless, looking off to the west, where the sun stained clouds the color of blood.

His Jeep already had been towed off, its front grille crumpled, its windshield blasted away. He didn't know how he'd get home. Or, if that was where he wanted to go. Then he heard a familiar voice.

"Hey, tiger. Need a lift?"

He turned to see Teresa leaning out the window of her little Toyota. She smiled at him, but her face was lined with worry.

"Yeah, I guess so. My Jeep was in an accident."

"So I heard. Goodman's got half the staff working on the story. And he wants to see you right away."

Drew shambled around the car and got into the passenger seat.

After he slammed the door, Teresa said, "You just don't get it, do you? We're supposed to cover the news, not make it."

He sighed. "Funny."

"Sorry, guess you're in no mood for jokes." She leaned over and kissed him on the cheek. "Are you okay?"

He shook his head, but said nothing.

"I talked to the cops," she said. "They said it was a clear case of self-defense. You didn't have any choice."

"I could've stayed home."

She smiled again. "I'll restrain myself from saying, 'I told you so.'"

"No, go ahead. You were right."

She shook her head and put the car in gear.

"It's all too ugly to gloat over," she said. "Besides, we're in a hurry. We've got a deadline to meet."

Drew leaned his head back against the top of the seat and closed his eyes. The car's movement made him feel woozy, but he didn't want to open his eyes. He wanted to sleep for a week, then wake up to find this was all a nightmare.

"Goodman wants to grill me again? Him and Felicia and Morrison?"

"They have a few questions." Her voice had a smile in it.

"I bet they do."

"Can you handle it?"

"I don't know. I feel like I've been dragged before the Spanish Inquisition already."

"Yeah, but that was just cops. This is for the front page."

Drew sighed heavily. He felt as if he couldn't get enough air. And it wasn't just the tape on his ribs. It was as if he'd squeezed his own lungs flat when the Jeep crushed Raj Davis.

They said nothing for several minutes, then Teresa said, "Want me to take you home?"

"I thought we had to go to the newsroom."

"That's what Goodman wants. But what do *you* want, tiger?"

"Take me to the paper. Sooner this all sees print, the sooner I'll be done with it."

Teresa pressed the gas and the car leaped forward. "That's what I thought you'd say."

Drew closed his eyes again. "We get the story, maybe Goodman will let me keep my job."

"Don't worry about your job, tiger. You're a hero. It's all going to be fine."

"I don't feel much like a hero. I feel like I've been hit by a truck."

He cringed at his own choice of words. Teresa giggled.

"Let's go talk to Goodman," she said. "Then I'll take you home, see if I can make you feel better."

There was a promising lilt in her voice. Drew tried to smile, but it didn't take. He kept his eyes closed, his head rocked back, until they arrived at the *Gazette*.

FIFTY FOUR

Hours later, Teresa lay naked beside Drew, one leg thrown over him, one hand toying with the hair on his chest. The room was flooded with moonlight.

"Feel better, tiger?"

He grunted, his eyes closed.

"I thought you'd be too tired, too beat up, but you did just fine."

"Oh, yeah," he said. "Before, I was only half-dead. Now I'm completely dead."

"You're still breathing."

"Not very well."

She let her hand slide down an inch until it reached the tape that stretched tight around his chest. "It's these bandages. Once they cut these off you, you'll feel like a new man."

"And who would this new man be?"

"Same old Drew."

"Too bad."

"But you'll feel better."

"I feel pretty good right at this moment. Turns out you're a good nurse after all."

She giggled and rearranged herself against his big body. "It's all a matter of the healing touch."

"Then I must be well, because we certainly did some touching."

She hadn't intended to sleep with him tonight. She'd planned to tuck him in, make sure he got some sleep after his ordeal. But she'd leaned over the bed to kiss him good-night, and one thing led to another. . . .

He was so tired. So frazzled. Goodman and the gang at the paper had treated him like a champion, kid gloves all the way, but he'd barely been able to mutter answers to their questions.

He'd dozed all the way to his house, and she'd figured he was ready to sleep for days. But Drew was a man, after all, and sex was never far from his mind. She'd done all the work, letting him lie on his back, his muscles limp against the bed. Well, most of his muscles. And now she wondered if sex had been the final blow, so to speak. If Drew had been pushed completely over the edge of exhaustion.

"Tiger?"

"Yeah?"

"Just checking. You still in there?"

"I'm asleep."

"I should go home."

He reached across and his hand found her shoulder. "No, stay. I want to wake up next to you. Assuming I ever wake up."

"Could be days from now."

"Stay."

She relaxed against him, wondering whether "stay" meant tonight only or forever.

A car door slammed outside. Nothing to worry about, not in Drew's neighborhood, where people came and went all night long. But she heard something else a few seconds later, a squeak of floorboards, the thump of footfalls. Sounded like they were coming from the front porch.

"Did you hear that?" she asked.

"Mm-hm."

"I think somebody's outside."

Drew blinked his eyes open, but he lay still, listening. Another noise came from the front of the house, a scraping against a window screen.

"That's what I need," he said, his voice muddled. "A freaking burglar."

He sat up stiffly and teetered on the edge of the bed, listening.

"Don't get up," she said. "It's probably nothing. I'll go peek out the window."

"No, I'll go."

He groped around in the dark, searching for his jeans. He pulled them on and padded from the room, headed toward the front of the house. She threw back the covers and swung her feet to the floor. As tired and beat-up as he was, he might never find his way back to the bedroom without her.

Teresa followed him into the short hall, then peeked around the corner. She didn't want to step out into the living room naked. She hid behind the door jamb, watching as he went to the front door.

Another noise came from the porch. Drew flipped on the porch light and snatched open the door.

"Shit," he said. "It's you."

Who? She peered around the edge of the doorway, trying to see past Drew's hulking frame. He raised his hands to shoulder height and walked backward a couple of steps. There, in the doorway, stood a tall, dark-haired man. Light glinted off the chrome pistol he pointed at Drew's chest.

Teresa caught herself before she made a sound and ducked back into the hall. She tiptoed toward the bedroom, panicky thoughts racing through her head. Call the police? Find a weapon? Scream? Do something!

She'd recognized the man with the gun in that instant before she ducked out of sight. She'd never met him in person, but she'd seen his photograph in the *Gazette* plenty of times.

Scott Cerf.

FIFTY FIVE

Drew shivered, and it wasn't because of the chill breeze that followed Cerf into the living room. The big shiny revolver was pointed right at his chest. A passing thought: He wished his chest were wrapped in Kevlar rather than adhesive tape. He took another step back as Cerf slammed the door shut with his foot.

Cerf flipped on the overhead light. He was as tall as Drew, but angular, thin. Drew could take him, even in his debilitated condition, if it weren't for that gun. Cerf's eyes looked wide and crazy, twitching around the room. Drew hoped he didn't know Teresa was there. Maybe Teresa was dialing the cops on the bedside phone. But what if she didn't even know they had company? He'd better make some noise.

"The cops are looking all over for you, Cerf," he said, louder than necessary. "What are you doing here?"

"Unfinished business." Cerf waved the pistol at him, gesturing him toward his reclining chair in the center of the room. Drew moved, but he didn't sit down. He stood next to the chair, hands still raised, hoping Cerf wouldn't check the rest of the house.

"I thought you left town. Your jet—"

"I sent it away without me. I wanted to wrap up some loose ends first."

Drew felt the shiver again. "And I'm one of the loose ends."

"One of them?" Cerf laughed, a joyless bark. "You're the main one, buddy. Since you came along, everything's gone to hell."

Drew kept his eyes on the pistol. It looked heavy, wobbling at the end of Cerf's outstretched arm. If only he could keep him talking . . .

"No," he said. "Things went to hell the day you decided to commit treason."

Cerf's mouth formed a straight line across his face, and his jaw jutted forward.

"Don't moralize to me, you pissant," he said. "It was all going well. People making money, deals being struck. I'd covered my tracks just fine—"

"Not well enough. DOD's after you. They know you sold that software overseas."

"Bullshit. They don't *know* anything."

"They're investigating."

"Let 'em. It'll take months to untangle it all. By then, I'll be long gone."

Drew took a step to the side, and Cerf countered. It was if they were dancing, separated by eight feet or so. The step brought Cerf closer to the hallway door, and that worried Drew. He hoped Teresa was smart enough to stay out of sight.

"I'm surprised you stuck around this long," he said, his voice rising. He wanted her to hear it all. "If I were you, I would've taken that jet and never looked back."

Cerf shook his head distractedly. He shifted the pistol in his hand, brought the other hand up to help steady it.

"No, you idiot, you don't get it," he said. "I could sit right there in my office, feet up on my desk, and never worry about the DOD. It's all buried too deep. They won't figure it out. But I *am* guilty of murder. And you're the witness."

Drew frowned. "You mean Sylvia Smith."

"That's right. And you told the police. That makes me a fugitive."

"But you didn't kill her," Drew said. "Edgewater did."

Cerf's face twitched and he nearly smiled. "You didn't see it?"

"See what?"

"What did you think I was doing while you and Otis wrestled around on the kitchen floor?"

"You got the hell out of there, soon as it looked like I had the upper hand."

The fractured smile danced across Cerf's face again. "Before that. She was still moving. After you jumped on Otis. I finished her off."

Drew's arms dropped to his sides. He felt stunned. Sylvia had still been alive. He escaped from his binds in time. He could've saved her. But Cerf crouched over her while Drew was busy with Edgewater, pressed the pillow harder to her face . . .

"I didn't kill the others," Cerf said, and Drew thought his protest sounded a little rehearsed. "I didn't order Otis to kill anyone. But you saw how he was. Once he got it into his head that it would help, he started taking people out."

"As he said—"

"Yeah, he said too much. And now you're trying to do the same thing to me. Keep me talking. Stall for time. But I'm not buying it, buddy. This conversation's over."

Cerf thumbed back the hammer of the pistol. The click sounded like a clap of thunder in Drew's ears.

☆ ☆ ☆ ☆ ☆

Teresa heard the click, too. She'd crept into the hallway from Drew's bedroom, her hands tight on the book she'd plucked off the bedside table after she called 911. She knew what Drew was doing, trying to stall the man until the cops arrived. But it wasn't working. Cerf was ready to shoot.

She took another step forward, almost to the edge of the doorway, the book raised over her head. She still wore no clothes—there hadn't been time—and she hadn't found much of a weapon. But maybe she could leap into the room, bring the heavy book down on his head. Even if she missed, it might buy them some time.

☆ ☆ ☆ ☆ ☆

Scott Cerf tightened his grip on the pistol, kept it pointed at Gavin's face. He felt like he wanted to say something else, a clever good-bye, but he was done talking. The time had come for action. He no longer had Otis to do his dirty work for him. From now on, Scott Cerf would take care of business himself. And the next order of business was to kill the man who'd ruined his life.

His tightened his finger on the trigger. Easy enough to shoot this fucker. He made a big target.

Then Cerf heard a noise behind him. He whirled to find a naked woman standing in the open doorway into the hall. A waif of a woman with short, black hair. She held a fat book over her head in both hands, as if she were offering it to the heavens.

Their eyes met as Cerf brought the gun around, and he saw fear there. She danced backward, her small breasts jiggling, her bare feet slipping on the hardwood floor. She dived sideways as the gun roared, and the plaster wall exploded in white dust.

Gavin. Cerf tried to turn back around. But a huge fist slammed against the side of his head and the world tipped and whirled. Another blow came down across his forearm, and the gun flew from his hand.

"Oh, shit."

☆ ☆ ☆ ☆ ☆

Drew was on top of Cerf before the pistol hit the floor. He punched him in the jaw with his left hand, then raked him across the face with his right, the metal splints breaking the skin, sending a fine spray of blood flying from Cerf's forehead.

Cerf lashed blindly at him, his fist catching Drew in the side of the neck. Drew shrugged off the blow and moved in, taking two shots to the ribs before he could get his hands around Cerf's neck.

He squeezed, hard as he could with two fingers out of the action. Cerf's eyes went wide, and his mouth opened, hunting air. Drew tightened his grip, pushing forward. Cerf bent backward, his face going scarlet, his hands clawing at Drew's arms, trying to get free.

Drew kept squeezing. This bastard had betrayed his country. He was responsible—directly or indirectly—for at least four deaths, including poor Sylvia Smith. He'd come to Drew's home, armed and ready to eliminate him. And he'd fired a shot at Teresa.

Cerf went limp, his eyes bulging. Drew braced against the weight as Cerf tried to crumple.

"That's enough, tiger."

Drew looked up, saw Teresa's head peeking around the

door jamb. Her eyes were wide.

"Let him go." Her voice was calm, an everyday voice, as if she was afraid to shout, afraid of what he might do.

He released Cerf, who fell to the floor in a heap. Cerf took a ragged breath, and a coughing fit wracked his body. Drew ignored him, still watching Teresa.

"Call the cops," he said. His voice sounded thick and fuzzy.

"Already did. They're on the way."

She stepped into the doorway, looking down at Cerf. The computer tycoon writhed on the floor, still trying to get his breath.

Drew stepped around him and picked up the revolver, where it had skidded to a stop against the wall. He pointed it in Cerf's general direction, then looked back to Teresa.

"If this place is about the fill up with cops, you might want some clothes."

FIFTY SIX

The front door burst open. Drew pivoted, bringing the gun around. The doorway was filled with men, one squatting, three others squeezing into the space above him, all pointing pistols in his direction.

"Drop it!" they shouted. "Drop it now!"

Drew did as he was told.

The men came through the door, fast and low, their quick eyes searching the room. Two stood over Cerf, pointing their guns at him. Another kicked the revolver away from Drew and started patting him down. Three others came into the room, pointing their pistols everywhere while they checked for hidden gunmen.

Drew could see right away they weren't local cops. These guys were lean and serious and well-trained. They wore military haircuts and combat boots and dark blue windbreakers.

"DOD?" Drew asked the one who'd finished patting him down. The man had dark red hair cut close to his scalp.

"That's right. Take a seat." He pointed at Drew's chair, just as Cerf had, but this time Drew obeyed. "Anyone else in the house?"

"My girlfriend's in the bedroom."

One of the Defense Department agents already had found

Teresa. He led her into the living room, a hand clamped around her arm. Her feet still were bare, but she'd put on some clothes.

The redhead left Drew in his chair and squatted next to Cerf, who rolled over onto his back and glared up at him. Some of the flush had vanished from Cerf's face and he appeared to be breathing normally now. But the scratch across his forehead still bled, and his neck bore purpling marks from Drew's fingers.

"We've been looking all over for you," the DOD man said.

"Fuck you," Cerf croaked.

"Cuff him."

The agent stood and stepped away. Two of the others holstered their guns and flipped Cerf over onto his face and handcuffed his wrists behind him.

"We called the cops already," Drew said to the redhead.

"I know. We waved them off. We'll be handling this guy."

Drew felt a scowl creep across his face. "But he's involved in several murders. Isn't that something for the locals?"

Agent Red stepped closer and rested a hand on Drew's bare shoulder. His face creased into a smile.

"We'll handle the cops, Mr. Gavin. Murder charges are the least of this guy's problems."

"But—"

"He'll be charged eventually. But we need to talk to him first. He's sold top-secret information to foreign powers. It's a federal matter."

"But the murders—"

"Forget the murders. Forget this guy." He tilted his head toward Cerf, who was being lifted to his feet by the others. "He'll be in a little room for a long time, answering questions about where and when and how he sold that software."

Drew felt dazed. He didn't want Scott Cerf spirited away. He wanted him tried in public, made to answer for his crimes, especially for the death of Sylvia Smith. He tried to think of an objection, but nothing came. These guys were in charge. And they didn't care a flip whether Drew got any closure.

Agent Red still watched Drew, looked like he was reading his mind.

"Don't worry," he said. "He'll get what's coming to him. All in good time."

The agents hustled Cerf out of the house, moving quickly and efficiently, forming a human box around him as they went out onto the porch. Cerf hung his head.

The redhead trailed them toward the door, but Drew stopped him by calling, "Hey."

"Yeah?"

"I've got to know: How long have you guys been onto Cerf? Did you hear about the software deals from Sylvia Smith?"

Agent Red shook his head.

"Sorry, pal. Wally Mertz sicced us on Cerf weeks ago. He and his private eye figured out what Cerf was up to, and called us."

"Then they both got killed."

Agent Red frowned. "Our mistake. We should've protected them. We underestimated Edgewater. Then you got rid of him before we could round him up.

"You made our job a little harder," he said, his face creasing into a smile again. "But you caught Cerf, and that makes it all right. We'll take it from here. Your government appreciates your help."

Then he was out the door, closing it behind him, and Drew and Teresa were left alone in the living room. Drew sighed, feeling incomplete. It was as if the showdown with Cerf hadn't happened at all, except that Drew had a bullet hole in the wall of his house and tremors of pain shooting through his ribs

"You hear that, tiger? 'Your government appreciates your help.' You're a hero again."

She danced around the chair, and leaned over until their faces were only inches apart.

"We've got to call the paper."

Drew groaned.

FIFTY SEVEN

It was past two o'clock in the morning by the time Teresa and Drew got back to his house. It had taken lightning-speed efforts by the staff to get Scott Cerf's capture emblazoned across the top of the next day's *Gazette*. They'd made it, though it meant missing all the late-edition deadlines and stalling delivery trucks for an hour.

Drew felt like he'd been through a Cuisinart, sliced and diced and pureed. He'd never felt so tired in his life, not even after the toughest football games he'd played. He took inventory of his injuries: the broken fingers, the aching ribs, the bruises, the bloodshot eye where Otis Edgewater had played hitchhiker. On top of all of those, he had the steady throb of exhaustion behind his eyes. His hands shook from stress and fatigue. He wanted aspirin and beer and sleep.

Teresa stopped the car in his rutted driveway, and he popped open the door. The interior light flared in his eyes. Teresa made no move to open her door, her hands still on the wheel. She turned to look at him, and he saw fatigue in her eyes, too, along with the glint of victory that comes from landing a big story. She gave him a weary smile.

"You're not coming in?"

"No," she said. "I want my own bed. Yours is too lumpy. This is one night when I'll be able to sleep soundly, and I want to enjoy every moment."

Drew nodded. He tried to smile back, but he was just too damned tired.

"I tell you, tiger, you sure know how to show a girl a good time."

"Yeah, well, I was trying to impress you."

"I'd never heard Goodman yell 'Stop the presses!' before."

"Usually, somebody just picks up a phone and mutters something to a pressman. Goodman was pretty excited."

"He wasn't the only one. God, what a night."

"It's one for the books all right. We may not be Los Angeles, but Albuquerque can be exciting at times."

The smile slid off her face. Drew felt his breath catch in his chest. He knew what was coming next, and he tried to will it away.

"I was going to talk to you about that, tiger. Earlier, before we got interrupted by Scott Cerf."

"You're going," he said.

She bit her lower lip, hesitating. Then she nodded.

"I can't pass up the opportunity. I owe it to myself, to everybody who's helped my career so far. Goodman. Elliott. You."

"Me?"

"Thanks to you, I've been involved in the biggest stories this town's had in years. Every time it gets slow around here, you go out and uncover some murders or something. Suddenly, we've got the big headlines and we're raking in awards. I'd never gotten the *Times'* attention, if not for you."

Drew was silent for a moment. He felt as if he were absorbing blows again, body shots that oofed the air out of him. He blinked rapidly against the sudden sharp heat in his eyes, then said, "Why doesn't that make me feel any better?"

"I'm sorry. I know it's going to be hard. For both of us. I don't know what I'll do without you. But I've got to give L.A. a try."

He nodded somberly. "I've been saying it all along."

"You've been a champ about the whole thing, especially coming when it did, with Curtis in jail and the whole world crashing down around you."

"Not around me. On me. Right on top of me."

Her lower lip quivered and tears welled in her eyes. "And now I'm making it worse."

He leaned across the car and gathered her in his arms.

"You're doing what you've got to do," he said. "Don't cry about it. It'll be fine."

She leaned back so she could look him in the eye. A tear had left a track down her cheek, and it glinted in the harsh light. Drew reached up with his thumb and brushed it away, her skin smooth and damp under his touch.

"Sure you won't come to California with me?"

He shook his head slowly.

"I can't. I've still got a lot to sort out with the cops and the feds. I've got to keep after this story. And then there's Pop and the house and, hell, I don't know, everything. This is my home."

Another tear rolled down her face.

"I know," she said. "New Mexico's my home, too. I don't know how I'll handle being away."

"We can still see each other. Flights are cheap. You'll fly home to visit the family. I'll come out there on vacation. It'll be fine. You'll see."

His mouth said all the right things, but on the inside, he felt as if he were falling, as if his world had been yanked out from under him. He kissed her, hoping she couldn't see his true feelings on his face.

"I hope you're right," she said.

"Yeah. Me, too."

FIFTY EIGHT

Two days later, Drew sat alone in the bleachers at a University of New Mexico practice field, watching Lobo football players sweating and grunting through their spring drills. The players wore gray practice jerseys over their shoulder pads and cherry-red helmets decorated with snarling gray wolves. Their cleats ripped at the damp sod.

It was a beautiful day, sunny and mild, a few cottony clouds drifting aimlessly around the turquoise sky. The mountains shrugged their shoulders as they looked down over the city. Drew tilted his face to the sun, his notebook loose and useless in his hands. He closed his eyes and sensed the world in other ways. The smell of new grass. The players' jocular banter and the coaches' sharp whistles. The sun's warm caress.

Feet banged on the metal bleachers as someone approached. He turned his head to the sound and opened his eyes. Curtis White climbed the bleachers toward him. He was dressed in blue sweats, and his body was all angles and lines as he stepped up the bleachers to stand over him.

"Well, look who it is," Drew said. "The free man."

Curtis smiled. With his long, skinny body and the snaky dreads all around his head, he looked like a happy mop standing there.

"Fresh air and sunshine, man. You don't know how much they're worth until they're taken away."

"What are you doing out here? I've got this practice covered."

"Yeah, man, looks like you're doing a helluva job, too. Lying there half-asleep. The watchdog news media."

"All bark, no bite."

"You got that right." Curtis sat beside him and looked out over the field.

"Nice day," he said.

"Yeah," Drew said glumly.

"Don't sound like you're enjoying it much."

"I'm all right. Still kinda sore all over. And I'm taking notes left-handed. But I'm getting better."

"How you feeling, though? Emotionally?"

He shot Curtis a look, but his friend was pretending to watch the action on the field.

"You know that's not allowed," Drew said sternly.

"What?"

"Guys asking other guys about their emotions. We don't play that shit."

Curtis laughed and shook his head, making the dreadlocks dance.

"Fuck you, man. See if I ever ask again."

Drew turned back to the practice in time to see a flying pass bounce off a wide receiver's fingertips.

"These guys can't play worth a damn," he said.

"Good to see some things never change," Curtis said. "Everything else can go crazy, but you can count on Lobo football."

They sat quietly for a while, watching the field. Drew

churned inside, his thoughts tripping over the events of the past few days. His emotions had taken a Tilt-a-Whirl ride, and he didn't know if he'd ever feel the same.

"I saw Teresa," Curtis said. "She came by the newsroom today, said she was on her way catch a plane."

"Yeah. We said our good-byes last night. She didn't want me to do the whole bit at the airport. Said it would be too hard."

"She's probably right, man. None of this has been easy."

"Tell me."

Curtis let a minute pass before he said, "Must be hard on you. Her leaving and all."

"It ain't easy, but we'll work it out. One way or the other. I was just thinking about it, before you got here. This should be a happy ending, right? Cerf's caught. Edgewater and Davis are dead. We've got the big headlines. But I feel like shit. It's all been dampened by Teresa leaving, by Sylvia Smith getting killed. Every time something like this happens, another woman or two disappears from my life."

Curtis reached up and rested a hand on Drew's shoulder.

"You saved my life, man. I wouldn't have lasted much longer in jail."

Curtis' bony hand felt comforting.

"So what are you saying? 'Thanks?' "

Curtis pulled his hand away and slapped his own knee with it, laughing. The sound made Drew smile. A few days ago, he'd wondered whether he'd ever hear Curtis laugh again.

"Yeah, that's what I'm saying, motherfucker. Thank you very damned much. I like being a free man."

"You're welcome. Glad to have you back."

They sat together a while longer, until the coaches sounded